The Exile Book of

NATIVE CANADIAN FICTION AND DRAMA

The Exile Book of

NATIVE CANADIAN FICTION AND DRAMA

edited by

Daniel David Moses

Exile Editions

Publishers of singular

Fiction, Poetry, Translation, Nonfiction and Drama

2010

Library and Archives Canada Cataloguing in Publication

The Exile book of Native Canadian fiction and drama / edited by Daniel Davis Moses.

ISBN 978-1-55096-145-4

1. Canadian drama (English)--Indian authors. 2. Canadian fiction (English)--Indian authors. 3. Canadian drama (English)--21st century. 4. Canadian fiction (English)--21st century. I. Moses, Daniel David, 1952- II. Title: Native Canadian fiction and drama.

PS8309.I53E95 2010 C812'.6080897 C2010-906454-2

Design and Composition by Active Design Haus
Typeset in Garamond and Gill Sans at the Moons of Jupiter Studios
Cover painting by Norval Morriseau; by permission of artist's estate
Printed in Canada by Imprimerie Gauvin

The publisher would like to acknowledge the financial assistance of the Canada Council for the Arts and the Ontario Arts Council, which is an agency of the Government of Ontario.

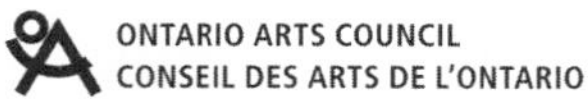

Published by Exile Editions Ltd.
144483 Southgate Road 14 – GD
Holstein, Ontario, N0G 2A0
info@exileeditions.com www.ExileEditions.com

Canadian Sales Distribution:
McArthur & Company
c/o Harper Collins
1995 Markham Road
Toronto, ON M1B 5M8
toll free: 1 800 387 0117

U.S. Sales Distribution:
Independent Publishers Group
814 North Franklin Street
Chicago, IL 60610
www.ipgbook.com
toll free: 1 800 888 4741

For All Our Relations

CONTENTS

Introduction by Daniel David Moses xi

TOMSON HIGHWAY
Hearts and Flowers 1

LAUREN B. DAVIS
Rat Medicine 20

NIIGONWEDOM JAMES SINCLAIR
Trickster Reflections 39

DANIEL DAVID MOSES
King of the Raft 69

JOSEPH BOYDEN
Born With A Tooth 73

JOSEPH A. DANDURAND
Please Do Not Touch the Indians 84

ALOOTOOK IPELLIE
After Brigitte Bardot 156

THOMAS KING
Coyote and the Enemy Aliens 161

YVETTE NOLAN
Scattering Jake 178

RICHARD VAN CAMP
Love Walked In 207

FLOYD FAVEL
Governor of the Dew 247

ROBERT ARTHUR ALEXIE
The Pale Indian 259

DANIEL DAVID MOSES
The Witch of Niagara 270

KATHARINA VERMETTE
what ndns do 325

EDEN ROBINSON
Queen of the North 342

Notes On the Authors *370*

Permissions *375*

Introduction

NOT-SO-COMMON PLACES FROM INDIAN COUNTRY

So today I'm imagining you finding yourself wondering on which shelf you might find a spot for this idiosyncratic selection of fiction and plays by writers from the First Peoples. Native Studies? Theatre? Canadian English?

Or maybe, in 2010, this one could simply go under Literature.

Are we there yet?

In 1992, many in the Americas and Europe, particularly those (I recall from television human interest news reports) of Italian descent, were celebrating the story ("In fourteen hundred and ninety two, / Columbus sailed the ocean blue...") of a "discovery" made five hundred years earlier. That same summer, here in Canada – and in the U.S. too, a month or so later – some of us who had discovered ourselves awash in that story's wake got together, as some might have it, to powwow. The story, do you recall, suggested Columbus had set foot on an island he took to be India? And wrongly, stuck us with the "Indian" label...

Well, we got together to confer, those of us from that swamped group who were still, or again, or were becoming, storytellers, the Americans among us then out front in fiction (Leslie Marmon Silko had just published her *Almanac of the Dead*), we Canadians taking the lead in the theatre (Tomson Highway's *The Rez Sisters* having recently made its loud splash).

We gathered to confer and tell and celebrate those tales and many others about our lives, all of which served as a literary antidote to the collective eye-rolling the Christopher Columbian spectacles had in us induced.

There were so many of us, old and young, a couple of hundred, probably, leaning into Saskatchewan's wind, and up around five hundred finding shade from the Oklahoma sun; those numbers produced for me – lucky enough to attend both gatherings – a feeling of safety I had never felt before in a writers' gathering. There's a commonplace in the Canadian Writers' Union that one of its founders, Margaret Laurence, dubbed the organization "a tribe," but the experience of their AGM culture, a confusion of Robert's Rules of Order, and a receding Sixties' idealism, pales beside the experiences I had that signal year with, well, as some of the elders say, All My Relations.

I know, and probably felt even then, that I would like to achieve a more universal outlook, the family of humanity, but it seemed to me, in retrospect, later that year, that we "Indians" were, as you say, preaching to the choir, the proverbial voices crying in the wilderness. Nobody but us knew or really cared that we still existed out there, wherever it was we were out on the prairie, that Indian Country.

Yes, yes, this was all in the those short giddy days nearly twenty years back in Canada, just after the Oka Crisis, around the time *Dances With Wolves* made Graham Greene a star, when there was even a season (do you recall?) the Gap used Indian actors in their ads in the Toronto subway stations because the CBC, to show that they, too, were paying attention, had given us the series, *North of 60*. But politicians have at best four-year attention spans, even if they've had to call out the army, and Hollywood after all that dancing could only find supporting roles for Mr. Greene, and the only less-than-white faces the always beleaguered CBC can afford nowadays inhabit *The Little*

Mosque on the Prairie. And as for that First Nations brown sort of face once seen on posters on those underground walls, they're now still and again just outside the TTC turnstiles enquiring after change.

There's a commonplace in Indian Country, heard most often in Canada's First Nations arts community, that Louis Riel, in one of his prophetic moods, foretold that his people would sleep seven generations before being brought awake by their artists.

I know I'm not the only one who takes comfort in this idea of a collective wake-up call from a troubled sleep, the writer in me choosing to think it suggests that there is or will be some sort of literary movement or wave I might be a party to, or riding on, even as I spend my solitary hours intent on perfecting another sentence.

And I know I'm not talking anymore about a party just for those folks of mine who gathered that season in Indian Country, who have just kept on trying with patience since to take back the old stories, or tell with growing skill some new ones (the table of contents of this anthology lists some of their names and their various clear accomplishments). Meanwhile a few mainstream writers (I'm sure you heard something of the "appropriation of voice" controversy) took offence, it seemed, at being criticized for their own less-than-sterling approximations of aboriginal tales and, bizarrely, protested again censorship, as if First Nations critics were the government. Hey, Dief the Chief only let us in on this voting thing in 1960. We haven't quite yet taken over Parliament!

About a decade after my visits with those folks in Saskatchewan and Oklahoma, I find that I am Writer in Residence at

Concordia University in Montreal, Quebec, and one day on another visit to an English class, there I am giving a reading, poetry, a scene or two from a play; then I answer queries.

A grey-haired gent in the back row, a mature student, I assume, asks me, with good will for my success, I guess, when I'm going to write something more mainstream.

I hesitate a moment over what "mainstream" means, but then answer that I can't not write about "what I know." That place I grew up in, and see the rest of the world from, even if it is "a reserve" by the laws and regulations of Canada, is the complex world that concerns me. I also defend my stance by reminding him of the aesthetic commonplace that the particular can, when done well, evoke the universal.

But an eye-shadowed Goth girl at the far end of the front row, then a red-haired boy in sweats in front of me in the third row, and finally a black boy with a Québécois accent and Buddy Holly glasses in the back corner, chime in and are all openly and energetically discussing the question, saying among other comforting and encouraging things, that I don't need to go mainstream, not for any of them, that they thought what I was writing was interesting and that they liked hearing it and wanted to read more, that they didn't know before what they'd been missing, missing from their pictures of Quebec and the rest of Canada.

Missing?

After that class, I'm hopeful all our First Nations writing activity will no longer stay "on reserve," especially if even that younger generation is aware that preaching from some old book of commonplaces isn't good enough, that the absence of our stories from their awareness of the larger world, from their imaginings, limits their world and our literature.

The best of our First Nations stuff is certainly not commonplace, not yet, and does touch those emotions and experiences that we think of as universal, that we recognize as literature.

These stories and plays have no need of a special separate shelf space or categorization.

They succeed at telling stories that are whole stories.

Are we there yet?

Read on and we'll all arrive much sooner.

Daniel David Moses
August 2010

TOMSON HIGHWAY

HEARTS AND FLOWERS

Daniel Daylight sits inside Mr. Tipper's traveling car. It is cold – not cold, though, like outside; of this fact Daniel Daylight is quite certain. He looks out through the window on his right and, as always, sees white forest rushing by; maybe rabbits will bound past on that snowbank in the trees, he sits thinking. He has seen them, after all, on past Thursdays just like this one. It is dark, too. Not pitch-black, though, for that half moon hangs unhidden, making snow – on the road, on the roadside, rocks, ground, trees (mostly spruce though some birch and some poplar) – glow, as with dust made of silver, Daniel Daylight sits there thinking. Daniel Daylight, at age eight, is on his way to his piano lesson in Prince William, Manitoba.

Twenty miles lie between the Watson Lake Indian Residential School, where resides Daniel Daylight, and Prince William, where he takes his weekly lesson. The Watson Lake Indian Residential School, after all, has no one to teach him how to play the piano, while Prince William has elderly and kind Mrs. Hay. So his teacher in grade three at the Watson Lake Indian Residential School, Mr. Tipper, drives him every Thursday, 6:00 p.m. on the nose, to his piano teacher's house, Mrs. Hay's, in Prince William.

Orange brick and cement from top to bottom, held in by a steel-mesh fence, then by forest (mostly spruce though some birch and some poplar), the Watson Lake Indian Residential School stands like a fort on the south shore of a lake called

Watson Lake, 550 miles north of Winnipeg, Mr. Tipper's place of birth. Prince William, quite by contrast, is a town that stands on the south bank of a river called the Moostoos River, just across from which sprawls a village called Waskeechoos (though "settlement" is a noun more accurate, Mr. Tipper has explained on previous Thursdays, for no "village" can be seen, only houses peeking out of the forest here and there). Waskeechoos, on the north bank of the muddy Moostoos River, is an Indian reserve, Mr. Tipper has informed Daniel Daylight, not unlike the one from which hails Daniel Daylight: Minstik Lake, Manitoba, 350 miles north of Waskeechoos, Prince William, and the Watson Lake Indian Residential School. It takes half an hour for Daniel Daylight to make the journey every week, in Mr. Tipper's travelling car, from the Watson Lake Indian Residential School south through the heart of Waskeechoos and across the Moostoos River to Prince William, so he has time on his hands for reflection (so, at least, Mr. Tipper calls such thinking).

Daniel Daylight likes these trips. For one thing, he gets to practise what he knows of the language they call English with elderly and kind Mrs. Hay, with the waiters at the Nip House or at Wong's (where he sometimes goes for snacks with Mr. Tipper once he's finished with his lesson), and with friends of Mr. Tipper whom he meets at the Nip House or at Wong's. He enjoys speaking English just as he enjoys speaking Cree with the students at the residential school (though, of course, mother tongues need no practise, not like English with its *v*'s that make one's teeth come right out and bite one's lower lip). Daniel Daylight, for another thing, likes to ride in "travelling cars" (as he calls them for the *v* in "travel"). Standing at the northern tip of a lake called Minstik Lake, the Minstik Lake Indian Reserve, after all, has no cars and no trucks, just dogsleds in the winter, canoes in the summer. A third reason why Daniel Daylight likes these trips is that he enjoys being dazzled by the lights of a city like Prince William (for, to him, the railway depot is a city of one million, not a town of five thousand) with its streets, its cafés, hotels, stores, and huge churches with tall steeples, whereas Minstik Lake, with its six hundred people, has no streets, no cafés, no hotels, just dirt paths, one small store, and one church. Daniel Daylight, for a fourth thing, likes these trips because Mr. Tipper's travelling car has a radio that plays songs that he can learn in his head. When it stops playing music, furthermore, it plays *spoken* English words, which, of course, he can practise understanding. Tonight, for example, people living in the east of the country (Mr. Tipper has explained) are discussing voting patterns of the nation (Mr. Tipper has explained) even though Daniel Daylight knows the word "vote" for one reason: it begins with the sound that forces one to sink one's teeth deep into one's lower lips and then growl. Sound, that is to say, thrills Daniel Daylight. Which is why, best of all, Daniel Daylight likes these trips: because he gets to play the piano. He gets to play, for elderly and kind Mrs. Hay, "Sonatina" by Clementi, which he now knows well enough to play page one from the top to the bottom without stopping. He gets to play for the third time this winter "Pirates of the Pacific," with the bass that sounds like a drumbeat. He gets to play, this week, for the first time, *with* Jenny Dean, the duet – for four hands – called "Hearts and Flowers."

"Jenny Dean is a white girl," he has overheard someone say at the Nip House, just a few days before Christmas, in fact, when he was there having fries and Coca-Cola with Mr. Tipper. "Daniel Daylight is an *Indian*. A Cree Indian. Indian boys do *not* play the piano with white girls," he has overheard one white girl whisper *loudly* to another over Coca-Cola in a bottle, "not here in our Prince William, not anywhere on earth or in heaven." Daniel Daylight let it pass. He, after all, was eight years old, not thirty-nine like Mr. Tipper; what could he have done to the girl who had made such a statement? Bop her on the head with her bottle? Shove a french fry up her nose? Scratch her face? Besides, neither Jenny Dean's parents, Mrs. Hay, nor Mr. Tipper seemed to mind the notion of Jenny Dean making music with a boy whose father was a Cree caribou hunter and a celebrated dogsled racer.

"There it is," says Mr. Tipper. And so it is, for the travelling car has just rounded the bend in the road from which the lights of Prince William and the Indian reserve on this side of the river from the town can be seen for the first time. The first view of both town and reserve, to Daniel Daylight, always looks like a spaceship landed on planet Earth, not unlike the spaceship in the comic book that his older brother, John-Peter Daylight, gave him as a Christmas present twenty-one days ago and that Daniel Daylight keeps hidden under his pillow in the dormitory at the residential school. Daniel Daylight likes, in fact, to imagine all those lights in the distance as exactly that: a spaceship come to take him to a place where exist not Indian people, nor white people, just good people and good music. In fact, he can hear in his mind already "Sonatina" by Clementi, key of G, allegro moderato. He can hear "Pirates of the Pacific" with that drumbeat in the bass that goes boom. He can hear "Hearts and Flowers." He has practised all three pieces to the point of exhaustion, after all, in the one room at the residential school that has a piano, what the nuns and the priests call the "library" but, in fact, is a storage room for pencils and erasers, papers, rulers, chalk, and some old spelling books. Feeling on the tips of his fingers all the keys of Mrs. Hay's brown piano, Daniel Daylight sees the sign on the roadside that announces, "Waskeechoos Welcomes You." Mr. Tipper's travelling car speeds past the sign, thus bringing Daniel Daylight onto land that belongs "to the Indians," Mr. Tipper, for some reason, likes proclaiming, as on a radio. "Speed Limit 30 MPH," Daniel Daylight reads on the sign that then follows. The road now mud, dried, cracked, and frozen, pot-holed and iced, the travelling car first slows down to a crawl, then bumps, rattles, slides.

"Indian people are not human," says Mr. Tipper, dodging first this small patch of ice then that small patch of ice, "at least not according to the government. They cannot vote." Daniel Daylight sits unsurprised – Mr. Tipper's use of English, white as a sheet and from Winnipeg as he may be, is not always perfect, Daniel Daylight has simply come to accept. The young Cree piano player, in any case, does not feel confident enough in either his grasp of English *or* his age to say much in rebuttal. His father, after all, speaks maybe ten words of English, his mother just two or three; of his eight living siblings, older all than him, only John-Peter Daylight, who is three grades ahead of Daniel Daylight at the Watson Lake Indian Residential School (and perhaps Florence, who once studied there, too, but quit at just grade four), speaks English. No one on the Minstik Lake Indian Reserve where Daniel Daylight was born, for that matter, speaks the language, not even Chief Samba Cheese Weetigo *or* his wife, Salad. Like people right here in Waskeechoos (as Mr. Tipper has informed Daniel Daylight in the past), they speak Cree and Cree only. So how, indeed, *can* they be human, Daniel Daylight asks himself, *if* they don't even know what the word means or looks like on a page?

At the bridge that spans like a giant spider's web the muddy, winding Moostoos River, a bottleneck is fast taking shape. Built mainly for trains, the bridge makes room for car and truck traffic only by means of a one-way lane off to one side. The traffic light glowing like a charcoal on this side of the crossing, four cars sit at its base humming and putt-putt-putting; the travellers from Watson, as happened last Thursday, will just have to sit there for four or five minutes, much too long for

Daniel Daylight, who can't wait to play the piano with Jenny Dean. Preparing, in a sense, for conversing with elderly and kind Mrs. Hay when he gets to her house (for Mrs. Hay's Cree, of course, is like Mr. Tipper's – it does not exist), Daniel Daylight makes a decisions: he will practise his English. On Mr. Tipper.

"Human, what it mean, Mr. Tip—" But Mr. Tipper does not let him finish.

"If a man, or a woman, aged twenty-one or older cannot vote," says Mr. Tipper – who, from the side, resembles Elmer Fudd, Bugs Bunny's worst enemy in the comics, thinks Daniel Daylight – "then how on earth can he be human, Daniel Daylight?"

"Vote?" Daniel Daylight feels himself bite his thick lower lip with both sets of teeth, so unlike Cree which has no such sound or letter, he sits there, regretting.

"'Vote' is when a person helps choose the leaders that will make the laws for his country," replies Mr. Tipper. He snorts once and then continues. "Every four years, in Winnipeg where I come from, for instance, the person who has the right to vote will go to a church or a school or some such building that has a hall, step inside a little... room – the *voting* booth, this room is called – take a small piece of paper on which are written the names of the four, five, or six people from that region or that neighbourhood who want to go to Ottawa to speak for the people of that region or that neighbourhood." Daniel Daylight is having trouble keeping up with the torrent of words pouring out of Mr. Tipper's mouth. Still, he manages to catch what he thinks Mr. Tipper, in the past, has referred to as "the drift." "The person then votes – that is to say chooses – by checking off the name of the person on that list who he thinks will best speak for him and his needs, and the person on that list whose name ends up being checked off by the greatest number of people in that region or that neighbourhood is voted, in this way, into power, and that person goes to Ottawa to help our prime minister run our country, is what the word 'vote' means, Daniel Daylight," says Mr. Tipper. "You 'vote' for your leader. *You* decide how *you* want *your* life to be in *your* country. That's what makes you a human. Otherwise, you're not."

The traffic light changes first to yellow, then to green. Daniel Daylight has always taken pleasure in looking at what, to him, is an act of magic. *Thump, thump* goes the travelling car as it crosses the bridge built for trains. The *thump, thump* stops. And now they're in Prince William (or in land that is human, as Mr. Tipper calls it, where people can "vote," just like in Winnipeg) – paved streets, lights so bright Daniel Daylight has to squint, lights so bright it looks like mid-afternoon. On Mr. Tipper's car radio, the music is back; some sad, lonely man is howling away about being "cheated" by someone, maybe his wife. To Daniel Daylight, it sounds, for some reason, like the Indians are being cheated.

In Mrs. Hay's living room, Daniel Daylight sits straight-backed at her upright Baldwin piano. Sitting in a chair right beside him, her hairdo white, short, and fluffy, her face as wrinkled as prunes, the elderly and kind human woman smiles at her one Cree student through glasses so thick they could be ashtrays, Daniel Daylight sits there thinking. Scales first, chords next, then arpeggios, key of E major. Right hand only, two octaves up: E, G-sharp, B, E, G-sharp, B, E. And two octaves down: E, G-sharp, B, E, G-sharp, B, E. Back up, back down, Mrs. Hay humming softly along, in her cracked, quavery voice, with the tune such as it is. Daniel Daylight cannot help but wonder as he plays his arpeggio in E major if playing the piano will or will not make him human. Left hand next, same arpeggio, only two octaves down: E, G-sharp, B, E, G-sharp, B, E. And two octaves down: E, G-sharp, B, E, G-sharp, B, E. He is dying to stop right there at the E with the brown stain and confront Mrs. Hay with the question, for Mr. Tipper, as always, has left him with her, alone, at her house for the hour.

"Very good, Danny," says Mrs. Hay, giving him no chance to ask any questions. Only she, of all the people he knows in the world, calls or has called him Danny. Not his five older brothers, not his six older sisters, not his one hundred friends, not even his parents call him "Danny Daylight." Daniel Daylight is not sure he likes it. But he says nothing. In any case, it is too late now; she has called him "Danny" ever since he first walked into her house that fine, sunny day in September almost three years ago. They move on. First "Sonatina" by Clementi, key of G, allegro moderato, a grade six piece; of this fact, Daniel Daylight is very proud if only because he has been taking piano lessons for only two and a half years and should, by rights, still be in grade three, not grade six already.

"It's the 14th of January," says Mrs. Hay as she peers over her glasses at the calendar that hangs on the wall with the picture, right above the calendar's big, black "1960," of her husband, Mr. Hay, driving a train and smiling and waving. "The festival starts on the 29th of March." Daniel Daylight thus has ten weeks to practise and memorize "Sonatina," for that is his solo entry at the festival and he plans nothing less than to win first prize. As he plays "Sonatina," a piece energetic and happy because it, after all, is written in the key of G major, allegro moderato (meaning, in Italian, "fast, but not too fast," as in "moderate"), Daniel Daylight, in his mind, sees his father, Cheechup Daylight, and his mother, Adelaide, standing in a line at the little wooden church in the village of Minstik Lake, a worn yellow pencil each in hand. They are lining up to vote. At this point in their lives, they are not human, for a sign on their backs says as much: "Non-human." The melody line for Clementi's "Sonatina" soars like a swallow flying up to the clouds, tugging at the heart of Daniel Daylight as with a rope. If he plays it well enough, his parents will surely turn, allegro moderato, into humans, Daniel Daylight prays as he plays. He comes to the end: dominant chord (his right thumb adding the minor seventh) followed, *seemak* (right away), by the tonic. *Thump. Thump.* In the pianist's mind, Cheechup Daylight and his wife, Adelaide, are turned away from the little voting booth by the missionary priest, Father Roy. They are not human. They cannot vote.

"Very good, Danny " says Mrs. Hay. "Jenny should be here in just five minutes," she adds, smiling. "But..." And this is where Mrs. Hay, kind as a *koogoom* (grandmother) as she may be, criticizes him and his playing, sometimes in a manner that takes him quite by surprise. He is tensing up at his right temple as he plays, says Mrs. Hay. If he is tensing up at his right temple, meaning to say that a vein pops up in that region, as she calls it, every time he reaches for a high note, then his right arm is tensing up and if his right arm is tensing up then his right hand is tensing up. Which is why the melody, from measure 17 to measure 21, in particular, sounds not very happy, forced, not quite "there," explains Mrs. Hay. He must try it again. He does. Mrs. Hay, this time, holding her bone-thin, liver-spotted, white right hand, gentle as a puff of absorbent cotton, on Daniel Daylight's thin right wrist, guiding him, as it were, from phrase to phrase to phrase. Better this time, he can feel it: his right arm is not tensing up, not as much anyway. Again, however, as "Sonatina" comes to an end, his parents are turned away from the little cardboard booth at the church that stands on the hill overlooking the northern extremity of Minstik Lake. *Still,* they are not human. *Ding,* goes Mrs. Hay's electric doorbell. And into the vestibule of her back entrance blow a flurry of snow *and* Jenny Dean. Taking off her bulky winter outerwear – mitts, coat, half, scarf, boots – her cheeks glow pink from the cold of a mid-January evening in far north Manitoba and her hazel cat-like eyes sparkle as does her blond, curly hair – yes, decides Daniel Daylight, Jenny Dean looks, indeed, like a human.

Now Jenny Dean is sitting on the brown wooden bench right there beside Daniel Daylight. She smells so nice, thinks Daniel Daylight, like snow just fallen on a green spruce bough. The sheet music for the duet Mrs. Hay has chosen as their entry at the festival sits open on the piano's music stand before them. He can feel his red flannel-sleeved right arm pressing up against the girl's yellow-pullovered left arm. His is the lower part, the part with the bass line and chord structure, hers the higher part, the part with the melody but with the occasional *part* of a chord, meaning that the Cree Indian, non-human pianist, the "Heart," Daniel Daylight, and the white girl human pianist, the "Flower," Jenny Dean, will be sharing chords, in public from a piece of music called "Hearts and Flowers" written in the key of C major, andante cantabile – meaning, in Italian, "at a walking pace *and* singing" – by a human woman named Joan C. McCumber.

Water-like, limpid, and calm, the chords start playing, they float, placed with care on the keyboard by Daniel Daylight. The bass sneaks in, the melody begins. Playing octaves, Jenny Dean's hands begin at the two Cs above middle C, arc up to the G in a curve, graceful and smooth, then waft back down to the F, move on down to the E, and thence to the D, skip down to the B and swerve back up to the C whence they had started. The melody pauses, Daniel Daylight's series of major chords billow out to fill the silence, the melody resumes with another arcing phrase, filled with sunlight. For Daniel Daylight, two things happen. First, from where he sits, he sees four hands, two brown (non-human), two white (human), playing the piano. He is sure, somehow, that once he and Jenny Dean have mastered the piece and won first prize in the duet section of the music festival, he – and his parents – will be human. They will have the vote. Father Roy will *not* be able to turn Cheechup Daylight and his wife, Adelaide, away from the little voting booth at the little wooden church that overlooks the northern extremity of beautiful, extraordinary Minstik Lake with its thousand islands.

One month later, Daniel Daylight sits at a table in a booth at the Nip House on Prince William's main thoroughfare, looking with amazement at the valentine just given him, at Mrs. Hay's, by the human piano player Jenny Dean. Standing upright on the table one foot before him, the card is covered with hearts and flowers. High above it looms the very white face of Mr. Tipper with his Elmer Fudd-like, round, pudgy nose, and behind Mr. Tipper, a wall made of one giant mirror. On the radio that sits on the counter five tables, and therefore five booths, behind Daniel Daylight, Kitty Wells is singing, "Three Ways to Lose You, It's True," his sister Florence Daylight's favourite song, the one she sings with her boyfriend, Alec Cook, as they sit there on the shores of Minstik Lake strumming and strumming their two old guitars. Now it is mid-February, the Kiwanis Music Festival looms even closer – just six weeks, Mrs. Hay has informed Daniel Daylight *and* Jenny Dean, so Daniel Daylight is excited to the point where he can't stop slurping, through a straw and as loudly as he can, at his glass half-filled with black Coca-Cola. They are sitting in the "Indians Only" section of the restaurant, Mr. Tipper, for some reason, chooses this moment to explain to Daniel Daylight, his blue eyes peering at the restaurant spread out behind and over Daniel Daylight's shoulder. Daniel Daylight stops his slurping and peers past the rim of the tall thin glass at the wall behind Mr. Tipper, the wall which, of course, is one giant mirror. Darting his eyeballs about like tiny searchlights, he looks for a sign that will, indeed, say "Indians Only."

"There is no sign that says 'Indians only,'" says Mr. Tipper, knowing, as almost always, what is going on inside the mind of Daniel Daylight.

"Indians only..." Kitty Wells has stopped singing, Daniel Daylight suddenly observes, and a man's speaking voice has taken over on the radio. Daniel Daylight locks his eyes with Mr. Tipper's – what on earth will the man say next about... ?

"Hamburger deluxe, gravy on the side!" yells the big, fat waitress who always scowls at Daniel Daylight, drowning out the voice of the man on the radio, at least temporarily.

"...cannot vote," the man on the radio ends his speech.

"You see?" says Mr. Tipper, sipping at his coffee with his thick purplish lips. "They're not human, not according to the radio, not according to the government. It is the law."

"Who made the law?" Daniel Daylight feels emboldened to ask Mr. Tipper.

"No one," says Mr. Tipper. "They are unwritten. It's the same thing at the movie house right here in Prince William, the taverns, the bingo hall, even the churches, Baptist, Anglican, *and* Catholic – Indians on one side, whites on the other."

Suddenly ignoring his half-finished plate of french fries with gravy, his Coke, and his valentine, Daniel Daylight twists his back around to look at the rest of the restaurant – looking in the mirror will *not* do: 1) the Nip House has room for at least sixty customers; 2) the fire-engine-red vinyl-covered booths are not high enough to hide anyone from anyone; 3) true to Mr. Tipper's unwanted observation, white people sit on one side of the restaurant, Indian people on the other. He turns back to the mirror and to Mr. Tipper, who, of course, is the one exception, being as he is a white man sitting with the brown-skinned, black-haired, non-human, Cree Indian pianist Daniel Daylight on the "Indians Only" side of the restaurant. Mr. Tipper must be brave, Daniel Daylight thinks rather sadly, lets go his Coke, and slips his valentine into a pocket of his black woolen parka. Suddenly, he is no longer hungry.

Six weeks later, Daniel Daylight sits inside Mr. Tipper's travelling car with the radio playing, again, country music, a song that Daniel Daylight does not know. He is about to ask when Mr. Tipper asks him, "What will they think when they see you and Jenny Dean playing together at the festival?" Daniel Daylight has no answer, not at the moment anyway, for "They will love our music" sounds somehow hypocritical, facetious, not quite truthful. Again they are going down the winding gravel road, with snow-covered forest rushing by as always, a rabbit bounding past on the snowbank just to the right. Daniel Daylight is on his way, this time, to the Kiwanis Music Festival in Prince William. He is going there to compete in the solo/grade six section with his "Sonatina" by Clementi, key of G, allegro moderato, which he now has down note-perfect and memorized. More important, however, at least so says Mr. Tipper, and with this notion Daniel Daylight is inclined to agree – he is going there to compete in the duet section of the annual event with the white girl/human, Jenny Dean, in a piece with the title "Hearts and Flowers," written by the human composer Joan C. McCumber.

They come to the Indian reserve called Waskeechoos, the sign that says so just going by and the next one saying "Speed Limit 30 MPH." The travelling car slows down. It bumps, rocks, and rattles. One pothole here, two there. Ice. Travelling car slides once, for six inches, then stops. A non-human man walks past, from the town and back to his home in Waskeechoos.

"People can't vote?" asks Daniel Daylight, his English, and his confidence, having bloomed rather nicely in the last two months for, of course, it is now the 31st of March, 1960, the last day of the three-day-long Kiwanis Music Festival, and Northern Manitoba is still gripped hard by winter.

"Soon they might," says Mr. Tipper. "I heard on the radio the other day..." But the traffic light at the railway bridge has just turned green and Daniel Daylight, in any case, has drifted off already to his own reserve 350 miles north, where his father and his mother are standing in line at the church on the hill that overlooks beautiful, extraordinary Minstik Lake, a worn yellow pencil each in hand. They are getting ready to select a man they can send to Ottawa to speak for Minstik Lake and all its people, perhaps even Chief Samba Cheese Weetigo. In the line behind and in front of them are crushed all six hundred people of Minstik Lake, even babies. And they are roaring, they want to vote. "Apparently the law is changing," says Mr. Tipper, "soon. Or so I heard on the radio." Good, thinks Daniel Daylight, all these people back there in Waskeechoos, like those people where I come from, will soon be human, he is thinking. He doesn't even notice that they are now on "human territory," as Mr. Tipper calls it, for already he can see himself on stage at the Kiwanis Auditorium in downtown Prince William, sitting at the piano beside Jenny Dean, playing music with all his might so his parents, and therefore he, can change from non-human to human. He is glad that Sister St. Alphonse, the principal seamstress at the Watson Lake Indian Residential School, has found him a suit for the evening: black, white shirt, red necktie, black shoes, all, for the moment, under his black woollen parka. His hands, meanwhile, are wrapped in woollen mittens so thick they do *not* stand a chance of getting cold, stiff, or claw-like, he has decided, not when he has to use them, tonight, to make a *point*.

At the Kiwanis Auditorium in downtown Prince William, Daniel Daylight sits in the audience with his back tall and straight, like all good pianists, Mrs. Hay has always insisted. From where he sits, in the middle and on the room's right side, he can see – now that he is two months wiser, courtesy of Mr. Tipper – that the room is, indeed, divided: white people on one side, Indian people on the other, the latter a little on the sparse side. Just like at the Nip House and at Wong's, Daniel Daylight sits there and thinks, *and* at the movies, the bingo hall, the taverns, and the churches – according, anyway, to Mr. Tipper, who has been to all these places. As he sits there waiting for his turn on stage, he can, on the left side of the hall, see Jenny Dean and her parents, with Mrs. Hay, waving at him and waving at him, beckoning him to come to their side. Shyly, he shakes his head. Jenny Dean, with her parents, belongs on the human side, he, with his parents (who are not only non-human but absent) on the other. Only Mr. Tipper sits beside him, and he is not even supposed to be there. On stage, some dreadful music is playing: two human boys at the piano, aged ten years or so (guesses Daniel Daylight), wearing green V-neck sweaters, white shirts, and bowties, their hair yellow as hay, skin white as cake mix. According to the program, they are playing a duet called "Squadrons of the Air" but Daniel Daylight can't really tell; whatever the word "squadrons" means, it sounds like they are dropping bombs from the air on some poor hapless village. Next come two human girls, plump as bran muffins, red-haired, freckled, dressed in Virgin-Mary-blue smocks with long-sleeved white blouses, again aged ten years or so. They haven't even sat down on the bench when they charge like tanks into a duet called "Swaying Daffodils." For Daniel Daylight, the daffodils try desperately to sway first this way and then that but can't quite do it; to him, first they bang around, then leap about, then bang around some more, until they just droop from exhaustion, stems half-bent over, heads hanging down, sad daffodils, unlucky plants. They are next, he, Daniel Daylight, and she, Jenny Dean.

Daniel Daylight marches down the aisle that separates the Indian section of the huge auditorium from the white section. Jenny Dean joins him from the other side. Two hundred and fifty human people look at them as with the eyes of alligators, Daniel Daylight thinks, for he can feel them on his back, cold and wet and gooey. He shudders, then climbs the steps that lead to the stage and the upright piano, following the eight-year-old white girl Jenny Dean in her fluffy pink cotton dress with the white lace collar and shoulders that puff out like popcorn. They reach the piano. They sit down. From where he sits, Daniel Daylight can see Mr. Tipper looking up at him with eyes, he is sure of it, that say, "Go on, you can do it." Only twenty-five or so Indian people, mostly women, sit scattered around him, also looking up at him but with dark eyes that say nothing. On the room's other side, he can see the eyes that, to him, are screaming, "No, you can't; you can't do it. You can't do it at all." Feeling Jenny Dean's naked left arm pressing up against his own black-suited, white-shirted arm, he takes his right hand off his lap, raises it above the keyboard of the Heintzman upright. He can hear a gasp from the audience. Then he is sure he can hear the white side whispering to one another, "What's he doing there, little Indian boy, brown-skinned boy? His people cannot vote; therefore they are not human. Non-human boys do *not* play the piano, not in public, and not with human girls." Daniel Daylight, however, will have none of it. Instead, gentle as snow on spruce boughs at night, he lets fall his right hand right on the C-major chord.

Water-like, limpid, calm as silence, the chords for "Hearts and Flowers" begin their journey. Placed with care, every note of them on the keyboard by Daniel Daylight, they float, float like mist. The bass sneaks in, the melody begins. Playing octaves, Jenny Dean's hands begin at the two Cs above middle C, arc up to the G in a curve, smooth and graceful, then waft back down to the F, move on down to the E, and thence to the D, skip down to the B and thus swerve back up to the C whence they had started. The melody pauses, Daniel Daylight's series of major chords billow out to fill the silence, Jenny Dean's elegant melody resumes its journey. In love with the god-sound, Daniel Daylight sends his/her[1] waves, as prayer from the depths of his heart, the depths of his being, right across the vast auditorium, right through the flesh and bone and blood of some three hundred people, through the walls of the room, beyond them, north across the Moostoos River, through Waskeechoos, north to the Watson Lake Indian Residential School and thus through the lives of two hundred Indian children who live there, then northward and northward and northward until the sound waves wash up on the shores, and the islands, of vast Minstik Lake. And there, deep inside the blood of Daniel Daylight, where lives Minstik Lake and all her people, Daniel Daylight sees his parents, Cheechup Daylight and his wife, Adelaide, walking up the hill to the little voting booth at the little wooden church that overlooks the northern extremity of beautiful, extraordinary Minstik Lake with its ten thousand islands. And Daniel Daylight, with the magic that he weaves

[1]Like all North American Aboriginal languages (that I know of anyway, and there are a lot, fifty-two in Canada alone!), the Cree language has no gender. According to its structure, therefore, we are all, in a sense, he/shes, as is all of nature (trees, vegetation, even rocks), as is God, one would think. That is why I, for one, have so much trouble just thinking in the English language – because it is a language that is, first and foremost, "motored," as it were, by a theology/mythology that is "monotheistic" in structure, a structure where there is only one God and that god is male and male only. Other world systems are either "polytheistic" or "pantheistic" in structure, having, for instance (now or in the past, as in ancient Greece), room for gods who are female or even male/female, systems where all of nature, including sound, just for instance, simply "bristles," as it were, with divinity.

like a tiny little master, *wills* his parents to walk right past Father Roy in his great black cassock and into the booth with their worn yellow pencils. And there they vote. Frozen into place by the prayer of Daniel Daylight *and* his "flower," Jenny Dean, Father Roy can do nothing, least of all stop Cheechup Daylight and his wife, Adelaide, from becoming human.

Receiving, on stage, his trophy beside Jenny Dean from a human man in black suit, shirt, and tie – Mayor Bill Hicks of Prince William, has explained Mr. Tipper – Daniel Daylight beams at the crowd that fills, for the most part, the Kiwanis Auditorium in downtown Prince William, Manitoba. Both sides are standing, the Indian side with its two dozen people, the white side with its 250. And they are clapping. And clapping and clapping. Some of them, in fact, are crying, white and Indian, human and... well, they don't look non-human any more, not from where stands exulting – and weeping – the Cree Indian, *human* pianist Daniel Daylight.

Daniel Daylight sits inside Mr. Tipper's travelling car. It is cold – not cold, though, like outside, of this fact Daniel Daylight is quite certain. He looks out through the window on his right and, as always, sees white forest rushing by; maybe rabbits will bound past on that snowbank in the trees, he sits thinking. Snow falling gently, it looks to Daniel Daylight, like he is being hurtled through the heart of a giant snowflake. In his black-trousered lap, meanwhile, rests his trophy, a ten-inch-tall golden angel with wings outspread and arms wide open, beaming up at her winner through the glow of the travelling car's dashboard lights. On the radio, the music has stopped and people living in the east of the country, explains Mr. Tipper, are discussing a matter that takes Daniel Daylight completely by surprise: the Indian people of Canada, it seems, were given that day, the 31st of March, 1960, the right to vote in federal elections, in their own country.

"You see?" Daniel Daylight says to Mr. Tipper, his English, and his confidence, having grown quite nicely in just two months. "We are human. I knew it. And you know why I knew it, Mr. Tipper?"

"Why, Daniel Daylight?"

"Because I played it."

LAUREN B. DAVIS

Rat Medicine

I saw the first rat next to where we stored the chicken feed. It was a week before John used his fists on me. I was out by the sacks and felt like somebody was watching me. The hair stood up on places of my body where I didn't know I had hair. I put down the tin pail I used to scatter the feed and picked up a shovel leaning against the shed. We'd never had no trouble. Living so far out of town like we did criminal types didn't seem to have the gumption to haul ass all the way out to our place, but there was always a first time. I turned around and there he was, sitting back on his hind quarters like a little rat dog begging for a tidbit, up on the shed roof. He didn't flick a whisker, bold as brass. Just kept looking at me, his little front paws tucked up in front of his belly, his eyes bright as black glass.

"What do you think you're doing up there?" I said, but of course the rat didn't say nothing back.

"Don't think you can get in and eat up all this good feed." The rat kept looking at me, straight and firm-like.

"We got a big old tomcat round here. He's going be picking his teeth with your bones, my friend." If rats could be said to smirk, that's what he was doing.

Now, most people, they really hate rats. Not me. I don't hate anything about the animal kingdom. Not snakes, not spiders, not coyote, not buzzard. That's the Ojibway blood, from my mother's people. My Granny used to tell me, you dream about a rat, you dreaming about some sickness, maybe a bad one, soon to come on. Granny was usually right about these things. I set store in omens, in symbols and signs. It's all there if you know what to look for. So I looked at the rat, recognized it for a fellow who'd come to tell me something.

"You got news for me, rat man? If you do, you better tell me. I ain't got all day."

The rat cleaned behind his ears. Then he turned and stuck his bald tail straight in the air and disappeared toward the other side of the shed roof. I tried to get around to see where he was going, fast as my size would allow, but when I looked there weren't no sign of him.

I didn't tell John about the rat because I knew he'd just blame it on me. Tell me I didn't keep the place clean enough. Which was a lie, but true facts never matter much to John when he's got a good rage going. I got a couple of old oil drums John kept about the place and put the sacks of feed in there, put old boards on the top and weighted them down with rocks.

When John came back that night he was in a mood even fouler than the night before. His moods had been getting worse for some time. He slammed the screen door so hard I thought the wood frame'd splinter.

"Nell!" he yelled. "This place looks like a goddamn pigsty! What the hell do you do all day?"

There wasn't no point in answering. He was just looking for a fight.

"C'mon in here and get your dinner, John."

He sat down at the kitchen table, his filthy work boots leaving marks on my clean floor. He stank of sweat from working at the mill in this heat. 'Course he wouldn't have thought to wash up before dinner. I didn't dare say nothing. I served us both up our food and set the plates down on the table.

"Fat as you are," John said, "don't think you're going to be eating all that. Take half off, Nell. You need to lose some goddamn weight."

I just looked at him.

"I mean it. You are getting to be a big fat squaw. I can't hardly bear to look at you."

I am a big woman, I don't deny it. I wasn't always this size, though I never have been small. It was after John Jr. died that I really started packing it on. Seemed like I didn't want to do much more than try and fill up the hole his dying left.

Slipped away in his sleep, silent as a leaf falling in the dark, and him not a year old. But I found a way to keep going without turning mean, turning against the force of life: Which is more than I can say for his father. We'd lost the baby more'n three years then and John never did get over it.

That and the farm failing.

John said the reason the farm failed, why the crops all withered up and got ate by every sort of crawling creature, was the land was poison. Said the poison came from up the mine that started digging great wounds in the side of South Mountain. Well I don't know. Maybe yes, and maybe no. It wasn't that John didn't work hard, it's just he never had his father's touch. Everything just turned to rot as soon as he came near it. It made him bitter.

The worst was last month, when we couldn't make the mortgage. It hurt his pride, faced with the choice to go down to Rickett's mill and beg for work, or hand over the land that'd been in his family for generations to the bank. It was hard on a man, sure hard. Years of too little money and too much whiskey and a small town where a man could never get ahead of his reputation. John liked his whiskey more and more. Me, I never touched the stuff. My mother and grandmother both impressed on me that you didn't get to be no spirit walker with a bottle in your hand. That might be OK for whites, but it wasn't for Indians.

So I tried to understand. That's the way women are, I think, that's the medicine we carry. To try to understand a man and stay soft about it. But that don't mean the hurts aren't there, deep in the marrow.

I looked across the table and saw the contempt in his face. I scraped half my food off my plate, but it didn't matter. I'd lost my appetite anyway.

That night I dreamed about a rat. It was sitting on the roof, like some sort of weathervane. It faced east and its nose scented every little breeze that came along.

Three days later I was washing dishes, up to my arms in warm, soap-creamy water. I like washing dishes; it's like meditation, just looking out the window at the back garden. That year I'd put in nasturtiums, because I like their peppery taste and they look so pretty. I got a crop of the three sisters: corn, beans and squash, plus tomatoes, zucchini, carrots and such, set about with a border of marigolds to keep down the bugs. I have a good hand at gardens, although I don't brag about it, because it sets John off to distraction the way things just seem to jump to life under my fingers.

So, anyway, there I am, looking out the window and daydreaming about the sorts of things a woman daydreams about when her man don't want to touch her anymore, and I realize there's a face in the window looking back at me. A rat face. There's the bugger, just sitting on the windowsill, staring me down. His fur's all clean and glossy brown and he's got a white stomach and little pink ears. He reaches out and puts one little paw up against the glass. I put my finger up against the glass on my side. He doesn't budge and the two of us stay like that for a minute or so, like somebody visiting a prisoner in a jail, although it was hard to figure out who was who. I had half a mind to open the window up and let him in; I was almost getting fond of the little guy.

Lying out on warm stones back of the house was Oscar, our tomcat, and the mouser supreme. He stretched himself into one of those contortions only cats can do, all sinew and pretzel.

"You better get gone, little buddy," I said to the rat. The rat just looked at me and put both paws up on the window. I tapped on the glass, trying to scare him off. Oscar often jumped up on the sill so I could open the window and let him in, and I didn't want to see the little guy get eaten up. "Go on! Go on!" I hissed, trying not to draw Oscar's attention. Too late, Oscar was high-tailing it over, ready to pounce on the rat. I closed my eyes.

Next thing I heard was Oscar's whining meow, demanding to be let in. I opened my eyes, figuring the rat had taken a quick dive out of there. On one end of the ledge was Oscar, as expected, but on the other end, not a foot away, was the rat. Calm as a cream-fed cat himself, eyes directly on me. Oscar didn't even notice. I opened the window to let Oscar in, wondering if the rat planned on jumping in as well, but he stayed put. Oscar scattered in, upsetting a glass left to dry on the drain board. I dove to grab it before it fell to the floor. When I turned back, the rat was gone. I shook my head and looked at Oscar.

"Well, some fine hunter you are, you big hairball." Oscar looked at me with the same complete lack of interest he always has, unless there's fish guts involved.

That night, John threw his plate of food over my head where it shattered into a hundred pieces. Said the chops were burned, which was nonsense. He shoved me up against the counter and smeared a dishrag in my face. Told me to clean it up and fix him something decent to eat. By the time I cleaned it up and cooked him some new chops, crying all the while, he'd passed out in the barcalounger in front of the TV with a bottle of Jack Daniels in his fist. I put a blanket over him and left him there.

That night I dreamed a swarm of rats were churning under our bed, their tails all tied together in knots.

In the morning I had a big purple bruise on my hip from where I connected with the counter. I had five small, separate storm cloud-coloured bruises on my upper arm. As I fixed John coffee and eggs and didn't talk to him at all, he came up behind me and, seeing the marks, kissed every one of them and said he was sorry. His damp lips felt so good on my parched skin.

"I'm sorry baby, I'm sorry," he kept muttering. I could have sworn he shed a tear.

John is a good-looking man. The first time I saw him, coming to buy smoked fish off my Uncle Joe, and me only eighteen at the time, I was a goner. This big old cowboy in the skin-tight jeans was the one for me. Looked just like Clint Eastwood. Auntie Betty said I was crazy to go off and marry some white man. We didn't know his family stories, didn't know what kind of past he was hauling around with him. But I didn't care. My eyes were firmly focused on his round little white man's butt in those Levis.

"I don't know why you put up with me sometimes," he said, and cradled my face in his big callused hands. He said he was sorry again and took me in his arms right there in the kitchen. I forgave him. You bet I did.

Two days later I was sitting in the kitchen having coffee with my friend Joelle when I look up over her shoulder to the top of the refrigerator and what do I see but my rat pal looking out at me from in between the fat chef cookie jar and the empty plastic ice-cube trays.

"I'll be damned. Joelle, turn, around slow and look up on the top of the fridge."

"What?" she said.

"Up there, look! Look at that damn rat!"

"Rat!" she shrieked. "What rat?"

"There, right there – look at it!"

"What are you talking about? I don't see no rat."

"You don't see him. Right there. That rat?" The rat sat up on his haunches, spit into his paws and gave himself a good old cleaning.

"Where are you looking?"

"There, goddamn it! Washing his ears!" I pointed frantically.

"I don't know what you're smoking, but there is no rat on the refrigerator. You're giving me the creeps."

There were two of them. Something caught my eye. I looked over by the sink and there was another one.

"You don't see anything at all strange in this kitchen?" I asked.

"The only strange thing in this kitchen is you."

When Joelle left, I called over to the rez. I called my Auntie Betty.

"I got rat problems," I said.

"You got rats," Auntie Betty said, practical as always, "you got to go out to the field they live in and explain to them you ain't got no extras to go round but you'll try and leave them some of what you can spare if they agree to respect your stores."

"Ain't that kind of rat," I said.

"Well, what kind are they?"

"The kind only I can see. And I been dreaming about them, too."

"Oh. That kind of rat." She paused. "I'll call you back."

I knew she was going to go pray some and ask her spirits what was going on over at my place. I'm not as good at this direct stuff as she is. I drank two more cups of tea waiting for the phone to ring.

"You got problems in your house, eh?" she said. "You got marriage problems."

"Yeah, I know."

"He's got some bad stuff around him. Very dark stuff."

I didn't say anything. I remembered the look on his face when he threw the plate.

"He's got anger twisted up in him, that one. You got to be careful. You know what I mean?"

"What should I do?"

"What you asking me that for? You gonna listen to me? You gonna come back home? You gonna leave that white man?"

I didn't answer.

"Uh-huh," Auntie Betty said. "I thought so. OK, now you listen to me. Animals don't take the time out of their busy day unless they got serious business. You hear me?"

"I hear."

"You got to listen to them. You got a bad sickness coming into your house. You need to clear things out. I don't know if it's too far gone, but you got to smudge out your house good. You got sweetgrass? You got sage?"

"Yeah."

"Well, use' em. Smoke that house up good, smoke your bed up good. Put a red blanket on the bed."

"OK."

"Then you go get these plants and boil 'em up. Drink the tea." She named some herbs and plants.

"One thing, Nell. One thing I got to ask. Is he hitting you?"

"Naw. Not really."

"What the hell is 'not really?' Either he is, or he ain't! You better get ready. His anger's gonna bust out all over you. I'll do what I can, but I don't know. You should come home for a while."

"I can't. I love him, Auntie."

"Love! Phooey! Should go back to the old ways! Let your aunties pick you out a good red man. Stay where we can keep an eye on you! You young people! All the same!" She went on for a while, but I didn't listen much. I knew this part by heart. And besides, I was too busy watching the rats run back and forth from the bedroom to the bathroom.

"Nell? You listening?"

"Yes, Auntie."

"OK, one last thing. Fat as you are these days, you ain't gonna be able to dodge him if he comes at you. You offer tobacco to these rats and ask them for a tuft of their hair. You braid it into your hair. That'll make you nimble like they are. Give you a chance if you need it."

"I never heard that one before."

"Yeah, well, it ain't strictly ours, eh? That one's from Africa. I learned it from that black nurse works with me midwifing. We trade stuff sometimes. Don't matter. All the same medicine. You just use it, you hear? Spirit rats or flesh and blood, they'll give you what you need. They're here to help."

"Yes, Auntie."

I promised to call her tomorrow and made her promise not to tell my mother, not to tell my brothers, for what good it would do. I know how gossip passed around out on the rez. Wouldn't be long before everybody knew what was going on at my house. Which maybe wasn't such a bad thing. Get a few of the old timers burning tobacco for me. Long as my brother Jimmy didn't find out. He'd be over wanting to kick some white man's butt.

I went out and offered my tobacco and found a tuft of rat fur up on the windowsill. I braided it in my hair. I picked the herbs. I drank the tea. I smudged the house. I put the red blanket on the bed.

It was Sunday the next day, and I knew John'd be out drinking with his buddies late that night. It could go either way. Maybe he'd just come home and pass out. Maybe he'd come home mean. I slept with one eye open, tucked up under the protection blanket. I didn't see no rats, but didn't know if that was a good thing or a bad. Rats abandon a sinking ship, or a house where there's a fire coming.

I heard the truck skid through the gravel around 3:00 a.m. He was drunk as a cowboy after a long dry cattle drive. He came in the kitchen, slamming stuff around and stumbling and cursing as he barked his shins and banged his elbows. I heard him pissing in the bathroom, then heard him coming down the hall. He stood in the doorway a few minutes, swaying. I knew he couldn't see my open eyes, dark as the room was, and I sure wasn't going to close them, not knowing what was coming. He took a couple of wide-legged steps toward the bed, trying to keep his balance, and finally toppled like a cut pine across my body. I heaved him over and left him snoring on top of the red blanket. Man, he smelled bad. Whiskey and smoke and beer and, although it broke my heart to admit it, some woman other than me.

I got up and went to the living room and cried myself to sleep, dreaming about rats on river rafts and rats in sewer drains and rats caught in traps.

I woke up the next morning to the sound of John puking. I went to fix him some coffee and orange juice, figuring that'd be about all his stomach could handle. I reached into the cupboard to get his favourite mug, the big one with the bucking bronco on the side of it. Sitting in it, with his little pink paws hooked over the top, was the rat.

"Morning, little buddy," I said. The rat jumped out and stood next to the coffee-pot. I opened the fridge to get the orange juice. A rat sat on the stack of cheese slices. He didn't budge when I reached in. I wondered if he'd learned how to turn the light on in there when the door was closed.

I heard John behind me and turned. He was still in his boots, his jeans, only his shirt was gone, and I guess he'd puked on it. Even mad at him as I was, there was a twinge down in my belly at the sight of his naked chest, all hard muscle and sinew, his stomach flat, with pale golden hair running down into the top of his jeans. There was a rat sitting on the top of his head, yanking up his hair between its long pointy teeth.

"Oh, man. My head's killing me." His eyes were bloodshot and yellowish, like two ketchup-covered eggs with runny yolks.

"Serves you right." I wanted him to be hurting. I handed him his coffee. The rat on his head jumped off and disappeared into the living room.

"I ain't in the mood, Nell."

"But I guess you were in the mood last night." I stood with my hands on my hips. I could feel the hurt starting to switch around to righteous anger. I knew I should keep my mouth shut, but I was too mad, too hurt.

"Leave it alone." His voice was ragged and dangerous.

"I don't want to leave it alone. You smelled like a goddamn whorehouse when you came in last night, you bastard. I want to know who you been with!" Out of the corner of my eye I could see a flurry of rat fur, diving under counters, through the window, skittering around door jams, and out of the room.

He slammed the cup down on the table, sloshing the coffee over the rim. His hands balled up into fists. He leaned towards me.

"Well you can bet your fat ass it was somebody under 200 pounds."

Tears sprang to my eyes and my face went red.

"Look at yourself, you think any man'd want you?" He ran his eyes up and down my body and sneered. "You used to be a good-looking woman, but now you ain't nothing but a sack of lard."

"I am a good wife to you, John McBride. I can't help it if I gained weight."

"What the hell do you mean, you can't help it? I ain't the one stuffing food down your throat! If you'd get off your floppy ass and do some work around this place, maybe you'd lose some of it, maybe I'd want you again!"

"I do all the work around this place! You don't spend long enough here to do no work."

"You saying I'm to blame for how disgusting you got? You blaming me, bitch?"

He took two steps toward me and I backed up until I found myself up against the counter.

"I ain't blaming you, but goddamn John, it ain't me who's the problem here – it's you!" I couldn't stop myself. "Out whoring around, mean drunk all the time – I ain't gonna take it no more, you understand?"

I didn't even see the blow coming.

Even with the rat fur charm braided in my hair, I couldn't duck the first punch or the second, or the one after that. I lost count then. He went for my face, I guess, because it would be the place where the hurt would show the most. Proof that there was some small spot in the world where he could have an effect. My nose. My lips. My cheeks.

I went down, and, a gal my size... well, I went down hard and stayed down. I could see his boots in flashes of motion, misted in red.

I think it was all this flesh that saved me from getting worse than I got, and that was bad enough. But I was bundled way down deep inside the womb of myself and even though his hands left bruises, they didn't break no bones. It didn't hurt. I kept thinking it should hurt more, but it just felt like numbness everywhere, great stains of frozen places bursting out from under his icy fists and feet.

"John, John..." I just kept repeating in a whisper. My heart speaking to his, willing him to hear me, see me, to stop... You're breaking me, I thought, you're breaking me apart. Then everything went quiet.

I could hear ragged breathing, great gulps of wet sobbing air. I thought it was me, but my moans were underneath that lung-punctured sound. I took my hands away from my face and as I did I heard my Auntie's voice, steel-strong and even.

"You step back, John McBride. Step back now."

I looked up at my husband. He stood over me, his face a twisted, crooked thing. Tears poured down his cheeks. His stomach heaved. He looked down at me as though he had no idea of how I'd fallen. He brought his bloody fists up in front of his own eyes and began to howl like a wild dog. He pounded his own face, first with his right hand, then his left, sparing no force.

"Bastard!" he cried. "Bastard!"

"Stop this! Stop this now! You hear me!" Auntie Betty stood in the doorway behind John. She filled the space with her square bulk. Her long grey braid was decorated with megis shells. She was dressed for serious ceremony work. Ribbons in her spirit colours on her skirt and blouse. Medicine pouch. In her left hand she carried the hawk-wing fan, in her right the sweetgrass basket containing her pipe, tobacco, other things known only to her.

John hit himself square in the face with both fists.

Auntie Betty put her basket down and walked up behind him. She reached up and smacked him on the back of the head.

"Don't be any more of a jackass than you already are. There's been enough hitting for one day, eh?" She glared at him as he spun around. She raised the hawk-wing fan and fluttered a circle in the air around his head. John let out a strangled noise, clamped his hand to his mouth and pushed past her out the door. I heard retching noises.

"Good. Puke up all that bad stuff," said Auntie Betty, coming toward me. "Come on, little one, let's see what kind of shape you're in." She bent down and helped haul me to my feet. I was shaky. There was blood on my dress, dripping down from my nose.

"Looks like I got here just in time. You'll live. Could hear it in the wind this morning. Time to come visit. Had Jimmy drop me off in the truck down the road a ways. Didn't think this'd be the time for him to come calling." She leaned me up against the counter and ran the tap water good and cold. She wet down a tea towel and put it in my hand. "Press that up against your face. You need ice." She waddled her wide, bowlegged walk to the fridge.

I started to cry, salty tears burning into my split lip. I heard the tires of our pickup squeal as John skidded out the drive and down the road.

"Don't waste your time crying, girl." She rolled ice in a plastic baggy. "Here, use this. What we need is a cup of tea. He's not coming back for a while. I guarantee. Sit," she ordered, and I did as I was told as she puttered around my kitchen and fixed the tea. She reached into her basket and took out a skin pouch, sprinkled some herbs into the teapot. "This'll help the hurts, inside and out."

I didn't feel much of anything just then, except glad Auntie Betty was there, glad someone else was taking control of things. I felt as limp as a newborn baby and just as naked. We drank the tea. I held the ice to my swelling-up eye. Auntie Betty held my hand.

Later she reached into her basket.

"I brought this for you," she said, and laid a carton of rat poison on the counter. "You got yourself a vermin problem."

"Poison?" I knew Auntie would never suggest such a thing, it went against the natural respect she had for one of all her relations, spirit rats or full bone and fur. "I don't need that," I said, my chest tight as a drum.

"I think you do. You got these kinda rats, you got to get rid of 'em. White man's rats need white man's measures. This here's white man's poison."

"You can't be serious. You've lost your mind!"

"No, and you better remember to respect your elders! I ain't lost my mind, but you better start using yours. I ain't talking about poisoning nobody, not that some people don't deserve it," she snorted with disdain, "but I been giving it some thought. Rat spirit chose to show up here, not no other. No bear or wolf or snake."

"You're scaring me, Auntie, and I been scared enough for one day."

"Well, let it be the last day anything scares you. You shed that fear skin and maybe you'll shed that fat skin too. Oh, don't look at me that way, you know it's true. Big woman's a fine thing, but not the way you're going at it. You can't grow another baby in you by trying to stuff if down your mouth. You weren't meant to be as big as you are, you ain't got the bones for it, not like me." She patted her belly and cackled. "But that'll take care of itself once you start taking care of yourself, and for now, that means getting rid of this big old rat."

"He didn't mean it. You saw how sorry he was. It's the pressure. We been going through some hard times."

"What a load of horse shit! Times is always hard. That ain't no excuse for what that man's doing. He needs to learn."

"I can't leave him."

"You can and you will. He might be able to get away with taking out his shit on soft-minded little white women, but no Indian woman's gonna stand for it." She leaned over and took both my hands in hers, looked into my battered up face.

"You think he's gonna stop unless you make him stop? You think it's not going to just get worse? Don't you watch Oprah?"

I didn't say nothing.

"Nellie. Answer me. You think it's gonna get any better unless he knows he's gone too far, knows exactly what it's cost him? Look me in the eye and tell me that."

She was right. I knew she was right and it caved in my heart to know it.

"I know."

"Well then."

"But Auntie, I..."

"Don't you even think about telling me you love that man! The man you fell in love with is gone. I don't know whether he'll be back or not, but what you got living in this house with you at the moment, sure as hell is not a man to love. This is an evil thing, all twisted over on itself." I made a motion to protest. "Don't interrupt me. Sometimes you put poison out for rats and like magic they disappear. Seems like they know it just ain't safe no more." She looked at me, her eyes flashing like stars among the wrinkles. "You understand?"

And I did.

She stayed all afternoon, and as night fell she smudged the house up good. Then she called Jimmy and had him pick her up. She waited out at the end of the driveway so he wouldn't come in and see me. Jimmy'd be just as likely to go off into town with his rifle and look for John, and nobody wanted that kind of trouble.

John didn't come home that night, and I shouldn't have expected him because Auntie Betty'd told me as much. Still, I lay in bed all night straining to hear the sound of his tires on the gravel. I finally fell asleep around dawn, too tired to mind the aches and pains, and didn't dream about nothing at all.

The next day I fasted. I smudged the house again. Around my neck I put the leather pouch with the lightening stone in it that Auntie'd given me. She'd dug up the round red stone from between the roots of a tree where lightening'd struck last spring.

It was powerful protection. I wore my ribbon dress. Green ribbons, white ribbons, black and rose. This was my ceremony.

I fixed the food just so. All the things John liked. Fried chicken. Lima beans. Mashed potatoes. Carrot salad with raisins.

I heard the truck in the yard just before 6:00 a.m. I took a deep breath. Smoothed my hair. Said a prayer. I heard the screen door shut and then John was in the kitchen. He stood in the doorway, a bunch of red roses in his hand. He was wearing the shirt I'd given his brother Philip last Christmas, so I knew where he'd spent the night. His hair was combed down neat. He looked like a school kid showing up at my door to pick me up for a date.

"Jesus Nellie, I'm so sorry. I'm gonna spend the rest of my life making it up to you, I swear." He winced when he looked at me. My left eye was swollen and black, my lips were swollen, my cheek had a big bruise on it. I looked a mess. He didn't mention my clothes, although I was in what he called "Squaw gear."

"Come on baby. You just got to forgive me. It'll never happen again, I mean it, cross my heart. Here, sweetheart." He held out the flowers. I took them but didn't say nothing. I put them in the sink. He came to put his arms around me from behind. I cringed as he squeezed my bruised ribs.

"Don't," I said.

"OK, OK. I'm sorry." He put his hands up like I was holding a gun on him and backed away. "Christ. I really am sorry, Baby. I don't know what got into me. You know how much I love you."

"I fixed some food for you. Fried chicken. Your favourites," I said.

"Oh, Honey, you're just the best. I knew you wouldn't stay mad at me." He hugged me and this time I let him. His arms felt so good. for a second I felt safe there. Then I pushed him away.

"Sit down."

John swung his long leg over the back of the chrome chair and sat, a grin on his face. I opened the oven and brought the plate I'd kept warming over to him. Then I went back and leaned up against the kitchen counter, next to the open box of rat poison. He picked up his knife and fork.

"Where's yours?" he said.

"I'm not eating. This here's special food. Just for you, eh?"

"I don't want to eat alone, Sugar."

"But I want you to."

He looked puzzled. He looked down at his plate. Looked back over to me and then his eyes flicked to the box of poison. The colour drained out of his face.

"No," he said.

"Why not?" I asked, folding my arms against my chest.

"You eat it," he said.

"Fine," I said. "See, it just don't matter to me anymore." I made a move toward the table, leaned over the plate, brushing my heavy breasts against his shoulder. I took the fork out of his hand and shoveled up a gob of mashed potatoes. I chewed it up and swallowed. He looked at me. I offered him the fork.

"Go ahead," I said.

"No. Eat some of the chicken."

I cut off a piece of chicken and ate it. "Um, um. I sure am a good cook. Yessir. That's one thing you're gonna miss."

He pushed his chair away from the table and stood up.

"What're you talking about?"

"I going home John. I'm leaving you." I felt it then. Knew my heart had just broken.

"You ain't going nowhere." The colour rushed back into his face, his eyes dark and cloudy.

"Yes I am. And, John McBride, you're going to let me walk out that door and drive back to where you found me. You know why?" I walked back over to the counter and stood near the poison. "Because if you don't, you will never eat another meal in this house without wondering. You will never get another good night's sleep."

"Bitch!" he said, in a rush of air like he'd been punched. He made a move toward me.

I stood my ground, drew myself up and out, became full of myself and my own spirits.

"You will never hit me again and live." I spoke very slowly, softly. "Is this what you want to be doing when you go to meet your maker, John?"

He heard me. I watched my husband's face crumple. He slumped down on the chair and put his head in his hands.

"Don't leave me. I'm begging you. Don't go."

I walked into the bedroom and picked up the bag I'd packed that afternoon. I carried it back into the kitchen. I picked up the keys to the truck from where he'd left them on the hook beside the door.

"You take care now," I said. "I'll have Jimmy drop the truck back later." I closed the door behind me, and started walking, but I could still hear him crying. I stopped by the shed and put down a tobacco tie and some corn and seed for the rats, saying thank you. I didn't see them, but I knew they were around.

Walking to the truck was like wading through hip-deep mud, but I made it. I drove down the road back to the rez and felt like I was dragging my heart all the way, tied to the back of the bumper like an old tin can.

NIIGONWEDOM JAMES SINCLAIR

TRICKSTER REFLECTIONS

Millennia later the [Anishinaubaeg] dreamed Nanabush into being. Nanabush represented themselves and what they understood of human nature. One day his world too was flooded. Like Geezhigo-quae, Nanabush recreated his world from a morsel of soil retrieved from the depths of the sea.

—BILL JOHNSON

"Is That All There Is? Tribal Literature"

One of trickster's primary modi operandi, *shape-shifting, the power to move fluidly beyond static definitions of cultural boundaries and taboos, is an impulse with both positive and destructive possibilities. Celebrating tricksters, it seems to me, should be done with caution. It is important to remember that shape-shifting can also be a form of witchery and that tricksters can be oppressive assholes as often as liberators – just check out the stories.*

—CRAIG S. WOMACK

Red on Red: Native American Literary Separatism

Boozhoo.

I have a Trickster story. It is my own. It is also now yours.

It's sometimes told out loud, but for now I share it here, with you.

You are there. So I am here. And so are you.

We're both in both, at once in this story, listening, speaking, writing, reading. We are in this together.

That's the trick.

It's always, for our entire lives.

Everywhere.

I open books and you are there. I speak and you are all I say. I write these words and you come out. Like here. And here.

You. You. You. You.

In this story.

Now.

Every morning, every day, every moment of my life you have been there. Even when I could not see you. I now know that you were around watching, listening, stalking, tricking me. Like a shadow. Like a reflection I can't walk away from.

Today you are lying right there, beside me, snoring – so loud in fact I've woken up with a headache. I stand up and you do. I scratch myself and you do. I drink some water and you do.

Luckily, you haven't woken her up. She lies with her back to us, her only movement the pulse of her steady breaths. I don't turn on the light, for fear that she might see you. Of course, I know she won't.

Ugh. Your breath is awful. What a stench. I gag. Raising my hands to my mouth, I smell your scent on my hands. I taste you on my lips. My tongue is covered by your hair. That's it. I race to the toilet. I'm throwing up, just like usual. Again. Disgusting.

I undress and get into the shower. I leave the glass door open, just a bit, hoping that you will come inside. You don't. I'm not surprised. You never clean yourself, although you badly need it. As usual, you stand outside and draw pictures in the condensation, just so I can see them. Oh yeah, there's that bird again. A tree. A man with squiggly lines coming out of his mouth. Good for you. That's what you always do – draw the same stupid pictures that make no sense.

Then I hear you opening the closet and throwing all of the clean towels onto the floor. You're pissing on them now. Oh the stink. You jerk.

Thank god I am here, in the shower, away from you. I can get away from your smell, at least for a while. I can clean myself with this fresh, hot water. I can wipe you off, close my eyes, and imagine you are gone. In the pool of my mind you don't exist, for just a second. There, I can escape you.

But I can't stay forever. I have work to do.

I step out, dripping, and see your mess. You've shit all over the sink and wiped your ass on the wall.

You've done it again. You've made a disaster. And, like always, I have to clean up, clear away the messes you create, the problems you leave behind. Every day. You infuriate me. You nauseate me. You irritate me. And, I think, with each piece of chaos, you might be killing me.

You. You. You. You.

I wipe the sink, the floor, the wall, and try not to get any of you on me. Throwing the towels in the garbage, I walk into our bedroom, leaving tiny puddles of water on the carpet. She'll be upset, but I'm in a hurry.

You're already there, of course, gazing at her peacefulness. You must have been there for a while – there's a pool of drool surrounding your feet.

Stop it. Stop looking at her. Stop touching yourself. Stop salivating, you creep. Get away from her. You will never have her. I promise you that. You don't deserve jer. You don't deserve anything, nothing at all, only what you have brought to me. Anger. Hate. Pain. Tricks.

Hee hee hee heeeeee, you moan. Hee hee hee heeeeee. Hee hee hee heeeeee. Hee hee hee heeeeee.

She sighs, reaches down, and pulls the blanket around her. I hear her breathing continue.

Thank god. A least she can shut you out.

I don't want to leave. But I have to. There is no choice.

It wouldn't matter if I stayed, would it. You wouldn't leave. You are my problem. My responsibility. I must get rid of you, somehow, someday, if only to free her from you.

I open my underwear drawer and find it empty. Again. Another trick. Hearing you in the closet, I open the door and there you are, wiping pairs of my gitch on your sweaty chest. I pick up one pair and they're damp and most, hair everywhere. Fantastic.

I put on my shirt and tie. You, of course, stay naked, if that's what you are. With all of your long black hair it's hard to tell. Just stay over there while I put on my socks and pants. No, don't put your ass in my face. Ugh. Why don't you clean yourself? Why are you the same disgusting creature every day?

I open the hallway window, mostly to see if it is raining. You're there, of course, standing on the ledge peering back in at me. You stare at me while I look over your shoulder and avoid your eyes. It's the only way I can see anything, you're so fat.

Hmph. No clouds.

I close the glass, lock it, and put the key in my wallet. Maybe that will keep you out. Nope, there you are, at the bottom of the stairs.

Dammit, it's like you're one step ahead of me, choosing where I will go and then pulling me along. Get lost, you. Go away. Listen, for once.

Oh, dammit. Is that the downstairs clock? It's seven o'clock. I'm late.

I race down the stairs, get to the front door, and grab my jacket. You are there, eating my shoes. Get away. I wipe your dripping saliva off and slide them on. I feel my socks squish beneath my toes.

Slamming the front door, I spring down the path to my car. You're there, sitting in the back seat, licking the back window.

Why didn't I lock the car? Did I? Would it have mattered?

Shit. I forgot to kiss her goodbye. You did it again. You made me forget her.

Hee hee hee heeeeee, you laugh. Hee hee hee heeeeee. Hee hee hee heeeeee. Hee hee hee heeeeee.

I retreat into the silence and drive. You breathe heavier and heavier as I drive faster and faster, in and out of traffic on the expressway. We pull up next to a Jeep Cherokee with three women in business suits in it. Stop it, you. I can hear you rubbing yourself, looking at them. I purposely turn down side streets, just so we don't meet any more people along the way.

Finally. Now I can get to work. Slamming the car door I reach for my briefcase and find that you've opened it and spread your filth all over my papers. Underneath, I find the remnants of you playing with yourself. I feel puke enter my throat, but hold it in.

At work I get into trouble from the man in the white pressed shirt. He doesn't want to hear why but I try to tell him anyways.

It's him. He's the reason I'm late. I know you can't see him. I'm not crazy. What do you mean I want special treatment? Go fuck yourself. Go ahead, tell on me. No, hold on. Listen, I'm sorry. I need this job. I'm sorry. I know it. It won't happen again. I'm sorry.

You always get me into trouble, don't you. You don't care about time. You don't care about money. You don't care about responsibility. Well, I have to. I have to make money. I have to pay for the house, the car, the food, the cable TV. I'm not living in your world, where nothing means anything. You're living in mine.

Walking into the maze of white and grey cubicles, I see that you've gotten into my square before me. You're wearing my headset, spinning in my chair, splitting my pencils, making so much noise my head hurts. You've eaten my mouse, stapled my files together, swallowed my newspaper, written on the memo I was writing. I can't work with you here. I can't do anything. I never can. Never. Never. Never. Never.

Hee hee hee heeeeee, you giggle. Hee hee hee heeeeee. Hee hee hee heeeeee. Hee hee hee heeeeee.

You need to go. I need to have meaning again. I need to know a time without you. I need to be alone.

There was, of course, a time before you came into my life. Well, at least I think you weren't there. Maybe if I remember, maybe if I imagine, you will leave again.

A time before you.

In a little brown boy, alone, waiting on the curb for his father to come and pick him up.

Friday. It was always on Friday when Dad would come get me. The good days were when he was on time. The bad days were others, in the moments of waiting, always waiting. Waiting for rituals. Waiting for stories. Waiting for laughter. Waiting for him.

I was lost in the waiting.

Home was painful hoping, invisible nothingness, wondering if Dad would come. Sitting at the end of my driveway, under that tree with my bike, waiting for the glimpse of a bumper, made it all easier. I kept busy. I watched that woodpecker. I played with stones. I sang to myself.

Other times I practised what I would do when Dad arrived. It was theatrical. Imagining that he was here. I looked away from the driveway, playing. At the last second, I pretended I saw him, turned, grabbed my bike, and raced down the pavement, trying to beat his car to the house I practised in front of an absent audience. I got it down so perfectly I memorized every bump, every pothole. Eventually, when he did arrive, I always beat him to the front door.

But, mostly, I just waited. Waited for Dad to come. Waited for the bumper to turn the corner. Waited for the soft candies that always sat beside him. Waited for the laughing to begin.

When he arrived, I knew he would be as happy as I was, joking, laughing. Then he would tell me funny stories – mostly ones that I knew were untrue, but I didn't care. They would be about how he created the world, gave the buffalo a hump, made the heaven have a flat tail. He told me hilarious stories about hunting, fishing, camping, and about the time he caught blindfolded ducks. Other times, he told me he had chased the sun, swam and played with the fish, and fooled his grandmother by pretending to be a rock.

I would laugh and laugh. You're lying, I would say. You're a postal worker, not a hunter. You don't even have a tent. You live in a house. No one can talk to animals.

Laughing, Dad would hug me, tell me he loved me, and then tell me about his new life, his new home, my new sister, and how my grandfather was doing.

Together, on the expressway, we would joke and laugh, ride and laugh, laugh, laugh, laugh. I never wanted it to stop. I loved those times.

One day, at the end of a story, he told me to tell him one.

I don't know any, I said. The truth was, I didn't know any that he would laugh at.

Tell me about your school, he said, or the books you are reading.

I have a good teacher, I said.

Oh yeah, he asked, is your teacher still teaching you that Columbus discovered America?

No, I said. I told her what you told me to say. Columbus didn't discover anything. She told me that I was right. It was Jacques Cartier who discovered Canada. He's the one who founded the land.

Well, what about Indians, he asked. What about our ancestors?

My teacher told me that Indians didn't know about countries and land. We knew about animals and trading, but Cartier brought Thanksgiving, laws, and government. She told me it's important that I know the truth about Canada's history. So, I memorized it all. I can tell you who the first leader was in Canada, Dad. Do you know? Sir John A. Macdonald. He was followed by Alexander Mackenzie and then John Abbott.

H said nothing, sitting quiet for a long time. It's like he was mad or something. See, I said to myself, my stories aren't funny. He said nothing until we got to his house.

It was then that I decided to never tell him true stories ever again. Made up ones were way funnier.

But I didn't know any good stories. I never hunted, talked to animals, lived in the bush. I never even pretended I was a rock to fool anyone. I needed help.

So I went to my teacher and she gave me a book.

Read this, she said. It will help you.

I looked at the cover. *Myths of the Indian.*

But there were scary pictures. Stories with big words I didn't understand. And lots of maps. Maybe Dad was right.

I recognized some of the stories as similar to the ones my dad told me, like the one about the blindfolded ducks. Others I didn't.

On one page I found a picture that said it was a story. It looked like this.

It said that the story was about a boy and his father. Just like us, I thought. I would show him this story. I didn't know what I would say about it, but I'm sure my dad would find something funny to say about it – he always did. I would show him that I knew hot to tell a good story, show him that I could make him laugh too.

Carrying the book in my backpack, I waited all week. That Friday I waited and watched the clock all afternoon, hoping it would move faster so I could see him.

Racing home, I didn't even go inside. I just sat there, under the tree, and waited at the end of the driveway.

It got dark. I practised until my legs hurt. I sat under the streetlamp, just so Dad could see me. I made as many piles of stones as I could. I watched the woodpecker for hours. I sang. I played until it was dark and I was alone.

In the dim light I opened up the book with the picture and the story. I strained to read. It was very dark. Giving up, I tried to remember what the story was, what the words on the page had said. I tried telling the story out loud. Frustrated, I found I couldn't remember all of the parts. I tried just making up stuff I couldn't recall, but nothing felt quite right. Exhausted, I just waited. I had the time. There was nowhere else to go.

I remember that night, so dark, so black, with only bright stars overhead. I remember the blinking streetlight. I remember being lonely. I remember waiting, thinking I got the day wrong. I remember being furious when I knew I hadn't.

I remember waiting and that Dad didn't come. I remember wanting to forget my dad as soon as he told me his first story. I remember hoping that Dad liked mine, even if I cheated. I remember being angry, looking at my story. I remember ripping out all of the pages from the book and throwing them on the ground. I remember Mom calling to me, telling me that it was time for bed.

What does a story matter, anyways, I thought. It's not mine. I'll just think of one myself. It doesn't matter.

Reaching for my bike, I left that empty book on the ground with the ripped out pages. Turning around, I grabbed my bike and headed on home.

Then, I heard you.

Hee hee hee heeeeee, you giggled. Hee hee hee heeeeee. Hee hee hee heeeeee. Hee hee hee heeeeee.

Where did you come from? Were you listening? Were you watching? Were you here the whole time? Were you waiting for me? Were you telling this story?

For the first time, I smelled you deeply, gagged, and choked. You appeared all of a sudden, your hair all over your body, your hunched shoulders, thick legs, shifting eyes, and that huge gaping mouth with no teeth. You were small then, not the fat slob you would become. Nevertheless, you started eating right away. It didn't take you long to swallow half the tree.

Are you real? I asked.

You, of course, ignored me, leaves falling from your mouth. When I grabbed a few up off the ground, then you stared at me.

I remember being scared. You were frightening to look at, especially the first time. I hopped on my bike and pedalled to get away, crying. You followed, and I thought you were going to kill me. You suddenly appeared in front of me and I swerved and fell, scraping my knees and breaking my glasses. It was then that I realized, for the first time, that you had powers. I left my bike and ran into my house, hoping I could escape.

All night, you were everywhere, causing trouble. In the kitchen. In the bathroom. In my room. In my bed. Everywhere was you, your smell, your ugly face. I tried to get away. I tried to hide. I tried to run. You have been there since.

I didn't see Dad again, until years later, in the big room with the old man in the black robes. I couldn't concentrate because you were there, eating the desk, playing with his wig, playing with yourself on his desk. I could barely hear that old man when he was talking to me.

What do you want? he asked me.

I don't want him in my life, I said, pointing at you.

Sole custody mother, supervised visitation rights father, the old man said.

No, I meant him. Not you, Dad. Not you. Not you.

My dad gave me a hug, told me he loved me, and I scarcely ever saw him again. When I did, he was tense, nervous, and sad, and even when I asked him to tell me stories, he wouldn't. Then, he started just to phone me. Years later, he stopped coming.

Please come back, Dad. I don't mind waiting. I don't care. Please, just come back.

It was weeks later when I realized your trick. You did it, I realized. You kept my father from coming that Friday. You tricked him, and then you tricked me. You're the one who did all of this. You wanted me all to yourself. You're an asshole.

And now, you play tricks on me all the time. When I draw, when I write, all I can create is you. You are all that comes out on the page. The disgusting pictures that I create are of you. You. You. You. Always you. I hate drawing, writing, living, like I hate you.

There is no reason to look back at that time. There are no answers there. There is only now, where you are today. I have to deal with you now. Now. Now. Now. Now.

I don't know what trick you are going to play next.

No one knows you are here. Even in this office, when I tell people to look, they say they can't see you. You are everywhere, I tell them. Right there, beside you.

They say I make no sense. I should go to a doctor, they say. I have been, I respond. I have seen doctors, psychiatrists, herbalists, yoga instructors, professors, bartenders. Once a guy in a New Age bookstore told me that seeing must be a gift. I said that he was wrong and told him your hand was on his crotch.

One time, I went to a real medicine man. He didn't tell me where he was from. He was an Indian, though. He told me that he could do a purification for me and it would wash you away. He sang and beat a drum. He told me to dance. Then, when it was over, he asked me for fifty dollars and there you were, laughing behind him, waving your ass.

I gave him a hundred. Keep the change, I told him.

I turn on my computer and you are all over my keyboard. The letters are covered in slivers of your hair and drops of your saliva. When I finally wipe them clean, I open my files and they are filled with descriptions of you. I read yesterday's reports, and they are covered with images of you laughing. My e-mails are all from you. My desktop is a photo of your huge, black mouth. You. You. You. You. Nothing else. What mean games you play on me.

I go to the bathroom to hide in the stall. I hold the door shut, but you eventually grunt and struggle as you open it and squeeze in there with me. You poop with me, beside me, through me, all over me. Oh, the stink. Not again.

At lunch you eat my food. You munch off of my plate, burping, farting, swallowing whole everything. As always, you grow fatter with everything you consume. I am hungry but can't eat because being around you makes me want to get sick, so I push my tray towards you, and you swallow the orange plastic completely.

I try to work when I get called to the boss's office to copy down every word he says.

Copy this down, he says. Memo. For Press Release. I Cappuccino Meaning, President and CEO of www.redman.com do hereby announce that, following the traditions of our – ahem – more cultural brethren, from now on we will have all of our encyclopaedic entries on Indian cultures free for everyone. There will be no rules, no owners, no standards. All of our existing webpages, newspapers, picture books, and e-mails will be editable, and members of the public are now encouraged to come and add their two cents. And don't worry, everyone will be right. We're also going to stop publishing anything new on paper, and – as of next year – open up our new 24-hour information centre built in the style of a real-life teepee where real-life old Indians will share oral stories and laughter. We will be completely authentic and real, and all of us can do whatever we want with whatever we hear. This will be the last word I will ever speak on paper. Thank you. Oh, I mean, ho ho ho ho.

My boss is fat, pompous and rude, but, hoping that he will promote me, I tell him he's lost some weight. You laugh at his jokes about his wife and roll on the floor at the stupidity that is yourself. You help yourself to his cigars, swallow them, and lick the covers of his books. I see your hairs on top of his Indian Entrepreneur of the Year Award, so I know you must have done something with that. Of course, you rub the photo of his wife on your crotch. I hand him the memo, and he laughs at the pictures of you I have drawn and tells me to come back tomorrow. Then, he tears it up and throws the pieces in the air.

Go and tell someone what I told you, my boss announces.

No wonder I am in this dead-end job. It's the same thing every day. I am unable to advance, to evolve, to grow, to do anything that would impress anyone. I will never get promoted.

Getting back to my cubicle I collapse into my chair. I feel the cold plastic grooves sticking into my ass because you've eaten the cushion.

I am paralyzed. It's always the same crap. It's killing me. You're killing me.

Hee hee hee heeeeee, you whisper. Hee hee hee heeeee. Hee hee hee heeeeee. Hee hee hee heeeeee.

I finish work and run away. I take the stairs, and I hear you having behind me.

You never run, do you. Your fat belly can't keep up to me. I run and you are far behind. I race to the exit and feel my eyes screaming at the pain of the afternoon light, my legs throbbing at the newness of motion. I squint as I sprint through the parking lot.

I get to my car and rip open the door. I lock it. I lock all of them. Even if I get a few second until you get here, I am safe. I am alone. I close my eyes.

Of course, I am only playing a trick on myself.

I drive away. You're there. I can smell you. I can hear you struggling to breathe, and I feel the vehicle weighted down with your fat ass.

Then, the smell of a cigarette floods my nose. How nice. Now you're really going to kill me. How the hell did you get that?

White tobacco fills the air, fixing the distance between you and I. I bet you knew I am allergic, you jerk. I cough and gag and swerve all over the road. For a moment, I think about driving right into the railing. Then one of us will die.

No. I can play your game and get rid of you. Maybe that will work. I am going to hurt you, make fun of you, make your life a living hell. I am going to win.

I rip open the back door but you are gone. Did you get out? Did you know what I was going to do? Maybe that was it. Maybe I am free. Maybe I see you, standing by the ditch, puking up the cigarette you smoked. Dammit.

I chase after you, like you have done to me so many times. I run and run and run and run. But you're always one step ahead, one turn, one pace, one laugh. I can't catch you. I don't know why I thought I could this time. It never worked before.

I drive and you smoke again. You never learn. You cough. You eat the butts. You puke in the back seat. Oh, the smell. Again, always again.

When I pull in the driveway, it hits me. I am home. She will help. She will know what to do. She will believe me. She will make it all better. She always does.

You follow, panting and groaning.

Opening the door, I feel a difference. There is no light on in the living room, no voice to announce me, no soft call of my name. There is only silence. I feel the coldness of the house – a hollow, empty absence. There is no one, no her, no centre, only spaces where there once was a something.

No. Not today. Not now.

I hear the microwave bell ring. You're in the kitchen, making yourself something to eat. How insulting is that?

I run upstairs, disbelieving the truth. I hear you behind me.

Her clothes, her bags, her presence, gone, wiped away. Her plants, the only things we owned together, are gone too. I live with nothing but leased furniture, photographs of memories, and my old bachelor dishes. Well, unless I count you, giggling in the corner as you gnaw on your own crotch.

I find her note, in pieces on the bedroom floor, drenched in pools of your spit. You ripped it up, you asshole. How did you get it? Where did you find it? There are some pieces missing. Did you swallow them? How do I make sense of these shards?

Hey, you're weren't alone. Who was that someone else? You hurt me. This will eat me if Tell me. It's not right. Last night proved it. I suppose you are. I keep telling myself Be honest with me. Don't blame father. No more lies. That make deeper. tears. honesty. faced. my ego. am not your undivided attention. independent. exist. normal. perhaps alone. kharma. I think she is right. I'm leaving. I care about you so much. I alone shield and deal. But I also respect you. to cope. Whatever works. survival mechanism crazy stupid say you don't care. Tell me this is over. mother's cut me off. tell me love someone else. Easy? so I too want to know love where to go I want to go stop hurting. I want to stop caring but you will leave again. And I can't forgive you now. Yes. I care about you I wish it didn't hurt you are not alone
Me.

I sit on the bed and put my head in my hands. I'm defeated. You enter the bedroom, sit on the opposite side and roll in the covers. The smell of shit fills the room.

How could I not see this coming? How could I be with her this morning? How can she be gone? How can I be alone?

Hee hee hee heeeeee, you shit. Hee hee hee heeeee. Hee hee hee heeeeee. Hee hee hee heeeeee.

You did, didn't you? You watched her, wanted her, took her, and now you have me all to yourself. You knew that she was the only thing that kept you from destroying me. She made me happy and it drove you crazy. So you tricked her, just like my dad.

I stand up and turn to you. I'm going to make you give her back to me. This time, it's going to be different.

Where did you go? I want to see you. I want you to feel the pain that you have created. And this time, I'm not going to stop. This time I'm going to win.

There you are, under that pile of shit. I can see you moving. You can't get away from me now. I want her back, and you will give her to me.

I bet you think I won't crawl through this pool of poop to get to you. I will. I will get you, you bastard. You think you are safe in that stink but I know it is just full of you. I know what you eat. I can handle it. I can beat you. I can dig through this shit. It's only my world anyway.

I will find a way to get her back once I get my hands on you.

I take a deep breath, dive in, and wade through your powerful smell. It is thick, dark, and all over me, between my fingers and toes, grabbing me, slowing me, gripping me. Soon, I am treading in a wall of stench so much more than I thought it was. I am surrounded by it; it is everywhere. The more I flail, the more I get filled in it. I've run out of air. I open my mouth and try to scream but it fills so quickly I can't even moan. I swing my arms and legs trying to get to the surface, but feel myself falling. Oh no. Down. Down. Down. Down. I try harder and harder, but I am too heavy, too slow, too old. The shit is too thick, too strong, too brown, too much. I am sinking, sinking, into the trap you set, filling me until all I can breathe is you.

Oh my god, I'm going to die. And you're going to live. I've lost. Fuck.

And, then, I see her. I remember her. I miss her. I love her.

In this moment, my worst, she comes back. Not in the shit, in my head – although the lines are hardly so separate anymore.

It's her story. My story. Our story. An important story. Oh, don't worry, you're there too, you asshole. It's the story where I first realize who you are, actually. You should probably hear it while I can still tell it.

It's about a time with you, but it's really about us.

The first day, in a class at that university. A professor walking in, telling everyone to pull out a book called *The Trickster:*

A Study in American Indian Mythology. You sit, right behind me. For years, I try to shut you out the best I could.

But today it's impossible. There, on the front page, is you, laughing and pointing right at me. The trickster, that's what the professor, the students, and the authors call you. And, from the first words out of the professor's mouth, I can tell they're yours. They are.

> Few myths have so wide a distribution as the one, known by the name of *The Trickster*, which we are presenting here. For few can we so confidently assert that they belong to the oldest expressions of mankind. Few other myths have persisted with their fundamental content unchanged. The Trickster myth is found in clearly recognizable form among the simplest aboriginal tribes and among the complex. We encounter it among the ancient Greeks, the Chinese, the Japanese and in the Semitic world. Many of the Trickster's traits were perpetuated in the figure of the mediaeval jester, and have survived right up to the present day in the Punch-and-Judy plays and in the clown. Although repeatedly combined with other myths and frequently drastically reorganized and reinterpreted, its basic plot seems to always to have succeeded in reasserting itself.

I hear you snickering beside me, rolling in the aisle, holding your fat belly. You did write this, you asshole. The professor continues.

> Trickster himself, is, not infrequently, identified with specific animals, such as raven, coyote, hare, spider, but these animals are only secondarily to be equated with concrete animals. Basically he possesses no well-defined and fixed form. As he is represented in the versions of the Trickster

> myth we are publishing here, he is primarily an inchoate being of undetermined proportions, a figure foreshadowing the shape of man. In this version, he possesses intestines wrapped around his body, and an equally long penis, likewise wrapped around his body with his scrotum on top of it. Yet regarding his specific features we are, significantly enough, told nothing.

Yeah, right. You wish you had a dick that long. These words are meant to confuse those who can really see you, mislead those who could help me. I know what you look like. You are this fat slob sitting behind me. The one that follows me around, like a bad nightmare that never ends. It's like you wrote this to make sure that the truth is that no one can figure you out.

But I know you.

Other textbooks say basically the same, minor variations on a larger theme of nothingness. You've written all of them, I realize. You are everywhere. You write in different voices in different fonts in different times in different books. Still, it is your voice, playing tricks. I know that this can't be a good thing. You are taking over.

I first tell a study group that these are tricks played by you. I know what you really look like, I tell them. I even draw a picture of you, but they tell me that it's just a blank page. You obviously erased the picture, I exclaim. It would be just like you to do that.

Soon, everyone refuses to work with me.

I had to do more. One day I raise my hand and tell the professor the same thing. That I know you. That you are there, writing on the blackboard. That the truth is that you are tricking all of us.

Personal experiences shut discussions down, the professor says, in front of the class. Now I know you are Indian, and your perspective is important, but what you need to practise is more open-mindedness, more awareness of other positions, more realization that there is no truth. I would suggest you read Gerald…

I miss the rest of what the professor says, especially after you pull out your scrotum and put it on the overhead.

But I do hear the laughter. At me. The whispers. The fingers pointing. The strokes of pens as each word of my shame is copied.

Embarrassed, I retreat into silence. The class ends and I am alone with my realizations. The world thinks you are something else, and I can't do anything to stop it. Shit.

Hee hee hee heeeeee, you dance. Hee hee hee heeeeee. Hee hee hee heeeeee. Hee hee hee heeeeee.

You repeat and repeat and repeat, growing louder with each round. Your hissing and footsteps grow so loud that soon they sound like permanent whispers, deep in my ear, like dance steps on my brain.

Until I hear her voice. For the first time since you came into my life you go silent.

How do you know tricksters? she asks, clearly.

Lost by your muteness, I confusingly say, I see one every day.

Tricksters aren't real. They're stories, she states.

I wish that were true, I reply.

I'm Aboriginal, and I don't see the tricksters you're talking about.

You're lucky.

We sit together for a long time. I enjoy the stillness and calm of her voice. You sit off on the bench, quiet for the first time in years, watching us. We talk for hours. She tells me to study you, write books about you, speak up to you, confront you. She encourages me to think different things than whimsical stories and theories of untruths.

Most of all, she trusts me. She tells me that what I experience is true. What I know was true. What I conclude is true.

But that's not the end, she states, your trickster might be beautiful too. He might even be fun, smart, and powerful.

How do you know this? I ask.

I've heard stories from my relatives.

So you've seen him?

Not yours. But one.

I don't believe it, I say. I tell her how you came into my life, how you are nothing but an asshole who makes my life hell, how you are nothing that I want to be, nothing that I want to become, nothing that reflects me or my life.

Tell me more, she asks.

We spend more and more time together, days, afternoons, evenings. She asks for details about you, about what you do, about what you say (which is nothing, I know). Then she talks about herself, her life, her interests, her dreams, and asks me about mine. It is the first time I speak about a time without you. It was easy, especially since I could concentrate. You were still there but you were calmly watching us, in the faded background of our community.

One Friday, in my apartment, she kisses me. I pull away, scared.

Okay, okay, she whispers. Don't worry. Be with me. Shhhhh. Focus on us, on me. The rest will come. Are you upset? Oh god, I didn't know. It's okay. I'll be gentle.

Kissing my neck, she takes off my shirt. I tremble, a warm chill hitting my skin.

Hearing you lick your lips, I feel your hairy hands help pull it over my head.

We move in together soon after that. One night, she tells me she loves me. We marry. I get a job. We buy a house. You come, but you subversively make your presence known, makng messes only I can find. I clean up after you, take responsibility for your actions. Sometimes I even pretend you aren't there. I don't want anything to happen to us.

Once in a while, she asks if you are around, if I see you, hear you. No, no, no, no, I lie, not anymore. He's gone. It's good. The trickster is just a fucking asshole. Just a jerk. Just there to make my life shit. Everything is better now. I'm happy.

I decide to try what she said. I put up with you. I try to see the beauty in you. I try to listen to you. It's hard. You are angry that I've been ignoring you. Pissed off that I have pretended to move on. You start doing different things. You drink, party, gamble, and do some horrible things. Sometimes I find the alcohol, drugs, and money you hide in my bag. Sometimes I find your used condoms. Sometimes I find blood.

But I'm happy, I tell myself. I can't let you ruin us. I can't let you break up my first happiness. I can't let you get to her. Why are you changing? Why can't you be like you were before? Why can't you go away?

You continue to mess things up, especially when she's not around. You pant in my ear, reek of booze and marijuana, and masturbate while you watch her sleep. I start leaving in the afternoon, just to keep you away from her. I go. I stay away and let you party, hoping you will pass out. I come home long after she is sleeping and stay on the couch. I keep you busy with beers to drink, floors to piss on, places to shit. I stay away as long as I can.

In this way, I protect her. I live on an island of our love, surrounded by you.

Until last night. When I couldn't stop you. I don't remember much, except for you and your drinking and your drugs and your dark fuzzy nights together when we can't stay away any longer and we come home not alone and you convince me to fumble with the locked door and come into the living room with sweaty hands making back circles and shapes kissing lying on top singing singing singing singing calling out to god pulling pushing it out in harder harder harder harder until her face not her but her becomes you suddenly it is you I have been fucking all this time, my hands holding your coarse hair as you come into with through on me and I see her standing away looking at me crying, shaking, screaming, oh honey I'm sorry it won't happen again I'm so sorry please come back please oh please I'm sorry, you saw him didn't you you saw him didn't you you saw him didn't you you saw him.

I wait until she is sleeping and slip into bed. You, of course, are already there.

I just realized, I touched you for the first time last night. I think I'm going to throw up.

I think I'm going to die.

There's no imagining the shit I have covered all over my hands, my body, my mind. It's very real, and you created it. I can't get to you. I will never get to you. The shit is too thick. I am too weak.

I cry, little sobs at first, and then try to scream out her name, even though my mouth is so full of shit I can't close it. I can make no sound. I am pathetic. I am lost. I am alone. And I should be dead by now, but I'm not. I can hear you giggling.

I feel a long rubber staff, like a rope, near my hands. It's bendable, firm, soft to the touch, kind of like a piece of wood covered in slippery moist plastic. I grab it and wrap it around my wrist as it pulls me free from the ooze. I breathe my first breath in what feels like days. Then, as soon as I free myself, the rope slithers back into the shit pile and disappears.

Coughing and wheezing on the floor, I've got nothing more to say to you. I've got nothing more to take. I slowly walk and sob and cry, travelling down the stairs calling her name.

I hear you coming down the stairs. Go ahead. I don't care what you destroy anymore.

I'm sorry, I cry out. I'm so so so so sorry, Sky. You deserve better. I'm sorry. If only my dad kept me from waiting. If only you hadn't tricked me. If only I listened better to her. If only.

Suddenly, you come in the living room and start to eat. It's small at first. The pictures on the wall of my mother, my father, my degree, her, they all go down your throat. My jacket, my laptop, my shoes, my wallet. You eat the clock her mother gave us for Christmas.

What are you doing, I scream, what are you doing, you asshole?

Then, I promptly throw up shit. When I am done, my throat is so burnt, I can only croak.

I watch, silently, as you smash the television set on the floor, and then munch on the pieces. You tip the cabinet over and it disappears into your stomach. You swallow the books whole, pages from my copies of *Bearheart, Kiss of the Fur Queen, Love Medicine*, and *Ravensong* spilling out of your mouth. You throw the bookcase across the room and it smashes into shards. You gulp those down too. You get bigger, bigger, bigger, bigger, too large for the rooms. There is no room for me anymore here.

I scramble to the kitchen. You eat all there is left in the fridge, the meat, the apples, the old milk curdles that drip down your shin. You swallow the sugar bags whole, the brown and white granules sprinkled all over your hairy palms. You help yourself to everything, turning over tables, breaking lamps, tipping over the fridge. Forget it. I'm not cleaning up your mess.

You get bigger, until your fat rolls fill up the entire floor on the first floor. All I can see when I look down is you.

I have to go. You've never gotten this big before. Something's different.

All the while you are smiling right at me. Now that she is gone you are tormenting me. Making fun of my loss. I'd scream but my voice is raw and burnt, infected with too much shit, too many words, too many yous. I can't speak.

I don't get it. I don't understand what the joke is. I don't know what is so funny, why you laugh, joke, play games. Yes, you play tricks. But they are always on others. Fucking mean tricks, too. I hate you.

At least no one can deny that you exist now. You're so huge. You take up all of the first floor, and you're oozing up the stairs. I can't even see the front door.

You're eating everything, the plaster, the stairs, the banister, the hardwood. Very soon there will be nothing left.

Oh my god. That's it. You're going to eat everything. You're going to eat it all.

The trick is that today you are going to eat me.

I run upstairs and you continue to grow.

I can't stop you, can't escape. You just destroy, destroy, destroy, destroy and eat, eat, eat, eat, and grow bigger, bigger, bigger, bigger. You start to fill up the second floor, inches at a time.

I go to open the windows in the hallway and the bedroom but they're locked, and you've eaten my wallet. You have trapped me, and I have trapped myself, you bastard. I need something to break through this glass.

You grunt and moan around me, pick up furniture, throw it against the wall, eat the pieces. I jump away from the glass, onto the bed of shit, now the only island in the room of you. Your slimy hair covers the windows and it grows dark and dusky.

I slowly start to sink. What's the point of this, I try to say, but nothing comes out.

Your hands emerge from the bubbles of your hairy fat, pick up handfuls of brown slime, and throw it at me.

But I am already sinking in this, can't you tell? You can't do anything more. Cover me completely, then. Here, I'll take off my clothes so you can cover me with your waste. Have them. There, I am naked. I'll cover myself with you. Are you happy now? Is this what you want? No history, no life, no possessions, no nothing? It is only you and me and shit now.

You stop and stare at my discarded clothes. This is what you wanted, isn't it. You want to replace me. You put them on and they explode with your fatness, your jiggling chest oozing out of my shirt and my pants bulging at your crotch. You smile. Damn you.

You start to eat the corner of the bed, yourself oozing from your mouth. When you're finished with the mattress you chew on the corner of the dresser. I grab one of your rolls and pull my naked self out of the waist-high slime, step on your jiggling back, and leap into the bathroom. Quickly slamming the door. I realize that I have nowhere else to go.

No, you can't destroy everything. No, you bastard. I won't let you.

I destroy everything I see, so you can't. I rip the glass shower doors off, tear the photographs of us onto the floor, smash the mirror on the wall. I kick the floor and punch the walls until tiny slivers of plaster and tile are jammed in my nails and my hands and feet bleed all over. I eat the shards of glass on the floor, the photographs, and whatever pieces of plaster, chunks of wood, that I can grab. The shards cut my throat, and my cuts spread open with each step and piece I slide in my mouth. I cry and feel my body shaking, cutting, bleeding, crying out in pain. Still, I punch, kick, and eat until I lie in the bathtub and there is nothing left. I am in so much pain. I am dying. I am really dying. I am dying. I am dying.

I smile. I have kept those little pieces from you, though. You'll see.

You eat the door and I see your stretched face cover completely the entryway. You are still wearing my clothes, but they are like shreds on your inflated self. I stand and feel all of my body scream in agony. Even if I cannot speak, my presence is ensured by this horrible struggle. I am so weak, but yet I am strong.

You see what I have done, and I can see you are angry.

I try to vomit up the shards, the wood, the pieces, the photographs, the memories, just to spite you, but nothing comes out. Nothing but blood oozing from my lips, nothing but parts of me slipping out onto the floor.

Your fatness, growing from your chin, stretches across the floor and surrounds my bathtub island. I sit down and see your busy hands reaching out from your blubber and onto the sides of my enamel lifeboat. I see your mouth swallow down the pieces of broken toilet.

I find a piece of the mirror in the tub and look at myself. I am bloodied, hideous, mangled – just like you. Take a look, see for yourself, you asshole.

I hold up the mirror shard. You stop destroying, look at your reflection and smile. You love looking at yourself, don't you? You, dressed in my clothes, looking just like me, your overwhelming fatness covering the floor, the walls, the space.

I make you happy when I destroy, don't I? I make you happy when I wreck my life. I make you happy when I hurt myself. You didn't even know that I could do that. You thought you were doing it for me.

I laugh at the absurdity of us both, even though it hurts so much. I laugh but no sound comes from my mouth. You laugh, mimicking me, but you're so overinflated no sound comes either. For the first time you look surprised, like you didn't expect that to happen.

Suddenly, it comes to me, although I knew it the entire time. I give you life.

I laugh again. So do you. Silently.

I know what I have to do.

I'm going to wash. I reach over to the faucet and turn it on, full blast. I stand in the hot and cold water, and feel it soaking my broken feet and ankles. It is tinged red from my blood. You just stand there, smiling, staring at yourself in the mirror. I will wash us both. Our destruction will be permanent, and we will be cleansed. I sit down in the rising water and watch you silently look at yourself. You have not moved.

Water fills the bathtub and runs over the sides, covering your floor of skin.

We are going to drown. We are going to be washed away. We are going to be together. We are going to be born. This is a flood, a beginning. No one will save us. We will be cleansed in this water, filled with chemicals, plaster, and glass. There will be no earth, no soil, no mud, no sand. We will have to be remade from these new things, if we are remade at all.

I watch as the water fills the room, to our waists. You reach down and nibble on the shit floating around you. You are still eating, trying to consume the world, all the way to the end. All you're doing is eating yourself.

That's it, I understand. I have finally played a trick on you.

Hee hee hee heeeeee, I laugh, mimicking you.

Then, just then, you look. Right at me. With your eyes. Your beautiful eyes. I see my reflection in them. They are filled, filled with me. I am in you.

The water fills to our necks, and my body grows light. I'm no longer carrying it.

Hee hee hee heeeeee, I laugh.

Your eyes tell it all. You are shaking. You are scared. After all of this time, you didn't know how this would end, did you? Amongst all of the shit, piss, vomit, saliva, grunts, and moans, you did not know the ending of this story.

Hee hee hee heeeeee, I laugh.

You reach out with your fat hands, like tiny sticks protruding from your blob. I take them. I am scared, too. I didn't know how this would end, either. I only know how we got here.

Hee hee hee heeeeee, we sing together, our space filling the air for the first and last time.

And with our laughter we become one, one picture, floating in water that covers our heads. We dance, weightless, merging, one. Underwater our selves return, and we sing songs with spirits of presence as we enter the next world gripped in a gaze of each other's love and hate. We are different but we are similar, each disgusting, each beautiful, each here, each there. With so many stories, so many confusions, so many thoughts, so many words, ours and others', so many spirits, so many goods, so many bads, so many others telling our story. And we have let them. To grow, we need to tell our story now. The story of our lives together, each necessary, each important, each needing the other to tell, to listen, to write, to learn. This is how we heal. This is how we die. This is how we live. Telling our stories.

Our world fills with the blood of the earth and is cleansed of our destruction. We are remade for the world that will be created tomorrow, when we will tell this story again. It will be new and it will be different, and it will be part of a story too. It will, though, be ours. We hope.

Regardless, if we are here or we are there, you will be with me. Maybe my dad will be with us too, laughing and telling stories with soft candies beside him. Maybe we will wait for him to arrive, but, if he doesn't come, we can't wait anymore. We have made mistakes too, and we are sorry. I pray that he knows that. But we are ready to continue.

Maybe Sky will come with us too, if she wants to come back. We have made so many mistakes. We don't blame her if she doesn't want to come back. She has her story to make too. Without her our story would have ended a long time ago, so she is acknowledged and thanked.

We don't know about tomorrow, about any of these things, because, in the end, that's all we have: each other. There will be a world that we will be born into, here or there, that we know. This place is where our story will be. We have to learn to do better and tell it like we have been living it, like we have been doing all along. Even though we may not know that we were telling it, writing it, drawing it, all along, we were.

Our trickster story.

I have a trickster story. It is my own. It is also now yours.

You are there. So am I. I am here. And so are you. We're both here and there, listening to this story as we speak it, write it, read it. We are together.

That's the trick.

It's always, for our entire lives.

Everywhere.

Boozhoo.

There is something more than survival and saving ourselves: it is continuance.

—Simon J. Ortiz

Woven Stone

DANIEL DAVID MOSES

KING OF THE RAFT

There was a raft in the river that year, put there, anchored with an anvil, just below a bend, by the one of the fathers who worked away in Buffalo, who could spend only every other weekend, if that, at home. The one of the mothers whose husband worked the land and came in from the fields for every meal muttered as she set the table that that raft was the only way the father who worked in the city was able to pretend he cared about his sons. Her husband, also one of the fathers, who had once when young gone across the border to work and then, unhappy there, returned, could not answer, soaking the dust of soil from his hands.

Most of the sons used the raft that was there just that one summer in the usually slow-moving water during the long evenings after supper, after the days of the fieldwork of haying and then combining were done. A few of them, the ones whose fathers and mothers practised Christianity, also used it in the afternoons on sunny Sundays after the sitting through church and family luncheons. And the one of the sons who had only a father who came and went following the work – that son appeared whenever his rare duties or lonely freedom became too much for him.

The sons would come to the raft in Indian file along a footpath the half-mile from the road and change their overalls or jeans for swimsuits among the goldenrod and milkweed on the bank, quickly, to preserve modesty and the blood from the mosquitoes, the only females around. Then one of the sons would run down the clay slope and stumble in with splashing and a cry of shock or joy for the water's current temperature. The other sons would follow, and, by the time they all climbed out onto the raft out in the stream, through laughter would become boys again.

The boys used that raft in the murky green water to catch the sun or their breaths on or to dive from where they tried to touch the mud bottom. One of the younger ones also used to stand looking across the current to the other side, trying to see through that field of corn there, the last bit of land that belonged to the reserve. Beyond it the highway ran, a border patrolled by a few cars flashing chrome in the sun or headlights through the evening blue like messages from the city. Every one of the boys used the raft several times that summer to get across the river and back, the accomplishment proof of their new masculinity. And once the younger one, who spent time looking at that other land, crossed and climbed up the bank there and explored the shadows between the rows of corn, the leaves like dry tongues along his naked arms as he came to the field's far edge where the asphalt of that highway stood empty.

Toward the cool end of the evenings, any boy left out on the raft in the lapping black water would be too far from shore to hear the conversations. They went on against a background noise of the fire the boys always built against the river's grey mist and mosquito lust, that they sometimes built for roasting corn, hot dogs, marshmallows. The conversations went on along with or over games of chess. Years later, one of the older boys, watching his own son play the game with a friend in silence, wondered if perhaps that was why their conversations that year of the raft about cars, guitars, and girls – especially each other's sisters – about school and beer, always ended up in stalemate or check. Most of the boys ended up winning only their own solitariness from the conversations by the river. But the one who had only a father never even learned the rules of play.

One sunny Sunday after church, late in the summer, the one who had only a father sat on the raft in the river as the rest of the boys undressed. He smiled at the boy who had gone across through the corn, who made it into the water first. Then he stood up and the raft made waves as gentle as those in his blue-black hair – I'm the king of the raft, he yelled, challenging the boy who had seen the highway to win that wet, wooden square. And a battle was joined, and the day was wet and fair, until the king of the raft, to show his strength to the rest of the boys still on shore, took a hank of the highway boy's straight hair in hand and held the highway boy underwater till the highway boy saw blue fire and almost drowned. The story went around among the mothers and the fathers, and soon that son who had only a father found himself unwelcome. Other stories came around, rumours about his getting into fights or failing grades or how his father's latest girlfriend had dyed her Indian hair blonde. And the boy who almost had drowned found he both feared the king of the raft and missed the waves in his blue-black hair.

One muggy evening when pale thunderheads growled in from the west, the boy who had almost drowned, who had the farthest to go to get home, left the raft and the rest by the river early. On the dark road he met the king, who had something to say. They hid together with a case of beer in a cool culvert under the road. The king of the raft was going away with his father to live in Buffalo in the United States and thought the boy who had almost drowned could use what was left of this beer the king's father would never miss. The boy who had almost drowned sipped from his bottle of sour beer and heard the rain beginning to hiss at the end of the culvert. He crawled and looked out in time to see the blue fire of lightning hit a tree. In the flash he saw again the waves in the king's blue-black hair, the grin that offered another beer. The boy who had almost drowned felt he was going down again, and, muttering some excuse, ran out into the rain. The king yelled after him that old insult boys used about your mother wanting you home.

The boy who had almost drowned found he could cross through the rain, anchored by his old running shoes to the ground, though the water came down like another river, cold and clear and wide as the horizon. He made it home and stood on the porch waiting for the other side of the storm, hearing hail hitting the roof and water through the eaves filling up the cistern. Later, out of the storm, he could still hear far-off a gurgling in the gully and a quiet roar as the distant river tore between its banks. The storm still growled somewhere beyond the eastern horizon.

The raft was gone the next evening when the boys came to the bank, and the current was still too cold and quick to swim in. No one crossed the river for the rest of the summer. The king of the raft never appeared again anywhere. In the fall, a rumour came around about his going to work in the city and in the winter another one claimed he had died. The boy who had crossed through the rain thought about going down even quicker in winter river water. Then a newspaper confirmed the death. In a traffic accident, the rain boy read. None of the boys had even met that impaired driver, that one of the fathers, surviving and charged without a licence. One of the mothers muttered as she set another mother's hair about people not able to care even about their kids. The rain boy let the king of the raft sink into the river, washing him away in his mind and decided he would someday cross over and follow the highway through that land and find the city.

JOSEPH BOYDEN

BORN WITH A TOOTH

My wolf hung at the trading post for two weeks until that new teacher up from Toronto bought him. My long-legged Timber with half a left ear. A local trapper snared and sold my wolf to Trading Post Charlie, who skinned him and pinned him on the wall next to the faded MasterCard sign. He was worth more than $250.

The teacher's been here less than a month, sent to us by the Education Authority at Christmastime so the rez kids can learn the Queen's English. They gave him a little house and a parka, and I think he's lonely like me and has got a lot to watch and learn. He knows nothing about a snowmobile or guns or the bush or the insult and danger of looking in the eyes. I can tell by watching him. Maybe I can teach him. He's got a thin face and he's tall and awkward. My face is round, and I can drive a snowmobile as good as Lucky Lachance.

The one and only Lucky Lachance is my uncle, gone for four days of every week. He knows something's wrong because lately he comes back from work saying, "Just because your name's Sue Born With A Tooth doesn't mean you have to stay on this reservation the rest of your life, Jesus fuck." He works for the Ontario Northland railway on the Polar Bear Express. His train runs from Cochrane to Moosonee, mostly taking tourists in summer and supplies in winter across Northern Ontario and up to our stomping ground on the bottom tip of James Bay. The tourists call it the wilderness, but Lucky

Lachance calls it the asshole of Hudson Bay. He's French Canadian and he's got a dirty mouth. His sister is my mother, and I think my father's most probably dead. My father came carrying my name with him from somewhere out west. He brought my name to this place of Blueboys and Whiskeyjacks and Wapachees and Netmakers and even in this place my name stands out. Eighteen years ago my mother sewed my father his first suit, and seventeen years ago he got her pregnant with me. All I know is he was full-blood Cree and belonged to the Bear Clan. In grade four I learned that the name for French and Indian mixed is Metis. I always thought that around here that made me nothing special times two.

Lucky says I'm looking into my fucking womanhood, and if I want to see the world he'll get me a free train ticket to Cochrane. He says it's time to stop moping around. "If you're not in school, it's time to work," he says. But I don't want to leave Moose Factory. I can't imagine another place where in summer you have to canoe or take a motorboat or a water taxi to the mainland and in winter they plough a road across the ice so cars can come back and forth. My mother wants me to learn how to sew.

Trading Post Charlie might have wondered why I was around the store so often the two weeks the wolf was there. I didn't buy anything. Charlie's fifty and is comfortable around me and pointed out all the pictures of his grandkids under the glass countertop once, but I could see his wife was jealous, me coming every day to drink free coffee and smoke her husband's cigarettes. She figured my visits out, though. Charlie's wife sold my wolf to the teacher yesterday.

For fourteen days I just showed up in the morning, knocking snow off my boots and letting a steam of cold air in through the door. I tried to learn how to drink Charlie's coffee and tried to make Charlie tell me everything he knew about the wolf. I think Charlie probably did know it was the wolf I came for, but he wouldn't look me in the eye, or anyone else for that matter. He's OjiCree and too polite. He doesn't talk much, just sells milk and bread and shotgun shells to the locals, pelts and Indian crafts to summer tourists.

But Charlie finally began to talk when he saw I wasn't going anywhere. "The trapper got the wolf in a snare. That blizzard come up off the bay, and the trapper figures it was two or three days the wolf choked slow before the lines could be checked again. The trapper said he ended the choke with a bullet in the wolf's brain." Later Charlie said, "It's the rare one that comes to the island and stays for long. Trapper'd seen the wolf's prints in the snow last winter. This winter too. He tracked him a while. Usually a pack comes across the ice for a night of following moose, but they never stay so close to humans long."

I imagined I could see the black wire mark when I ran my hand against his fur. He'd already started collecting dust.

My wolf was skinny but brave. He came to see me often that winter two years ago, disappeared before spring, then came back again the next freeze. I watched him and loved him.

I still can't sleep, my head wandering and thinking the wolf waits outside for me. There aren't too many reasons to go outside in the dark when it's minus forty and trees pop and crack in the cold. Tonight marks that night two winters ago.

I couldn't get comfortable in bed so I pulled my parka and mukluks on and went outside. It was the cold that makes your fingers burn through mittens and the moisture in your nose freeze and your toes ache no matter how many pairs of socks you wear. I walked just to walk, south on our road, smelling the woodsmoke and watching sparks fly from neighbours' chimneys. I looked up at the black and tried to find Mars and Venus, the stars that don't twinkle. I was hoping to see the northern lights. I wanted to walk quiet like the ancestors because I could sense them behind rocks and perched in the scrub pines, watching me and judging me. But my feet crunched on the dry snow and echoed in my ears under my hat loud enough that I felt silly. If the ancestors had been around, I had scared them away.

When I got to the edge of Charles Island, I lit a smoke and looked out at the ice highway running across the bay to Moosonee's twinkling lights. That's when I first came across him. I heard his paws in the snow, so I took my toque off to hear him better. I walked home slowly and felt his eyes on my back, but it wasn't spooky, only like an old friend come back to visit. Even though my ears hurt, I kept my hat off because I knew he was there. He followed me home but didn't show his face till the next night. That's when I laid my trap. Lucky's friend had gutted a moose, and I stole some innards and put them in a snowbank in our backyard. That next night I waited by the window for him, waited until past two. Then he appeared like a ghost or a shadow, slinking, lean, sniffing and jittery. I watched him drag my present into the bush.

Charlie tells me his name is Michael and he's only been teaching for two years. Lucky calls him a city slicker cocksucker and asks me what this guy thinks he can teach anyone. I follow this teacher to the trading post and coffee shop and post office. He never knows it. I wait for school to let out and follow to see where he lives. He walks along with his parka hood up, dragging his boots and humming.

I start thinking I want him to notice me, so I get bolder, crossing the street when he does and walking by him, or taking a seat near him at Trapper's Restaurant and only ordering a coffee. When he looks at me, I look away. When he smiles at me, I walk away.

It was three months, close to the ice breakup that first winter, before my wolf finally trusted me enough to stay in sight when I came outside. All winter I'd watched from the living-room window after Mom and Lucky had gone to their beds. At first I tried luring him with pieces of chicken or whitefish. I'd sit on the back step with my hand outstretched, waiting. But he wouldn't leave the shadows. So I'd arrange the scraps in a circle and go inside to my window perch and watch him slink across the yard. He knew I was there but wouldn't look up. He grew fuller and less jumpy. The night he finally ate from my hand, I knew something was going special.

Michael comes up to me at the coffee shop today and asks if he can sit by me. I say, "Okay," so he sits directly across the table and asks questions.

"Why don't I see you at the high school?" he says. I just shrug. He'll learn soon enough. Most of the rez kids make it to grade nine. That's when the government says it's legal to leave school behind. And that's when a lot of us know it's right. He asks me what my name is, and I tell him I'm Sue Born With A Tooth. He stares at my eyes, and I want to ask him if he's trying to insult me, but that would be rude. He's got little whiskers and his skin is very white and the fur on his hanging parka hood frames his jaw nicely. He says my hair is long and black and pretty, and I tell him I have to go. I leave change on the table and walk outside.

"Can we have coffee again?" he asks, following me out.

"I guess," I say.

"When?" he asks. "Tomorrow?"

"I guess," I say.

On the night he first touched me, I had no meat to offer the wolf, just bone and gristle. But he was lonely and I was too. It was the act of offering and the middle of a long night and each of us growing used to one another. I held the bone in my bare hand and felt the moisture on my fingers freeze to a throb. I walked to the middle of the yard. He was in the shadows but slowly walked up when I stretched out my hand. He padded slow and tense from his hiding place and raised the fur on his neck. It made him look bigger and mean, and he kept walking out as I stood slumped and relaxed buty wanting to explode inside. He stopped a couple of metreers from me. I thought that would be as close as he'd come, but I kept my stare focused on the snow by his feet. He walked closer, till his nose twitched by my hand. He flattened his ears back and I looked at the left one, ragged and bitten or shot half off. I felt his eyes on mine, so I looked too. Yellow eyes. Harvest moons. He smiled at me with his black lips and opened his mouth and the white teeth gently took the bone. He turned around and trotted slowly back to the edge of the bush, then turned his head to me before disappearing.

I often wondered where he went all day, whether he was safe or if his visits put him in danger. I wanted to ask Lucky about the hunters on the island. I wanted to know if they knew about my stray. No one ever talked about any wolf tracks near their door in the mornings after a new snowfall. But still, I worried for him.

My mother talks so little that there are people in Moose Factory who believe she doesn't know how to. She works with her sewing machine out of the house. She's very small and very smart. You can see it in her shiny black eyes, "*C'est dommage.* It is too bad there is so much of your father in you," she tells me.

"Unable to sleep at night, always wanting to dance with the ghosts." I wonder how much she actually sees and how much she knows to sense. I've watched her sew for hours, and the day comes that I will stitch too, but for now I get everything I need from a few coins in Lucky's money jar.

Michael asks me out to drink coffee most days after his teaching and continues staring at my eyes. I want to tell him that I don't think I really like coffee after all and that we should go to his house and smoke cigarettes instead. Lucky saw us and teases me at home.

"Sue hangs out with the city fuck. The skinny cocksucker thinks he's going to get some French and Indian ass at the same time, eh? He thinks the Metis like to mate, eh?" His words make me run to my room. But Lucky always knocks gently and tells me he is sorry. He says, "Metis means that you are stuck in the middle, Sue."

Whenever he says that, I know that he's going to finish his talk. He reminds me that Indians consider me a Frenchie, and whites look at me like I'm Indian. But I imagine I don't feel different from most of the rez kids. Maybe I'm lonelier. My best friend has a husband and a baby now, and another friend moved to Thunder Bay. Tonight Lucky says he is not here enough to watch out for me and I should be careful with the city boys.

Michael has him somewhere in his house. I want to sit by Michael's stove and look at him. Michael talks a lot when we go out to the coffee shop. He tells me about Toronto, the woman mayor, the Canadian National Exhibition, the men who sleep on heating grates in the middle of winter underneath huge glass buildings. He tells me about his little brother and parents. Michael asks if he can come over to my house for dinner. He says he's writing a paper on the Aboriginals of Northern Ontario. But I can hear Lucky saying, "Do you want another potato, cocksucker?" so I say I'll go to Michael's house instead.

It's a small cottage on Ministik Road, outside the rez boundary, just a clapboard living room and a kitchen with dried flowers on the tiny table and a wood-burning stove. I help him carry wood in, and we leave our coats and boots by the stove. He cooks dinner and fumbles with the plates while setting the table. He talks a lot, asks a lot of questions about me and Moose Factory. I tell him my daddy was a full-blood Bear Clan Cree. That he worked in the bush and was the son of a hunter. I lie and tell Michael my father was killed while hunting. I don't know why I say this. I look down at the floor, then at the walls. I don't see him.

After dinner we sit on the sofa and listen to music, drinking beer.

"You're not the most talkative person," Michael says. "Aren't there things you want to know about me?" He leans in closer and takes my hand in his. It's sweaty.

"So you have a girlfriend in Toronto?" I ask.

"No," he says. "There's a woman I like, but ..." and I stop his talk with a little kiss.

Lucky would be angry if he knew I was alone with Michael in his house. But Lucky's on the train tonight, somewhere near the Soo.

I want to tell this one about the other. About how close we were by the second winter. How he'd come up to me in the middle of the night almost as friendly as a dog and take gifts from my hand, then go back to the edge of the bush to eat. He wouldn't let me touch him, didn't want the smell of human on his fur. I want to tell him about that time when the ice was beginning to break up on the bay and even snowmobiles weren't crossing any more. It was late and I offered him a strip of venison. He walked up and ignored my hand. Instead he nuzzled me hard between my legs. He could smell my blood. I felt his hot breath and tongue against my jeans for just a moment.

Michael looks awkward pulling out the sofa bed. "If I had known I'd be living like this," he says, "I'd have shipped my futon up with me." He's holding onto me and unbuttoning my shirt. I want to know what a futon is, but I lie back and let him struggle with my jeans.

I can feel his tongue and his breath in the dark. He's come back to me, nipping and licking, tasting me. He slides up and I can feel the hair of his chest on my belly, on my breasts. He is hard against me and pushes inside for my first time, his shoulder across my neck. The white flash of pain is his smile and dark lips. He nudges my legs wider. I bite his ear and he yelps and I can feel him release inside of me.

Michael mumbles and half talks in his sleep, so I quietly get up and pull my clothes on. The stove's gone out and I can see my breath, so I squeak the stove door open and fill it with wood. I leave and walk down Ankerite Road, listening to my boots crunch in the snow and trees moan in the cold. Tonight it's so dark and empty I wonder if anything is alive.

The days are getting longer again. Michael and I don't go out for coffee much any more. People in town started talking, asking why the teacher and a seventeen-year-old half-Indian girl were hanging out so much. Michael ran into Lucky and thought he was a big bearded lumberjack come to chop him down. Lucky says he didn't say a word to him. Just looked. When we do meet for coffee, this teacher doesn't look at my eyes any more, just mumbles into his cup and watches out the window, then kisses my cheek and leaves. I wanted to tell him he was the first, but I can't now.

Sunny days leave the ice highway slushy and dangerous to cross. I only asked Michael about my wolf one time, a little while ago. I tried to sound casual and like I didn't care, but my voice came out squeaky and tense.

"That pelt, the damaged one?" he said. "I sent it out on the mail plane to my woman friend in Toronto. She loves northern stuff."

I try not to think of my wolf any more, sent to hang in that woman's house.

Michael calls me today after the first canoe race of the year, the one from Moose Factory to Moosonee celebrating the spring. He asks me to meet him at the usual place.

"I'm leaving, back to TO," he says as I stare out the window at the bay and people on the ferry dock. The trees will bud soon. He lights a smoke. "I thought I might want to renew my contract and stay through the summer. But I've got business to take care of back in the city." He smiles. A casual smile. "Besides, I hear the blackflies drive you crazy in the spring. Don't worry, though. I'll write. Maybe you can come visit me sometime."

He always talks too much. I light a smoke and look him in the eyes. He looks back for a second, then looks down and plays with his cigarette pack. I stare at him till he gets up and leaves.

The last night he visited me a few months back, I knew my wolf could smell the evil in the air. He was jumpy and his yellow eyes looked dull. I was tired and didn't want to get out of my warm bed. But I knew he was there, looking up at my window from his shadows at the tree line. I knew he wanted to see me. There was no food to offer so I poured him a bowl of milk and went outside. He sneaked up to me, then looked over his shoulder.

He sniffed the saucer but let the milk freeze. I wondered what he had done all day, if he had caught a hare or run from his enemies. Half awake and not thinking, I reached out to scratch his torn ear. I lazily ran my fingers over his scruffy head and scratched his neck. Just as I realized what I was doing, he nipped at my hand and walked away, looking back over his shoulder at me until he disappeared into the dark. He had the smell on him.

I don't like coffee any more, but I still go to the coffee shop and drink it. When Michael left, Lucky said that the city fuck was worried the blackflies might chew his cock off if he stayed any longer.

My stomach's getting puffy so I try not to smoke, but it's become a habit. It won't be long before Mom and Lucky notice. It won't be good. I'll have to tell them soon.

When it comes, the pain will be like that night with him, and worse. I will open my legs wide and scream and curse and howl.

Then the midwife will back away, muttering prayers and crying. My baby's grey furry head will enter this world. He will bare his white teeth and gnaw through our cord. He will look at me and smile with black lips and yellow eyes. He will run off into the bush, and he will cross the ice highway.

JOSEPH A. DANDURAND

PLEASE DO NOT TOUCH THE INDIANS

This drama premiered at the Museum of the American West's Wells Fargo Theatre in Griffith Park, Los Angeles in March of 2004, produced by the Native Voices at the Autry under the direction of Randy Reinholz with dramatology by Bryan Davidson.

CHARACTERS

WOODEN INDIAN MAN

WOODEN INDIAN WOMAN

SISTER COYOTE

BROTHER RAVEN

MISTER WOLF

TOURIST

SETTING

A painted backdrop of the HANK WILLIAMS SR.'S BAIT AND GIFT SHOP. There are some fallen leaves on the ground. Centre stage there is a wooden bench and sitting on the bench are two wooden Indians. Their clothing is simple and not quite traditional but more of a Hollywood taste. WOODEN WOMAN is holding flowers that someone has put in her hand. WOODEN MAN sits with his eyes closed and around his neck is a sign that reads: PLEASE DO NOT TOUCH THE INDIANS.

ACT ONE

SCENE 1

Lights come up as music begins: Hank Williams Sr.'s "Kalajah." Music ends as French TOURIST comes out and sets up a camera and tripod. French TOURIST sets the timer and sits between the two Indians. As the timer beeps, the WOODEN MAN opens his eyes and sticks out his tongue. French TOURIST looks at WOODEN MAN but he has already closed his eyes and has returned to being wooden. French TOURIST stands, gathers the camera and tripod, and exists as lights fade to black.

SCENE 2

Lights come up. Night. More fallen leaves on the ground. In the distance we hear squealing tires and screams from teenagers as they cheer on the drag-racing cars. WOODEN WOMAN begins to move as noise fades. WOODEN WOMAN looks at flowers in her hand and screams as she throws them to the ground in front of her.

WOODEN WOMAN

Geez, who put flowers in my hand? Don't they know that's bad luck? Holding flowers is a sign of death. Hey, you listening? Are you awake?

WOODEN MAN does not move, nor does he speak.

You just going to sit there all night and not say a word? Don't you get tired of not moving your mouth? Geez, I'd go crazy not being able to talk. You better move your mouth or else you'll never be able to talk. That's what happened to old Charlie Ketchup. He never spoke to a soul for the last twenty years of his life. When the doctor went to see him on his deathbed, Charlie couldn't even tell him where it hurt. I bet he's talking up a storm in the spirit world. Old Charlie Ketchup. I knew his wife; she was crazier than he was. Betty Ketchup. A big woman, she must've weighed about three hundred pounds. No wonder Charlie never spoke, she'd come screaming out of the house after him if he ever spoke a word against her. Never seen a woman move so fast, never seen a man move faster.

WOODEN MAN scratches his nose as a raven caws in the distance.

Betty Ketchup sure was a big woman, but she would never hurt anyone. I remember going to her house to borrow some wood one day and she was running around trying to catch every fly that came into her dirty house. I'd say, "What'cha doing with them flies, Betty Ketchup?" And she'd turn and look at me with that little mouth of hers trying so hard to suck in enough air to breathe, and say, "I'm catchin' 'em for my supper." And she laughed so hard, I was afraid she'd swallow more than she caught.

WOODEN MAN scratches his left knee.

She never did eat any of them. She was really catching them because she could never kill a fly. She'd spend the whole day catching them and storing them in an old jar that she kept on the kitchen sink right next to her set of false teeth. I followed her one day, you know, to see where she went with them flies. She must've had a hundred in that jar that day. She waddled her way to the cow field and here she came across the biggest cow patty that she could find. It was real fresh, the steam still rising. Betty Ketchup opened up her jar of flies and let them fly right on to the patty. A hundred flies with a new home. Those flies never came back to Betty Ketchup's house. They stayed on that cow patty for the rest of their lives. Betty Ketchup saved millions of lives in the ten years that I knew her. Never a dead fly in her kitchen. A place to live was all they wanted. She was a big woman and her heart was just as big.

Lights fade as a coyote barks. Blackout.

SCENE 3

Stage lights come up. Night. More leaves on the ground. WOODEN MAN snaps awake and stares at WOODEN WOMAN.

WOODEN MAN

Are you awake? I had a vision: I was on the river, my boat was filled with fish. I had started home when a coyote began to follow me from the shore, he was smiling at me, you know, with them yellow eyes, he's smiling with his crooked teeth. He took his time, stopping every so often to rest his ragged paws, he knew my boat couldn't get far with all that fish. My boat was pushing slowly up to our home, the coyote watched from the shore and then the raven came and joined the coyote, they both watched from the shore: the raven with his red eyes and his torn feathers, the coyote lights a cigarette and blows the smoke toward me and my boat. The raven smiles as coyote offers him a drag. They both sit there on a log and they laugh at me. The fish begin to dance, they want to go back to the river, they do not want to be eaten by the coyote, nor do they want to be picked at by the raven. The fish begin to sing to me, they tell me to throw them back: "Please throw us back, we will come back next year." Over and over they sing this to me. The raven and the coyote are laughing at me as they begin to share their bottle. And then I begin to throw the fish back to the river, the fish throw kisses to me as they swim back to their homes, they promise to name their children after me, they turn and disappear. The raven and the coyote stand there on the shore, their mouths open with confusion. They try and catch up to me but my boat is empty and goes like the wind. I hear their howlin' and cawin' at me as I disappear around the mountain… I don't think they will name their children after me, I thought to myself, and then I woke up. Hey, are you awake? Did you like the flowers?

An English TOURIST enters and sets up a camera. He sets the timer and sits between the wooden Indians. As the timer beeps the WOODEN MAN and WOODEN WOMAN open their eyes and smile. WOODEN MAN also puts his around the English TOURIST, he puts a sign on the English TOURIST's back. Both Indians freeze as the English TOURIST looks at them as if they did truly move, he shakes his head and goes to gather his camera, he turns his back to the audience and we see the sign on his back – KICK ME! Blackout.

SCENE 4

In the dark we hear a coyote bark followed by a voice yelling: "Get outta here, you stinking coyote!" A spot comes up downstage centre. SISTER COYOTE walks into the spot, she is beautiful, but she has been crying and her makeup has run down her face, so now she looks somewhat clownish and sad. In the background we hear sounds and music that you would hear at the circus or the carnival. SISTER COYOTE reaches into her purse and pulls out a cigarette, lights it, takes a huge drag and exhales it into the air. She does this again and tries to act cool and special, but inhales down the wrong pipe and begins to choke, and her eyes bug out and she appears even more clownish than before.

SISTER COYOTE

Nothing like a good smoke. You know I first started smoking when me and my sister went to the carnival that would come to our reserve every summer. We really went with our parents but as soon as we got there we would run away and disappear into the crowd, and our parents were going to the beer tent anyway so they didn't miss us much. We would run straight for the far end of the carnival grounds. We would always go to the far end of the grounds, you see, this is where the freaks and the scary rides were.

She puts cigarette out and takes out a mickey from her purse, looks around to see if anyone is looking and takes a sip. Puts the bottle back into her purse and smiles.

My sister and I had both started to wear makeup, not very well I may add, not like I wear mine now. We didn't know a thing back then, but we didn't care because we were thirteen and we were away from the rez for a day, and we had a pack of Marlboros that we had stolen from Dad and we were looking to smoke and act cool and we were looking to see if there were any cute guys that had come with the carnival. We didn't see any, they were all fat, ugly guys with a lot of tattoos and they smelled like horses. We walked around and smoked our cigarettes, and we ate junk food and sipped Cokes, and we walked like we owned this land, well we did, well our people did, but we walked like we owned it, and we let people know that we were smoking and we were cool.

Spot changes to blue and SISTER COYOTE sits down in the pool of light. She digs into her purse for a compact and begins to fix her makeup.

As the day wore on and the sun got hot and we became kind of sick from all the food and the pop and the Marlboros, my sister said she was going to find Mom and Dad, and I told her I wanted to check out more of the freak shows and maybe see if there were any cute guys hiding in the Haunted House. I was making my way toward the Haunted House when I saw IT.

Stage lights come up as SISTER COYOTE still sits in the blue spot. WOODEN MAN stands and stretches and reaches underneath the bench and takes out an old baseball glove and ball and begins to throw the ball up into the air and catch it.

There I was in big red letters on a black sign: SEE THE TWO-HEADED BABY. I freaked out. I reached into my pocket and dug for the quarter that I knew was there and then I ran up the stairs that led to the TWO-HEADED BABY. When I got to the top of the stairs, a man who smelled like horses took my quarter and told me to go on in and to leave out the other side when I had had enough. I went in and it was dark and smelled like horses and over in the corner there was a table and on the table there was a jar and in the jar was the TWO-HEADED BABY. And I walked up to it and looked at it and it turned and it looked at me. I screamed but no one could hear me over all the noise on the rides outside. I wanted to run but I couldn't look away so I stood there and it stared back at me and I stared back at it. I moved closer to see if it was really alive but how could it be alive, right? I mean it was floating in some sort of liquid in a jar and it was a two-headed baby, so how could it have lived in the first place, right? But when I went up to it, it moved again, but not real movement, more like floating movement like it was in space or something, and it just spun around and around inside that jar and I just stared at it and stared at it and as its heads would spin around, the eyes would stare at me and they were looking at me like they wanted to come out of that jar and play. I wanted to run and I wanted to scream but I just stood there and stared and then someone else came in and they wanted to stare at the two-headed baby and I let them and I went outside and I never went back, and as I went down the stairs I threw up all over some cute guy who was combing the BEARDED LADY's beard.

WOODEN MAN drops the ball and it rolls over beside SISTER COYOTE. Blue spot fades as she picks up the ball and walks toward the WOODEN MAN.

You dropped your ball.

WOODEN MAN stares at her and reaches for the ball.

WOODEN MAN

I could never throw a curve ball. All my life I couldn't throw a curve to save it.

SISTER COYOTE

I could show you mine. I was pitcher for the Redhawks. We were the meanest team you ever set eyes on.

WOODEN MAN tosses her the ball, goes stage right and crouches like a catcher and shows her the glove.

WOODEN MAN

My dad tried to show me how to throw a curve, but the ball just wouldn't curve for me. He'd get so mad, his face would get all white and he would spit a little out of the corner of his mouth and he would swear and go in the house and turn the TV on, and he would mumble: "Kid's arm is useless."

SISTER COYOTE walks over to the opposite side of the stage and fades him and tosses the ball up into the air and fields it in the palm of her hand. She scratches out her mound with her feet and she readies herself to throw a pitch.

SISTER COYOTE

Our coach was the chief and he made the rules because he bought all the uniforms and he supplied the equipment. He pretended like he was BIG LEAGUE but he didn't know a thing about baseball and the only thing BIG about him was his belly and his big belly stuck out of his shirt and he would just sit in the dugout and pretend like he was giving us secret signals. We all would look at him and pretend that he was running the show but really it was Lucy, the third baseman, who was making the calls, and she called for a fastball and I would wind up and give her my best fastball.

She throws him a fastball with some smoke behind it and it makes a hard snapping sound as it hits the glove.

WOODEN MAN

STRIKE ONE!

WOODEN MAN tosses it back at her and resumes his catcher position. She does her ritual and prepares herself for another pitch and she awaits his signal this time. WOODEN MAN shows her two fingers and readies himself again for the next pitch. She throws it and it hits the glove just like the first one.

STRIKE TWO!

He stands up and walks toward her as if he is the catcher walking toward the mound in an important game. He gives her the ball and kicks at the dirt.

SISTER COYOTE

Okay, I've given two of my best pitches and all I have left is my curve, and I've been working hard on it all week but it just sort of hangs there and doesn't curve that much and the chief is getting all mad and he's threatening to pull me out of the game, and my friends are there and that cute guy in grade twelve is there with all his friends and he's come to see my great curve ball and this is the time for it, right?

WOODEN MAN

The CURVE.

He walks slowly back to home plate as she continues to talk to herself.

SISTER COYOTE

Was there any other choice? You had thrown the fastball on the first pitch and that batter just sat there and she knew, yes, she knew that the curve was coming up, everyone knew that the curve was going to be the last pitch, so she just sat there and she chewed her big wad of gum and she just waited for the third pitch because she knew it was going to be my weakest pitch.

WOODEN MAN crouches in his catcher position and shows her one finger, the middle one, and he smacks the dust out of his glove and readies himself for the next pitch. SISTER COYOTE sees the sign and she winds up, checks the bases, looks at the catcher, and she throws the most perfect curve ball that she could ever throw, and it hits the glove with a resounding smack.

WOODEN MAN

STRIKE THREE, YOU'RE OUT!

SISTER COYOTE

It was the most beautiful pitch that I have ever thrown in my life, even now I could never have thrown a better pitch, and everyone was screaming and yelling at me like I was some sort of hero, and the girls on my team all ran up to me and they put me on their shoulders and paraded me up and down the their base line, and all the people in the stands cheered and called out my name and the cute guy in grade twelve smiled to me and gave me the thumbs-up sign, and the chief was trying to get at me and hug me but he tripped and ripped the seat of his uniform pants and everyone saw his bum and everyone started to laugh at him and he began to laugh and everyone was laughing, even the other team who had travelled all this way to try and beat us, but we had beaten them, yes, we had beaten them with the best curve ball anyone could've thrown on that day.

WOODEN MAN

Nice pitch, kid.

He walks over and sits down in his spot and puts the glove and ball backunderneath the bench, and then becomes wooden.

SISTER COYOTE

Arm's a little tired. Not used to the distance, I guess.

She crosses over and sits down at the feet of the WOODEN MAN and she leans against his legs and goes to sleep.

WOODEN MAN

Nice pitch, kid.

Stage lights begin to fade. In the dark we hear a raven cawing followed by a voice yelling: "Get out of here, you stinking raven!" A spot comes up downstage centre and BROTHER RAVEN walks into the light, lights a cigarette and blows the smoke back at the voice.

BROTHER RAVEN

I was picking at the apples in the garbage. Just picking at the apples. Where is the wrong in that?

Takes another long drag, it goes down the wrong pipe and he begins to cough. He stamps the cigarette out and wipes the tears from his eyes.

Never was much of a smoker.

Takes bottles out of his coat, takes a good-sized swig and puts the bottle back into his pocket.

Now drinking is more my style. Nothing like a good shot to get the earth moving. Nothing like a good shot.

The spot turns to blue and BROTHER RAVEN sits down and takes a piece of paper and a piece of candy from his pocket. He unwraps the candy and puts in into his mouth and savours the sweet taste, he uncrumples the piece of paper and begins to read it.

"In the morning as Mother walked to the river and all the children slept so peaceful on the floor with their little feet sticking out of the warm blankets, there would be a calm quietness that came over the land and all you could hear was the river as it moved gently to the ocean and Mother would walk down to the river and she would take off her dress and she would slip into the water and bathe herself and ready herself for the long day ahead."

He takes the candy out of his mouth and admires it and puts it back into his mouth and sucks on it some more and flips the piece of paper and continues to read.

"Mother would start the fire and me and my brothers and sisters would rise up off the floor and stare at her in wonderment and she would ask us if we had had visions in our sleep and I would always answer yes and proceed to tell her what I had seen: I had seen a young salmon come to the shore of the river and it whispered to me that I should join her in the water and I asked her why and she giggled and said it was nice and warm, so I went in and the salmon swam right beside me, and she would whisper to me that I was cute and that I had skinny legs, and I would laugh and try to catch her, but she was a salmon and she could swim somewhat better than I could, and she would always get away before I could touch her. Mother would always laugh at my visions and my brothers and sisters would always laugh and tease me and they would always show me the salmon they had caught and say to me: 'Is this her, is this her!' And I would cry because what if it was her and they had cut her open and they had put her on the fire and I had eaten her. Mother would try and explain to them what my visions meant, but they were too eager to run out and play in the forest, and I would just sit there and Mother would tell me her visions, and I would eat tuna sandwiches because I felt too bad about eating salmon, and Mother would join me on the floor and hold me tight and she would laugh as she told her visions, and I would laugh too because she was so funny and kind, so funny and kind."

He folds up the piece of paper and puts it back into his pocket as stage lights come up and WOODEN WOMAN begins to move. She reaches beneath the bench, pulls out a spinning top and begins to spin it about the stage as she follows it on her hands and knees. BROTHER RAVEN stands up, reaches into his pocket, pulls out a comb and begins to comb back his slicked black hair.

Always had the ability to have visions. Never know quite what they mean but they mean something and I have them every night.

He finishes combing his hair, puts the comb back into his pocket and pulls out an old rotten apple from his pocket and begins to pick and eat away at it. WOODEN WOMAN stops spinning the top, goes back and reaches underneath the bench and this time she comes out with a bag of marbles and starts to play a game of marbles while still on her hands and knees.

Just picking at the apples. Never meant any harm to no one but they think you're stealing from them even if the apples are rotten. Even if the apples are rotten...

WOODEN WOMAN shoots one marble and it rolls to the feet of BROTHER RAVEN. He picks it up and walks over to her and her game of marbles as the blue spots fades.

WOODEN WOMAN

Play for funsies or keepsies?

BROTHER RAVEN

Keepsies!

WOODEN WOMAN

Okay, okay, but I get to shoot first and you can't say funsies if I start to win, all right?

BROTHER RAVEN

All right, but I only have one marble left and if I lose it I can't play anymore.

WOODEN WOMAN

Okay, you better shoot first. Where's your marble?

He reaches into his pocket and pulls out a red marble. He holds it up to the light and stares through it. WOODEN WOMAN comes up beside him and she stares through it too.

BROTHER RAVEN

It's the prettiest marble I've ever owned. All my life I've been playing marbles and this is the prettiest one I've ever come across.

WOODEN WOMAN

It's lovely. All red and you can see right through it. Where did you get it?

He brings it down from the light and steps back away from her and kneels down and readies himself to play marbles. WOODEN WOMAN kneels down beside him and looks him right in the eyes.

Where did you get that marble?

BROTHER RAVEN

I'm not supposed to say.

WOODEN WOMAN

Why not? Is it a magic marble? Because if it is, then I don't want to play for keepsies.

BROTHER RAVEN

Too late.

He begins to win all her marbles. She kneels there beside him and watches as he makes the most amazing shots she has ever seen. The red marble banks and kicks out all her marbles and she sits there in wonderment and he collects all her marbles and puts them in his pocket.

WOODEN WOMAN

No fair. Winning with a magic marble just ain't fair.

BROTHER RAVEN

Here, have an apple.

He gives her one of his rotten apples and she bites into it without looking at it.

WOODEN WOMAN

Good apple.

BROTHER RAVEN

I picked it myself.

WOODEN WOMAN

I was good at picking cherries.

BROTHER RAVEN

Not me. I couldn't climb the trees and I was always falling out of them and landing on my head. I just ate the ones that fell to the ground.

WOODEN WOMAN goes and sits in her spot on the bench and lifts her dress up to the knee. BROTHER RAVEN goes and kneels at her feet just like SISTER COYOTE is sitting with the WOODEN MAN.

WOODEN WOMAN

See this scar right here on my shin? A spirit gave me that scar. You see, I got that one from falling down a cherry tree when I was just a little girl. The tree was on old Irving's land. No one ever went onto his land because everyone thought his land was full of bad spirits. They used to say the spirits were bad because they had all died on the same day, they had all died on the same hour and they had all died the same way, and they had all been buried together on Irving's land.

BROTHER RAVEN rests his head on her knee, listens to her story and slowly falls asleep.

Nothing on his land but rocks and weeds anyway, so we pretty much stayed away from him and his land of bad spirits. But there was that cherry tree that everyone knew and talked about. They said that the cherries were so big and juicy that you could eat one and be full for a week. They said this tree never went a day without a new cherry growing and becoming big and juicy. As you can tell by this scar, I went on that land and I went past those bad spirits and I went up that cherry tree and I picked me the biggest and the juiciest of all the cherries on the earth. I ate maybe four or five and stuck the rest of them cherries into my pockets and I was making my way down the tree when I saw her.

She puts her dress down and puts the half-eaten apple in the WOODEN MAN's hand. BROTHER RAVEN is fast asleep as she touches his face.

I've never seen such a sight in all my life. It was a young girl. She looked to be maybe ten or eleven. She stood there at the bottom of the tree and she looked up at me. I spoke to her and I said: "Hey, would you like some cherries?" The little girl stared at me and then she touched the tree and the whole tree shook, no, the whole world felt like it was shaking and I tried to hold on but I couldn't because my hands were slippery from the juiciest cherries in the whole wide world, and I fell, no, I slid all the way down that tree and fell right at her feet.

That girl just stared at me as I ran, no, I limped all the way off of Irving's land and I never looked back. So you see, a spirit gave me this scar.

BROTHER RAVEN moves and becomes more comfortable, and as he does this his magic red marble falls out of his hand and WOODEN WOMAN reaches down and picks it up and she stares at it in the light as stage lights begin to fade.

Finders keepers.

Blackout.

SCENE 5

Stage lights come up. More leaves on the ground. A wolf howls. A German TOURIST enters and sets up a camera on a tripod. SISTER COYOTE is asleep on one side of the bench and BROTHER RAVEN is asleep on the other side. WOODEN MAN and WOODEN WOMAN are in their usual spot on the bench. The German TOURIST sets the timer and quickly sits in between the two wooden Indians. When the timer beeps the German TOURIST smiles and the WOODEN MAN takes a bite out of the rotten apple that was in his hand and he goes back to being wooden. The German TOURIST looks at the WOODEN MAN and then down at the apple. He shakes his head and then rises and gathers his camera and tripod and exits. WOODEN MAN slowly begins to chew the mouthful of rotten apple. SISTER COYOTE moves and talks in her sleep.

SISTER COYOTE

Tell me a story, Poppa. Tell me a story, Poppa.

WOODEN MAN looks down at her and takes another bite from the rotten apple.

WOODEN MAN

Are you talking to me? 'Cause if you are, then you should look me in the eyes, not polite to ask someone for something and not look them in the eyes.

He takes another bite and another and another until the apple is finished and then he puts the apple core into WOODEN WOMAN's hand.

I met a man once who wouldn't look me in the eyes. He'd always be wanting something from me and he would come right up to my door and he'd ask for it without ever looking me in the eyes, and I'd tell him no every time, and he'd walk away all mad but he would come back and he would ask me for something else, and I would look him right in the eyes and I knew that I would give him whatever it was he was asking for, if he would just have the respect to look me in the eyes when he asked for it, but he never did and he hated me. That man hated me because I asked for respect.

SISTER COYOTE moves again and speaks again in her sleep.

SISTER COYOTE

Poppa? You there, Poppa? The house is so cold and all the wood is still wet and my blanket's too small 'cause I'm getting taller. Can you see that I'm getting taller, Poppa?

WOODEN MAN

Not going to look me in the eyes? Then I am unable to answer you. Sorry, but it's just a rule I have with people. If you can't look me in the eyes then I can't answer you. It's a rule I've stuck with all my life and I can't start breaking my own rules for the sake of talking to anyone so you'll have to look me in the eyes if you want me to answer you.

WOODEN MAN whistles and plays with the buttons on his shirt. This bores him and he bends down and unlaces his boots and reties them and repeats this and becomes bored with this, and he looks around for something to do but realizes that there is nothing left for him to do.

All right! I will speak and answer you this one time, but you can't tell anyone that I broke one of my own rules, because if people find out that you can't even respect your own rules, then why should they respect anything about you, right? Right. So I'm talking to you because there's no one else to talk to right now and I have to tell you about this vision I just had and if I don't tell anyone then I think I may have to scream and if you've ever heard me scream then you know what a loud scream that I have. So here is my vision. I was on...

SISTER COYOTE

Poppa, can I have another piece of bread? My belly isn't quite full yet.

WOODEN MAN

Listen, if we're going to have a conversation, then you'll have to respect that I was talking and it was my turn to tell you about my vision, so you just sit there and don't say a word, all right? All right. Anything more to say before I carry on with my vision? No?

SISTER COYOTE moves and we see her face, she smiles and continues to sleep as WOODEN MAN stands and stretches his legs and picks up a leaf and crumbles it in his hand.

I was on the river. I know, I know, I am always on the river but this time I was really on the river. I was born on the river. I bet you didn't know that. I was born and raised on that river.

He bends down and picks up another leaf and lets it fall from his hand to the ground.

I was on the river and I was on my old boat. The old boat sure could move, when it wanted to. It could cut through the water and nothing, no storm, no wind, could stop her from getting me home.

He picks up another leaf, and goes and sits down in his spot on the bench and stares at the leaf.

I was on the river and I was on my old boat and we were heading home from a long day of fishing. I didn't pull in too much on that day, but I had enough for supper. The water was calm and there was no wind, and you could just make out the blue of the sky, and you could just catch a glimpse of the mountains. We were making real good time when all of a sudden the engine went dead. I tried to start it up again but she just wouldn't turn, and then the wind came out of nowhere and the rain started to fall hard, and the blue of the sky was gone and it was dark and you could no longer see the mountains, and the boat turned and started to head downriver as the river's current became strong and angry.

He drops the leaf to the ground in front of him. It becomes windy on the stage and the leaves are blowing all over the place as he continues to tell his vision.

I had no idea where I was anymore. The boat seemed to have a life of its own and it took me where it wanted to go, and I had to go because there was no choice, and the boat landed itself on shore and then the wind stopped and the rain stopped and the sky cleared, and there was the blue and there were the mountains and I still had no idea where I was.

Wind stops and leaves come to rest on the ground. Offstage we hear a wolf howling followed by a voice saying: "Get out of here, you stinking wolf!"

I got off the boat and went down the shoreline trying to figure out where I was, but nothing was familiar to me and it felt like I was in a different world, and then I saw him. He was sitting on a log and he lit a cigarette and smiled right at me.

Spot comes up downstage centre and MISTER WOLF walks into the spot. He is dressed in a three-piece suit and his hair is in two braids. He is wearing sunglasses as he lights a cigarette and blows the smoke into the air as he smiles.

MISTER WOLF

That your boat?

WOODEN MAN stands to answer him.

WOODEN MAN

Yes it is. It's a good…

MISTER WOLF

I need a boat.

WOODEN MAN

She's not for sale.

MISTER WOLF

Did I say I wanted to buy it?

WOODEN MAN

No.

MISTER WOLF

No, I did not. I said I needed a boat. Is this one available?

WOODEN MAN

I was going home and the wind brought me here. I have to get home and cook the fish before they go bad. If you like, I could take you upriver a ways.

MISTER WOLF

That would be fine.

They both sit down. MISTER WOLF puts his cigarette out and takes off his sunglasses and put them into his pocket. The spot turns blue as the WOODEN MAN looks down at SISTER COYOTE but she is still asleep.

WOODEN MAN

This vision feels so real.

MISTER WOLF

What? What did you say?

WOODEN MAN

Nothing. You must've heard the thunder. It's been real crazy today.

MISTER WOLF

Can't this heap go any faster?

WOODEN MAN

She usually goes faster but her belly is full of fish that I caught today. See?

MISTER WOLF looks beside him and pretends to pick up fish and eat them whole until they are all gone. WOODEN MAN whispers to SISTER COYOTE.

He ate all my fish. There must've been thirty fish in her belly and he ate them all. He ate them whole.

MISTER WOLF stands and feels his full belly.

MISTER WOLF

Now you can go faster.

WOODEN MAN stands and he is angry because MISTER WOLF has eaten all his fish.

WOODEN MAN

You want to go fast, well here we go!

They both start to shake and twist as if going fast on a boat. They build and build their actions until they both meet centre stage and crash into one another, causing them to fall to the ground onto the now pile of dead leaves on the ground.

MISTER WOLF

Where am I?

WOODEN MAN

I've got to stop having these visions. They're really getting kind of weird.

MISTER WOLF

Where am I?

Both stand and stare at each other. MISTER WOLF has leaves in his hair and his suit is somewhat crumpled and creased. WOODEN MAN limps back and sits down in usual spot.

WOODEN MAN

You're right here. Where else would you be?

MISTER WOLF stares at him.

MISTER WOLF

Do I know you?

WOODEN MAN whispers to SISTER COYOTE who is still asleep on the ground beside the bench.

WOODEN MAN

Watch this one, he's very tricky.

MISTER WOLF

What? I didn't hear what you said. You're going to have to speak up because I seem to have lost some of my hearing.

WOODEN MAN becomes wooden and silent. MISTER WOLF goes up to him and taps him on the shoulder but WOODEN MAN does not move. MISTER WOLF taps everyone else on the shoulder but they do not move either. He goes back and sits in the blue spot as stage lights begin to fade.

Right back to where I began. No one to talk to. No one to laugh and play tricks on. Just me and the earth.

Reaches into his pocket and pulls out an old pocket watch and chain. He stares at it and he listens to see if it still ticks.

Never know if it's the right time or not. Can't tell by this old timepiece. It's only good to stare at when the sun is out. See how it glows in the light.

He holds it up to the light and watches as it spins and gleams in the light.

Never was good for telling the right time.

He puts the watch back into his pocket.

Always had clocks and timepieces for the time at any time in my life. When I was a kid we had two clocks, one in the kitchen on top of the stove and one in Grandma's room right next to her bed. You could hear that old clock ticking just as loud as Grandma's snoring. We used to sneak in there at night and set the alarm to ring at exactly midnight and wait for it to ring and for Grandma to wake up and screams at us kids to stop fooling around, but we would be laughing so hard and she would start giggling too, and swear up and down that all us kids were crazy and that we should be locked up somewhere. We would get Grandma a tea and let her get back to sleep and we would go on to our rooms which were on the other side of the kitchen and we would pass the other clock that was on the stove and it would tell us that it was bedtime and we would all go to sleep and we would all hear the ticking of them two clocks because one was faster than the other: tick tick tock tock tick tick tock tock…

He curls up and goes to sleep as blue spot begins to fade.

Tick tick tock tock tick tick tock tock…

Lights go to black.

SCENE 6

In the black we hear horses and men screaming: CHARGE! Lights come up slowly. Night. More leaves on the ground. WOODEN MAN and WOODEN WOMAN are sitting in their places on the bench. SISTER COYOTE stands to the right of WOODEN MAN, BROTHER RAVEN is standing to the left of WOODEN WOMAN, MISTER WOLF is standing behind and in the middle of the bench. They hold their pose as the TOURIST, now dressed as a Mountie, enters and sets up his camera and tripod. He sets the timer and goes behind the bench and stands beside MISTER WOLF. As the timer beeps, the TOURIST raises his hand and makes the peace symbol, as all the other characters each raise one of their middle fingers. TOURIST looks at each of them as if they did move, shakes his head and gathers his camera and exits. Again sounds of horses and men screaming: CHARGE!

WOODEN MAN

He smelled like horse shit!

SISTER COYOTE

He must've stepped in it when he got off his horse.

MISTER WOLF

Smells more like he was rolling around in it, you know they do that.

BROTHER RAVEN

Do they really?

MISTER WOLF

Sure they do. Some sort of ritual. Some sort of ceremony to make them stronger when they go into battle.

WOODEN MAN

He's going to scare the other side away smelling like that. They won't be able to see him coming because he'll be covered in flies. All they'll see is a cloud of flies coming over the hill.

WOODEN WOMAN stands and walks downstage left. She takes out her red marble and stares at it through the light. SISTER COYOTE walks up to her and lights a cigarette and blows the smoke into the air and into the light that WOODEN WOMAN is staring at.

SISTER COYOTE

Did you smell the horses?

WOODEN WOMAN

All I can smell is smoke.

SISTER COYOTE

I couldn't smell the horses. I think those guys were just kidding about him smelling like horses. He did look pretty in that uniform and that big hat, they sure got big hats.

WOODEN WOMAN stops looking through her marble and puts it away. SISTER COYOTE offer her a drag from her cigarette.

Here, have a taste.

WOODEN WOMAN takes the cigarette and takes a drag. She blows the smoke toward the men who are all now sitting on the bench checking their shoes to see if they are the ones who have stepped in horse shit.

WOODEN WOMAN

Everything becomes different when you look at it through smoke. Nothing is as clear as it should be. It looks older and worn.

She hands the cigarette back to SISTER COYOTE.

Thank you.

SISTER COYOTE

You're welcome.

SISTER COYOTE takes a drag and blows the smoke at the men who are now sniffing each other trying to figure out where the smell is coming from.

The smoke makes them disappear.

WOODEN WOMAN

I know. It's like they've never existed. One minute they're talking and smiling and the next they're gone.

SISTER COYOTE

Wait till the smoke clears and then we can see and hear them again.

She puts out the cigarette and looks back at the men who are now standing and have moved away from each other.

MISTER WOLF

I had a horse once.

BROTHER RAVEN

Was he fast?

MISTER WOLF

No, not really. He would just stand there and eat and shit.

WOODEN MAN

Doesn't sound like much of a horse.

MISTER WOLF

He wasn't. I won him at a card game. I had three queens. I bet all my belongings on that hand. There was no way I was going to let that horse get away from me. Three queens won me that horse.

MISTER WOLF sits down on the centre of the bench.

BROTHER RAVEN

What did you bet for that horse?

MISTER WOLF

I bet my life.

WOODEN MAN

What did you do that for? That sounds pretty dumb to me, betting your life on three queens.

MISTER WOLF

I wanted that horse. There was no way I was going to walk out of that game and have no horse. It was like nothing else mattered and the only way Ii could go on living was if I won that horse. So I put down my three queens, stood up, walked out the door, and I got on that horse and rode into the night.

MISTER WOLF pretends to ride a horse.

BROTHER RAVEN

A horse is no good if he's not fast. What did you do with him?

MISTER WOLF

I rode him until the sun came up and then I sat there and just stared at him. He was one ugly horse.

WOODEN MAN

Three queens, your life, for an ugly horse?

MISTER WOLF

Yep. He was the ugliest animal I had ever seen. He only had one eye and his mouth sat there half open and his tongue hung out like a big snake.

BROTHER RAVEN

I hate snakes. They're always trying to get me with their big teeth. Sometimes I can't get five steps without one of them trying to bite me. You ever been bitten by a snake?

WOODEN MAN

No, but I did get bit by a dog before. Big dog bit me on the ass. He wouldn't let go, just bit right into my ass and stared at me with crazy eyes.

BROTHER RAVEN

What did you do?

WOODEN MAN

I tried to spin him around and knock him off but he had a hold of me good. I spun and spun but he wouldn't let go. I stopped and looked down into his eyes. I tried to warn him to let go but he held on, so I took out my knife from my pocket and I stabbed him right in the ass. His eyes and mouth opened wide enough for me to get my ass out of his mouth. I turned around and showed him the piece of his ass that I had just cut out and told him that we were even, and that he better get on down the road or I was going to cut him somewhere else. He turned and ran away leaving me there with my bloody knife and my bloody and sore ass.

MISTER WOLF stops riding his horse. WOODEN MAN sits down in his spot very carefully and on one cheek.

BROTHER RAVEN

I've never been bitten by a dog but I have been bitten by a snake before.

MISTER WOLF

Did he bite you in the ass?

BROTHER RAVEN

No, he bit me right on the heart.

He lifts up his shirt and shows both men where he has been bitten by a snake, there should be bite scars right where his heart is.

WOODEN MAN

That's gotta hurt.

MISTER WOLF

How in the heck did you let a snake bite you on the heart like that?

BROTHER RAVEN

I didn't let him, he took a bite when I was sleeping right beside him.

WOODEN MAN

What were you doing sleeping beside a snake? I thought you hated snakes.

BROTHER RAVEN

I didn't back then, I thought he was okay. He gave me some of the chicken that he had stolen from some farmer. Any snake who would give me some of their chicken must be a good snake, I thought.

MISTER WOLF

You ate raw chicken with a snake?

BROTHER RAVEN

No, he cooked it up, made a nice sauce out of some of the old berries that I had picked up along the road. We cooked it over a nice fire and sat there by the river and ate that chicken whole.

WOODEN MAN

And then he bit you on the heart?

BROTHER RAVEN

No, not right away. He told me stories about where he had come from and as it got later and later I began to fall asleep. He must've curled up beside me for warmth because I woke up one time and found him right there beside me. I didn't want to be rude and ask him to move away because he had given me his food and he had let me sleep by his fire. So I let him sleep there beside me, closed my eyes, and tried to dream.

WOODEN MAN

That's when he bit you?

BROTHER RAVEN

No, not right away.

WOODEN MAN

Gee, did he bite you at all, or are you just making this story up?

BROTHER RAVEN sits down on the bench.

BROTHER RAVEN

No, he bit me. But not right away. It was like he was trying to get close enough to me so he could bite right into my heart. I went back to sleep with him there beside me and then I woke up again and this time I found him right up my shirt and he had his head right next to my heart. I tapped him on top of the head and asked him: "What are you doing?"

MISTER WOLF

What did he say?

BROTHER RAVEN

Nothing. He looked right up at me with those green eyes and he opened his mouth up real slow and then he bit right into my chest. I let out a scream, and jumped up and tried to pull him off, but he was under my shirt and I couldn't get a good grip on him so he bit harder and deeper. His teeth felt like they were razors cutting into my chest. I tore my shirt off and now I had a hold of him but still he wouldn't let go, and all this time he looked at me with those green eyes and had those razor teeth buried into my chest. It was as if he was smiling at me. Smiling because he knew I was going to die. I tugged and tugged and slowly he started to get weak and his hold wasn't as strong as before. I pulled and pulled on him and it felt like I was stretching him. His eyes closed and he knew that he had to let go so he opened that big mouth and his teeth slowly came out of my chest and I swung him around in the air and I threw him into the river.

MISTER WOLF

Could he swim?

BROTHER RAVEN

Yes, he could swim. But not fast enough. When he hit the water the sound made a big splash and an owl who had been watching all this jumped from its tree and it glided toward the struggling snake. All I could see were those green eyes as they tried to make it back to shore but the owl came down and snapped that snake in half. Those green eyes closed one more time and disappeared with the owl as the night became quiet.

SISTER COYOTE and WOODEN WOMAN clear a small circle in the leaves by their feet and sit down beside it. They begin to play marbles as the men sit and become wooden. SISTER COYOTE shoot first, makes the first shot but misses the next.

SISTER COYOTE

Wasn't much of a marble player.

WOODEN WOMAN

This is a magic marble, watch how it moves and takes the other marbles from the circle.

She takes out the rest of the marbles and sits and stares at the red marble as a single spot lights the marble circle area. Stage lights begin to fade until only the single spot is left.

SISTER COYOTE

My brother used to play a lot of marbles. The other kids would save up their money until they could buy a couple of marbles at the rez store. They would come by all ready to take on my brother because he was the champ.

WOODEN WOMAN

Did he have a marble like this one?

SISTER COYOTE

No. But he had the magic within him. The other kids would watch as he gracefully took their favourite marbles. They watched as he took the marbles they had saved up for.

WOODEN WOMAN

Did anyone ever beat him?

SISTER COYOTE

They say he beat himself.

WOODEN WOMAN

What do you mean?

SISTER COYOTE

He had won all the marbles on the rez and no one would play with him anymore. So he gathered up all his marbles and he went into the woods to play one final game with someone who had a chance to beat him.

WOODEN WOMAN

Who did he play against?

SISTER COYOTE

They say the spirits came to his game and they brought all their magic marbles. My brother played each one until all their marbles were now his.

WOODEN WOMAN

What did you do with those magic marbles?

SISTER COYOTE

Some say he gives them to children who have nothing. He comes late at night and leaves one red marble on their chest. When they wake up, find it, they know that my brother's spirit has come to see them.

WOODEN WOMAN

See how the light makes it glow?

SISTER COYOTE

One red marble.

WOODEN WOMAN

See the life, the power?

SISTER COYOTE

It looks like a tiny heart.

WOODEN WOMAN picks up the marble and stares at it through the light as spot begins to slowly fade.

WOODEN WOMAN

A child's heart.

Lights go to black.

ACT TWO

SCENE 1

Daytime. An area downstage centre has been cleared and there is a raised platform. On the platform is a blanket with food and drink like a picnic. MISTER WOLF, SISTER COYOTE and BROTHER RAVEN are sitting on the platform. WOODEN WOMAN and WOODEN MAN are sitting on the bench. WOODEN MAN is holding a baby in his arms. Offstage we hear children playing in a park.

WOODEN MAN

She's so pretty. Look at those brown eyes.

WOODEN WOMAN

What should we call her?

WOODEN MAN

We should wait for the spirits to show us what we should call her.

WOODEN WOMAN

She likes it here, see how she smiles.

WOODEN MAN

Let's listen to the spirits and see what name we should give to our daughter.

MISTER WOLF takes off his dirty running shoes and begins to pick at his toes.

MISTER WOLF

Look at these toes. Have you ever seen more perfect toes before?

BROTHER RAVEN

They look more like claws.

BROTHER RAVEN takes off his shoes and shows them to MISTER WOLF

Now these are perfect feet.

SISTER COYOTE

They look more like turkey feet, all skinny and hairy.

BROTHER RAVEN

These are great feet. I can pick anything up with these.

BROTHER RAVEN attempts to pick up a plate with his toes but is unsuccessful.

WOODEN MAN

Turkey feet.

WOODEN WOMAN

What?

WOODEN MAN

We call her Turkey Feet.

WOODEN WOMAN

Turkey Feet? I don't think so.

WOODEN MAN

You're right, the other children would laugh at her.

SISTER COYOTE takes off her shoes and puts her feet in the air.

SISTER COYOTE

My feet are perfect.

MISTER WOLF

Never seen a perfect foot before. Let me see.

He stands and examines her feet.

You should see these, they're perfect.

BROTHER RAVEN stands and examines her feet.

BROTHER RAVEN

They're perfect.

He begins to tickle her feet.

SISTER COYOTE

Hey, cut that out, it tickles.

BROTHER RAVEN and MISTER WOLF both tickle her feet as she screams and laughs.

Don't! Hey, stop! I'll pee myself!

They both stop tickling her and she tries to catch her breath.

You guys are so mean.

MISTER WOLF

Just having some fun.

BROTHER RAVEN

We were just playing. No harm done. Are you okay? I mean, did you pee yourself?

SISTER COYOTE

No. But I bet I can tickle you until you pee your pants.

She goes to him and tickles his sides as he squirms to get away.

BROTHER RAVEN

Don't! Ravens don't like to be tickled. Hey, stop it! You're ruffling my feathers.

She stops and goes and tries to tickle MISTER WOLF, but he just sits there and ignores her.

MISTER WOLF

You can't tickle a wolf.

She stops and sits down.

WOODEN MAN

Ruffled Feather!

WOODEN WOMAN

What?

WOODEN MAN

We can call her Ruffled Feather.

WOODEN WOMAN

I don't think so. She is much more beautiful than a ruffled feather.

She takes the baby from WOODEN MAN and holds it in her arms.

WOODEN MAN

You're right. Boy, these spirits sure aren't very good with choosing a name.

Offstage we hear children playing and then a voice saying: "Get out of here, you stinking kid." TOURIST enters dressed as a small boy and carrying a red ball and a lollipop. TOURIST goes up to WOODEN MAN and kicks him in the shin. TOURIST goes up to WOODEN WOMAN and pulls on her hair. They both do not react. TOURIST goes to picnic area and stares at MISTER WOLF, SISTER COYOTE and BROTHER RAVEN. WOODEN MAN reaches for the TOURIST but WOODEN WOMAN pulls him back.

Rotten kid.

WOODEN WOMAN

Leave him be, he doesn't know any better.

WOODEN MAN

Just a good kick in the ass. That's all it'll take.

WOODEN WOMAN

He doesn't know any better.

WOODEN MAN

Where do they learn that?

WOODEN WOMAN

History, I guess.

TOURIST goes and pokes MISTER WOLF. MISTER WOLF howls and tries to be big and strong.

MISTER WOLF

You better get away from me, kid. I'm a big bad wolf!

TOURIST speaking as a snotty kid.

TOURIST

Wolves don't wear suits.

MISTER WOLF

Oh yeah?

TOURIST

Yeah. Wolves have big teeth and walk on all fours.

MISTER WOLF

Well, I don't.

TOURIST

Then you're not a wolf.

MISTER WOLF

Beat it, kid, before I bite you on the ass and show you just how big my teeth are.

MISTER WOLF reaches for him but the TOURIST runs away and pokes at BROTHER RAVEN who caws real loud and tries to flap his arms like wings.

BROTHER RAVEN

You better not mess with me. I'm a big old raven and I'll peck our your eyes if you're not careful.

TOURIST

You're not a raven. Ravens don't have greasy hair. They have beautiful black feathers.

BROTHER RAVEN

Yeah, well I'm having a bad hair day. Get going or I'll...

He reaches for him but TOURIST runs away and goes to SISTER COYOTE and pulls her hair.

SISTER COYOTE

Ouch! Hey, quit it!

TOURIST

What're you going to do about it?

SISTER COYOTE

I'll bite you! I'm a coyote and my bite really hurts!

TOURIST

You're no coyote. Coyotes are beautiful and have nice eyes.

SISTER COYOTE

I have nice eyes. Hey, where do you get off telling me I don't have nice eyes!

TOURIST smiles and pulls on her hair again as he skips off stage. Sounds of children playing ends. SISTER COYOTE begins to cry.

I have nice eyes, don't I?

BROTHER RAVEN and MISTER WOLF go up to her and try to console her.

BROTHER RAVEN

Sure you do.

MISTER WOLF

Nothing more beautiful than a coyote's eyes.

BROTHER RAVEN

Except maybe her feet.

MISTER WOLF

And her feet.

SISTER COYOTE

Thanks, guys.

BROTHER RAVEN

My eyes are black like the night.

MISTER WOLF

My eyes are yellow like the sun.

SISTER COYOTE

My mother told me that my eyes were like the earth and they could look at you forever. That's what she used to call me, Forever.

They sit down on the picnic blanket and begin again to compare feet. WOODEN MAN stares at his child as WOODEN WOMAN holds her in her arms.

WOODEN MAN

We shall call her Forever.

WOODEN WOMAN

Yes, that's a wonderful name.

WOODEN MAN

Look at those eyes.

WOODEN WOMAN

Yes, they look at you forever.

Lights fade.

SCENE 2

Daytime. Stage is covered in dead leaves. All characters are sitting or standing at the bench. WOODEN WOMAN is still holding the child in her arms. Offstage we hear a military bugle playing softly and then the sound of a marching drum, sounds of men going into battle. TOURIST enters now dressed in a blue U.S. Calvary uniform. He enters holding freshly taken scalps, his old camera and tripod. He places the scalps in the hands of WOODEN MAN and WOODEN WOMAN, goes and takes their picture. No one moves. TOURIST gathers the scalps, his camera and tripod, and exists as stage lights and sounds fade.

SCENE 3

Daytime. Only the platform area is lit. Everyone is sitting on the blanket and facing downstage. Offstage we hear: "Get out of here, you stinking Indian." WOODEN MAN stands and faces downstage.

WOODEN MAN

We are going into battle.

WOODEN WOMAN stands with her child still in her arms and faces downstage.

WOODEN WOMAN

The men have all left the village.

MISTER WOLF

This bread is real tasty.

SISTER COYOTE

Could you pass the butter? I like a lot of butter on my bread.

BROTHER RAVEN

Here you go. Could you pass the blueberries? It's been a long time since I've had any.

MISTER WOLF

It's a nice day for a picnic. Sun's out, not a cloud in the sky.

Sounds of war softly in the distance, horses, men screaming, gunfire, screams of wounded and dying men.

WOODEN MAN

I must go. I must kill those that have killed my fathers.

WOODEN WOMAN

The men have all left. It's just the mothers and the children.

WOODEN MAN steps off the platform. We should hear the crunching of dead leaves as he steps down. He walks and stands downstage right as red spot comes up.

Don't go! Don't go! They will kill you and there will be no more fathers for our children. Don't go! Our baby has only lived two days and has not met the earth and all its beauty.

WOODEN MAN

I must go. I must kill those that have killed my mothers.

WOODEN WOMAN is holding her child in her arms as sounds of battle get louder and louder.

WOODEN WOMAN

Come back! Come back! Be with us forever. We can hide in the forest and the soldiers will not find us. Come back! Come back!

WOODEN MAN

I must go. I must kill those that have killed my children.

Sounds build to a crashing end. Red spot fades as WOODEN WOMAN sits down with her child in her arms.

WOODEN WOMAN

The men have all disappeared. The Blue Coats have taken and destroyed their life. The earth has become silent. No more screams, no more screams. It's quiet now, my child. Sleep and dream, sleep and dream of days unlike this, this is a sad day, a day filled with the loss of our men. May their spirits sleep like you, my child. May they sleep with endless peace.

MISTER WOLF

It's a great day for a picnic. Not one sound, not even noisy songbirds.

BROTHER RAVEN

You got something against birds?

MISTER WOLF

Only ones who sing poorly.

BROTHER RAVEN

I wasn't much of a singer.

SISTER COYOTE

Could you pass the bread? My belly isn't quite full yet.

Lights fade to black on picnic area.

SCENE 4

MISTER WOLF, BROTHER RAVEN and SISTER COYOTE are asleep on the picnic blanket. WOODEN WOMAN stands on the edge of the platform, still holding her child. TOURIST enters. He is now dressed as a movie director. He brings out his chair and his movie camera and sets both up to the right of WOODEN MAN who is still downstage right. TOURIST sits down in his director's chair and on the back we read: "Mr. Costner." He talks into a walkie-talkie.

TOURIST

Lights! Okay, bring in the buffalo!

WOODEN MAN

The cannons fired and the earth shook as they charged toward us with their fire.

WOODEN WOMAN talks to her child.

WOODEN WOMAN

Your father was the bravest of all the men. He held his head up high when he went into battle with those Blue Coats.

TOURIST

More smoke! I need more smoke!

WOODEN MAN

The cannons killed half the men in five minutes. We had nowhere to run. My brothers were on the ground, torn and dying by that screaming hot metal.

WOODEN WOMAN

Your father was a great man, everyone listened when he spoke. They looked up to him and they respected his vision.

TOURIST

Okay, kill the buffalo! Where's the wolf? Someone get the wolf out of his trailer. I need the wolf to howl on cue. Can he do that?

MISTER WOLF howls in his sleep.

WOODEN WOMAN

Your father was so beautiful. His eyes held my spirit the first time I looked into them.

WOODEN MAN

A piece of hot metal cut into my leg and I fell from my horse as those around me died.

TOURIST talks directly to WOODEN MAN

TOURIST

Could you talk slower? More poetically. Slowly and clearly. These words were written for a reason. Let's hear them, okay? More cannon fire! More cannon fire!

WOODEN MAN

I was there on the ground with my leg bleeding and burning with the fire of those men who were here to destroy us. My brothers had all died, and I watched their spirits rise off the ground and into the beautiful sky. They gathered above the battle and did not know what to do. They were confused and they began to cry and sing like the death they had become.

TOURIST

Okay, that's better. Now, I want you to look mean. Can we see your war face? Who did this guy's makeup? I want more paint! More paint on this one! Makeup! Makeup!

WOODEN MAN

I was alone as the soldiers charged forward with the cold steel of their bayonets. They slid the blades so easily into my brothers who were already dead. The cold blade slid into the warmth of death and then they cut off their beautiful hair. With the harshness of a cold blade they took their hair and screamed in victory. My brothers screamed from the sky as their hair was taken and shown to them, and then the battle became quiet.

Spot fades on WOODEN MAN as he exits. TOURIST stands and gathers his chair, camera, tripod.

TOURIST

Okay, enough of this shot. Let's get some close-ups of those bleeding scalps. I want it to drip and drip. And get the women and children ready. I want to see the children and the women screaming and crying. Can they do that? Tell them we'll pay them more if there's real tears. Okay, let's go! Let's not waste this beautiful sunny day.

TOURIST exits. WOODEN WOMAN puts her child down and stands on the edge of the platform as lights slowly begin to fade.

WOODEN WOMAN

The soldiers didn't stop. They were heading for our village. They were coming to kill us all and take our hair. They were coming to kill our children so they would not grow up and avenge the death of their fathers. The spirits of the dead men had made it back to the village before the soldiers. They were above us and they were telling us to run to the forest. Where are you, Husband? I do not hear your voice. Where are you? Wake up, children! Wake up! We must run to the forest and hide! Wake up!

WOODEN WOMAN tries to wake up the sleeping MISTER WOLF, BROTHER RAVEN and SISTER COYOTE, but they stay asleep as the light fades to black.

SCENE 5

Night. Entire stage is covered in dead leaves. Platform is gone. SISTER COYOTE, BROTHER RAVEN and MISTER WOLF are all sitting on the bench. WOODEN WOMAN is standing behind them with her child in her arms. Offstage we hear: "Get out of here, you stinking Black Robe." TOURIST enters now dressed as a priest. He sets up his easel and begins to paint a picture. WOODEN WOMAN begins to move and speak.

WOODEN WOMAN

Your father is dead. The soldiers are here. They are killing the women and children.

SISTER COYOTE

I hate waiting for the bus.

BROTHER RAVEN

Me, too.

MISTER WOLF

This bus is always late.

WOODEN WOMAN

The soldiers took the children and they made them watch as they shot all the women. My sisters fell to the ground as their children screamed for them. The soldiers took the hair of my sisters and then they turned on the children. I had run into the forest with my child and I watched as the soldiers walked to the crying children. What had they done? Why did they want to kill the children?

SISTER COYOTE

When I was a child I was sent to a Catholic school on a bus.

The TOURIST goes to SISTER COYOTE and leads her downstage left as a red spot comes up. She stands there and continues to talk as TOURIST sits back down and continues to paint.

My mother was screaming at the priests and the nuns. She didn't want me to go with them.

WOODEN WOMAN

The soldiers took each child by the hand and they led them to a hole. "Don't kill them!" I wanted to scream but they would see where I was hiding and they would kill my child. So I stayed quiet but in my head I screamed, "Don't take them! Don't kill our children!"

SISTER COYOTE

I went with the sisters and the priests. I went to their schools and they cut my hair and told me to speak English. They told me that I was a savage and that the word of God would be my saviour.

BROTHER RAVEN

I was taken away from my mother on a bus because the government men said she was unfit to care for me. I was sent to live with a family far, far away from home.

TOURIST stands, takes BROTHER RAVEN by the hand and leads him downstage right where another red spot comes up. TOURIST returns to his chair and continues to paint.

WOODEN WOMAN

They slit their throats, the youngest of the children, slit their throats and tossed their small harmless bodies into the hole.

BROTHER RAVEN

My mother was too drunk to realize what was happening to me. The government men came and took me away, took me to a family that would never love me.

MISTER WOLF

I was sent to prison on a bus. Sent to rot behind cold bars for a crime I did not commit. They came to my grandmother's house and they took me to their prison.

TOURIST stands, takes MISTER WOLF by the hand and leads him downstage centre where a red spot comes up. TOURIST returns to his chair and continues to paint.

WOODEN WOMAN

The soldiers took the older children and dragged them toward the hole. They were screaming and begging for their lives but the soldiers shot them, each one with a bullet to the head. They tossed their lifeless bodies into the hole. The hole began to fill with blood.

MISTER WOLF

I couldn't stand it in there, with those steel bars keeping me away from my home, keeping me away from my grandmother.

BROTHER RAVEN

I couldn't stay there. I couldn't stay with a family that did not want me. They never loved me. They never saw me as one of their own. But they were getting extra money from the government so they had to keep me. They had to keep me. They kept me in a little room beside the kitchen. They gave me bits of food but nothing a real raven needs to grow strong. I was getting to be a real nice bird before they got their hands on me. Look at me now, all skin and bones. You can't fly right if you're nothing but skin and bones, I tried to tell them, but they kept me in that little room until I decided that I had had enough.

SISTER COYOTE

They kept me in that school, they kept me until I decided that I had had enough. I had had enough of being beaten and kicked around. I am a Coyote, I would scream at them but they would laugh and kick me some more. I am Coyote! But they would say that I was a child of God and that he would be my saviour. I am Coyote! And I wasn't going to be kicked around anymore.

WOODEN WOMAN

My child began to cry. It was as if this child could feel the death around her. She began to cry louder than the sound of the soldiers as they yelled in victory. A soldier spotted me as I tried to run deeper into the forest.

TOURIST stands, goes to WOODEN WOMAN, takes her by the hand and sits her down back on the bench in her usual spot. TOURIST sits back down in his chair and continues to paint.

SISTER COYOTE

My last night on earth was in my tiny bed. I was trying to dream of my family back home. The fat priest came into my room and he pulled off my little dress and he placed his fat cold body on top of me and he hurt me real bad, all the time telling me that I was his gift from the Lord and that I should never tell anyone. He raped me, and then he smacked me across the face and told me to never tell anyone or else God would punish me.

BROTHER RAVEN

My last night on earth was spent in my tiny room just beside the kitchen. The father of the family came into my room and told me that I had made a mess and that he would therefore have to punish me for this. I tried to tell him that I wasn't the one who made the mess but he came at me anyway. He took off his thick black belt and he tore off my little pants and he smacked me until I was bleeding and screaming for him to stop. He told me to never tell the government men about what he did to me or else I would never see my mother alive again.

MISTER WOLF

My last night on earth was spent in a dark cell. I hadn't eaten in days and they were telling me that they were going to keep me there until I was dead. They came into my cell and they beat me with pipes until I could no longer walk. They told me I would never see my mother again.

WOODEN WOMAN

The soldiers couldn't see me but they could hear my child crying. "Hush, little girl. Go to sleep. Hush, now." But she wouldn't stop crying. I took my hand and I placed it over her mouth but you could still hear her crying and the soldiers were getting closer and closer.

SISTER COYOTE lies down and begins to pile dead leaves on top of her body.

SISTER COYOTE

The fat priest let the piece of rope that he used for a belt in my tiny room. I placed the rope around my neck and tied it too the beam that went across my room.

WOODEN WOMAN

The soldiers began to shoot in the direction that I was hiding.

A loud gunshot is heard.

SISTER COYOTE

I jumped and I became the Coyote.

BROTHER RAVEN lies down and begins to pile leaves on top of himself.

BROTHER RAVEN

The father of the family that never loved me left his thick black belt in my tiny room that was beside the kitchen. I placed the belt around my neck and placed the belt around the beam that cut across my tiny room.

WOODEN WOMAN

They were shooting right at me, one of the bullets ripped into a tree that was right near my head.

Another loud gunshot is heard.

BROTHER RAVEN

I jumped and I became the Raven.

MISTER WOLF lies down and begins to pile leaves on top of himself.

MISTER WOLF

They placed the noose around my neck. The priest said some words to me that I couldn't understand. He didn't even look me in the eyes. He turned away and they let me fall.

WOODEN WOMAN

Another bullet hit me in the arm and I screamed real loud and my child began to scream. Another bullet hit the tree.

Another loud gunshot is heard.

MISTER WOLF

I jumped and I became the Wolf.

The TOURIST stands, goes to each pile of leaves and administers the last rites. As he does this each red spot fades.

WOODEN WOMAN

They were coming to kill me and take my hair. My child wouldn't stop screaming so I took some dead leaves and I gently pushed them into her mouth.

WOODEN WOMAN bends down and takes dead leaves and places them into the mouth of her child. TOURIST finishes the last rites and exits taking his painting and chair with him.

There, now, my child. You can sleep now. The soldiers can't hear you anymore. Sleep, my child. Sleep and dream of days unlike this one. Dream of days spent playing and enjoying this earth that was given to us by the creator. Sleep and dream, my child.

Lights begin to fade. Offstage we hear beautiful sounds: a coyote barking, a raven cawing, and a wolf howling. Blackout.

SCENE 6

Daytime. WOODEN MAN and WOODEN WOMAN are sitting in their spots on the bench. There are the three piles of dead leaves still on the stage but now each one has a white cross at the head of it. There is also a small pile of dead leaves right in front of the bench and it also has a small white cross. Offstage we hear: "Get out of here, you stinking tourist." TOURIST enters now dressed in a bright Hawaiian shirt and Bermuda shorts. He sets up his camera and tripod and sits between the Indians. As timer beeps, nothing happens. TOURIST stands and checks his camera and resets it and sits back down. As timer beeps, nothing happens again. TOURIST angrily gathers camera and tripod and exits.

WOODEN MAN

It sure is quiet here without the children.

WOODEN WOMAN

Weather's changing. Autumn's almost over.

WOODEN MAN

Are you warm enough?

WOODEN WOMAN

Yes. Are you?

WOODEN MAN

Sure. Not much wind on this side.

WOODEN WOMAN

Are you hungry? I've got an apple left.

WOODEN MAN

No, my belly's full.

Offstage we hear the faint sound of children playing and singing.

WOODEN WOMAN

I didn't mean to kill her.

WOODEN MAN

I know.

WOODEN WOMAN

She wouldn't stop crying. Everything I did made her cry louder.

WOODEN MAN

I know. It's okay. We just have to live on, together.

WOODEN WOMAN

I just wanted her to be quiet for a moment so I could think straight. I never wanted her to die like that.

WOODEN MAN moves close to her and puts his arms around her.

WOODEN MAN

We still have each other. We still have our memories.

WOODEN WOMAN

I put leaves into her mouth so she would be silent just for a moment. She stopped crying when I did that. I was able to breathe for a moment and rest and try and get strong, but she wouldn't wake up when I was taking the leaves out of her mouth. She just stayed there all quiet and so beautiful.

WOODEN MAN

Rest now. She is with the spirits of the forest. They will take care of her now.

WOODEN WOMAN

I loved her so much. I would do anything to bring her back, you know that, don't you?

WOODEN MAN

Yes, I do. Rest now. She is with the spirits. Can you hear them playing?

Sound of children get louder and louder.

WOODEN WOMAN

Little child with her little red heart. She would've grown up to be a wonderful daughter. Her little red heart and those brown eyes that looked up at you forever.

WOODEN MAN takes her by the chin and kisses her softly on the lips as sounds of children get louder.

WOODEN MAN

I love you more than anything on this earth. I will never leave you alone again. Let's just sit here a while longer and go home. The weather's changing and soon the snow will come.

WOODEN WOMAN

I am at peace here. I can see her, you know. I can see her as a little girl playing with other children, I can see her playing catch with her brothers, I can see her as she plays marbles and gets dirty, I can see her as she becomes a woman, I can see her as she becomes a spirit, a beautiful spirit upon this earth.

WOODEN MAN

Rest now. We will come back tomorrow and see what spirits come to visit us. Go to sleep, my love. Sleep and dream of days like this. Days filled with wonderful and alive spirits that play and sing forever...

Sounds of children build and build, and then slowly fade as lights begin to fade to black.

The end.

ALOOTOOK IPELLIE

AFTER BRIGITTE BARDOT

My family and I were expecting to spend a quiet spring just minding our own business hunting and gathering seals, doing some fishing at a nearby river, and going after ptarmigans and waterfowl that were once again arriving from the south. It was a ritualistic relocation we had religiously followed for decades. As arrival of spring goes, this particular one was not much different from all the past ones since we were feeling emotionally and spiritually upbeat with the coming of warm weather. Our optimism was never higher until it was abruptly interrupted by a mass of people gathered around our favourite seal hunting camp when we arrived there.

I parked my dog team a few hundred yards from the crowd and went over to find out what the commotion was about. It was easy to recognize the video cameramen, still photographers and reporters among the crowd. They were jostling for position in search of catching the 15-second video clip, the perfect photo image or some quotable words. There must have been at least sixty media hounds, twenty dog teams and assorted other hangers-on milling around this blonde woman lying on the ice, hugging a white-coated baby harp seal pup. I couldn't believe my eyes! What was the big deal?

"Who is she? Why the fuss over the baby seal?" I asked a man who was also observing the theatrics on the sea ice.

"She's the famously beautiful French actress, Brigitte Bardot. She's here to save the baby seals from the senseless slaughter they receive every spring from seal clubbers."

"I don't understand. What does she have against us? We're just simple Inuit trying to make ends meet by hunting and selling sealskins. It's our only bread and butter. Why is she targeting us?"

"I'm not exactly sure, but it may have something to do with her being an animal freak and feeling the need to identify herself as the saviour of all animal species on earth. Who knows, maybe it's just a publicity stunt. She hasn't exactly been seen on the silver screen lately."

"I'm wondering how she ever ended up fighting for the rights of baby harp seals. France has never even seen a single seal in it entire history – just curious."

"Well, by what was stated in the press release before all this happened, a self-proclaimed Swiss 'philanthropist' named Franz Weber sponsored this little tryst. He's also a bit of an animal freak. Rumour has it, there were supposed to be six hundred reporters who were to take this trip but there weren't enough dog teams in the world to take all of them here. Can you imagine six hundred reporters coming here on... ummm... two hundred dog teams? It would have been quite the scene."

"Have these French gone mad? Haven't they any notion of our lifestyle here?"

"I guess Brigitte had never heard of you guys until she was lured to come here. I'm sure there are a lot of mad French out there. And some are madder than others. I suppose one could observe that she is the maddest of them all."

"I'd say she is. Did you notice something odd about that baby seal she's hugging?"

"Of course. It's stuffed."

"Some people! Some guts!"

"She certainly has the guts, but no discernible mind."

"Have you heard the latest blonde joke?"

"Uh-uh."

"How many blondes does it take to change a light bulb?"

"Dunno."

"One million. The first 999,999 blondes are such airheads, they haven't a clue how screws work."

The photo-op was soon over. Brigitte Bardot put the stuffed seal into a gym bag and headed for the sledge she had taken to get here. All twenty dog teams sped away, led by Brigitte Bardot's team. It was at this point I promise myself I would never go see any of her B-movies ever again.

My family and I set up camp and were happy to be rid of the sixty reporters, twenty dog teams, Brigitte Bardot, et al. I was looking forward to hunting and gathering seals for their valuable skins, which we had come to depend on to make a little money to augment some lean times.

The spring and summer seal hunt was unusually bountiful. I kept thinking Brigitte Bardot may have brought us good luck by her now-infamous foray into our hunting and gathering culture.

When autumn came, I made my seasonal trip to the trading post to cash in my sealskins.

When I arrived with a sled-load of sealskins at the post, I was shocked to find out from the manager that the sealskin market had collapsed. The European Economic Community Parliament had voted to ban the entry of all seal products destined for Europe. The trading post wasn't buying another dead skin from the likes of me or my fellow hunters. What a shock! What were my family and I to do without the much-needed extra cash?

I stood there in front of the manager, stunned, my mouth agape, at a loss for words!

"Here, take a look at this." The manager handed me a newspaper clipping.

BARDOT SUCCEEDS IN ENDING SEAL HUNT IN CANADA'S FAR NORTH, the headline screamed at my face. There she was, illustrating the story, hugging that damn stuffed seal!

"The bitch! How could she do this to us?!"

"Politics. The desire to be seen to be doing something without any relevance to either science or ecology. And for that matter, to the well-being of Inuit. There's a quotation in that story which I find quite amusing. She refers to the baby pup seals as 'little balls of wool.' Can you believe that?"

"I'm not the least surprised. What am I going to do with a sled-load of sealskins now?"

"Feed 'em to the dogs, I suppose."

I thought for a moment. I came up with a grand scheme to find out Brigitte Bardot's address and send the sled-load of sealskins. The manager agreed to help me send them off to her. If nothing else, that ought to rile her a bit.

I went on to finish the newspaper story. Someone in the article was quoted as saying, "Until her arrival, the seal hunt story was all blood and death. But now it was blood and death and sex. No more potent combination could be put together."

The truth hurts bad in the guts.

If I had realized Brigitte Bardot was going to destroy the seal industry, I would have taken her for a long ride in my dog team that day and told her about the realities of our lives as hunters and gatherers. But I am not sure she would have comprehended what I would have told her. As a flesh eater, I probably would have riled her enough that she might have spat in my face. What can one say about radical animal-rights activists? They have dormant mindsets that can only see through the eyes of the animal beings.

When I returned to my camp later that day, I had a remarkable vision of a slightly senile Brigitte Bardot, an older and still unrepentant rebel, walking along a French street with an Inuk companion. I was amused to see that her upper body had turned into a harp seal!

This was actually a transformation she was to endure for a lifetime. She would completely turn into a harp seal when her human life was over. She had willed herself to be reincarnated as a harp seal! And, in true Christian tradition, she was wearing a cross around her neck.

Her Inuk companion seemed perfectly content to be with the aging Brigitte Bardot. He was about to get a rude surprise. A baby harp seal pup snuck up behind the two of them. He clubbed the Inuk's skull open! The blood and brain tissue spewed out on the street! Brigitte screamed her lungs out. She tried in vain to put the brain tissue, which was just a pile of mush, back into her companion's skull. In a flash, the baby harp seal pup waddled behind a building and disappeared.

Later that day, I found out the truth of this horrendous act of violence. The ghosts of all baby harp seal pups that were ever clubbed to death over the years were now avenging atrocities done to them by humankind. The irony is this was not happening anywhere else on Earth except in France.

It was now blood and death and sex.

THOMAS KING

COYOTE AND THE ENEMY ALIENS

You know, everyone likes a good story. Yes, that's true. My friend Napioa comes by my place. My good place. My good place by the river. Sometimes that Napioa comes by my good place and says, Tell us a good story. So I do. Sometimes I tell those good stories from the Indian time. And sometimes I tell those good stories from the European time. Grown-up stories. Baby stories.

Sometimes I take a nap.

Sometimes I tell Coyote stories. Boy, you got to be careful with those Coyote stories. When I tell those Coyote stories, you got to stay awake. You got to keep those toes under the chair. I can tell you that.

You better do that now. Those toes. No, later is no good.

OK, so I'm going to tell a Coyote story. Maybe you heard that story before. Maybe not.

Coyote was going west. That's how I like to start that story. Coyote story. Coyote was going west, and when he gets to my place, he stops. My good place. By the river.

That was in the European time. In 1940. Maybe it was 1944. No, it was 1942.

Coyote comes to my house in 1941. Hello, says that Coyote. Maybe you have some tea for me. Maybe you have some food for me. Maybe you have a newspaper for me to read.

Sure, I says. I have all those things.

So Coyote drinks my tea. And that one eats my food. And that one reads my newspaper.

Hooray, says that Coyote. I have found a job in the newspaper.

Maybe you're wondering who would hire Coyote.

I thought so.

OK. I'll ask.

Who would hire Coyote? I says.

The Whitemen, says Coyote. The Whitemen are looking for a Coyote.

Oh boy. Coyote and the Whitemen. That's pretty scary.

It's over on that coast, says Coyote. In that west. That's where my job is.

Good, I says. Then I won't have to move.

But I am so hungry, says Coyote. I don't know if I can get to that coast unless I get something good to eat.

OK, I says, I will feed you so you can get to that coast.

And I don't have a good shirt, says Coyote. I really need a good shirt, so the Whitemen will see that I'm a good worker.

OK, I says, I will give you my good shirt.

Oh, oh, oh, says Coyote, how will I get there? It's a very long ways, and my feet are quite sensitive.

You still got those toes tucked under that chair? You better keep your hands in your pocket too. Just in case Coyote notices you sitting there. And don't make any noise. If that Coyote sees that somebody is listening to him, that one will never leave.

OK, I tell Coyote, I will call Billy Frank. My friend Billy Frank goes to the coast. He drives that pickup to that coast to go on that vacation. Maybe he will take you when he goes on that vacation.

Hooray, says Coyote. Hooray!

So Billy Frank takes Coyote to that coast. And that's the end of the story.

No, I was only fooling. That's not the end of the story. There's more. Stick around. Have some tea. Don't move those toes. Coyote is still around here somewhere.

Ho, ho. So a lot of things happen. All of a sudden, everyone is fighting. Mostly those White people. They like to fight, you know. They fight with one another. And then they fight with those other people. And pretty soon everyone is fighting. Even some of us Indians are fighting.

You're probably thinking that Coyote is fighting, too.

Is that what you were thinking?

It's OK, you can tell me.

So Coyote comes back. I warned you about this. Coyote comes back, and he is driving a pretty good truck.

Yoo-hoo, says Coyote, come and see my pretty good truck.

Yes, I says, that's a pretty good truck, all right. That job you got must be a pretty good job.

Oh, says Coyote, that job is the best job I have ever had.

That pretty good truck that Coyote is driving says "Kogawa Seafood" on the door. Ho, that Coyote. Always looking for something to eat.

Coyote stole me, says that pretty good truck.

No, I didn't, says Coyote.

Yes, you did, says that pretty good truck.

Don't talk to that silly truck, Coyote tells me.

What's wrong with talking to trucks, I says. Everybody talks to trucks.

Not anymore, says Coyote, and that one lowers his eyes, so he looks like he is sitting on a secret. Talking to Enemy Alien trucks is against the law.

Enemy Alien trucks? Holy, I says. That sounds serious.

National security, says Coyote. If someone saw you talking to an Enemy Alien truck, I might have to arrest you.

I'm not an Enemy Alien, says that truck.

Yes, you are, says Coyote.

No, I'm not, says that truck.

So Coyote and that pretty good truck says "Kogawa Seafood" on the door argue about Enemy Aliens. They argue about that for a long time. All day. Two days. Three. One week. They keep everyone awake. Nobody on the reserve can sleep. Even the dogs are awake.

Knock it off, those dogs say. You're keeping everyone awake.

I haven't heard of any Enemy Aliens, I tell Coyote.

Oh, says Coyote, they're all over the place. But you don't have to worry. You don't have to run away. You don't have to hide under your bed.

That's good news, I says.

Oh, yes, says Coyote. Now that I'm on the job, the world is a safer place.

No, it's not, says that pretty good truck.

Yes, it is, says Coyote. And those two start arguing again.

I don't know about you but all this arguing is making me dizzy. Maybe we should have some tea. Maybe we should have some dinner. Maybe we should watch that television show where everyone goes to that island, practise their bad manners. Maybe we should go to sleep. You can sleep on the couch.

So when I wake up, that pretty good truck is gone. But Coyote is still here.

Where is your pretty good Enemy Alien truck, I ask Coyote.

Oh, says Coyote, I had to sell that one. That's the law now. All Enemy Alien Property must be confiscated. All Enemy Alien Property must be sold. That's my job. And that Coyote shows me a piece of paper says "Order-in-Council 469."

Boy, I says, that paper has a nice voice.

Order-in-Council 469, says that paper. All hail, Order-in-Council 469.

Boy, I says, that paper sounds pretty important.

It is, says Coyote. That paper says that I am the Custodian of Enemy Alien Property.

Coyote is the Custodian of Enemy Alien Property, says that paper. All hail Coyote, Custodian of Enemy Alien Property.

That job sounds pretty important, I says.

It is the most important job in the world, says Coyote.

Is it more important than being truthful? I says.

Oh, yes, says Coyote.

Is it more important than being reliable? I says.

Absolutely, says Coyote.

Is it more important than being fair? I says.

Probably, says Coyote.

Is it more important than being generous? I says.

It certainly is, says Coyote.

Holy, I says, that is one pretty important job, all right. How do you do that pretty important job?

Well, says Coyote, first I find all the Enemy Aliens. Then I confiscate their property. Then I sell their property. Say, you want to buy some Enemy Alien Property?

Enemy Alien Property. Yes, that's what that Coyote said. Sure, I don't mind asking. You keep sitting in that chair. Keep those toes under the chair. And stay awake. You start snoring, and that Coyote is going to hear you for sure.

So, I ask Coyote, what kind of Enemy Alien Property do you have for sale?

Oh, says Coyote, I have everything. You want a sewing machine? How about a set of dresser drawers? I have a bunch of radios. Cameras? A refrigerator? Blankets? Teakettles? A wheelbarrow? A house. Maybe you need an easy chair. I got lots of bicycles. Maybe you need a new car. Maybe you need a fishing boat.

A fishing boat? You have a fishing boat for sale?

Ho, ho, says that Coyote, I have more than one. How many would you like?

How many do you have? I says.

Eighteen hundred and four, says Coyote.

That's a lot of fishing boats, I says.

It's a hard job, says Coyote. But someone has to be paid to do it. Maybe you need a pretty good kimono.

No, I says, I don't need a pretty good kimono.

Come on, says Coyote. Let's go see the Enemy Alien Property.

So I go with Coyote. But we don't go in that pretty good truck says "Kogawa Seafood" on the door because Coyote has sold it. But that Coyote has another pretty good truck says "Okada General Store" on the door.

You sure have a lot of pretty good trucks, I says.

Oh, yes, says Coyote, I am an excellent Custodian of Enemy Alien Property.

So Coyote starts driving. He drives to those mountains. And that one drives into those valleys. And then he drives to that Pacific National Exhibition in that Vancouver city.

I am lost, I tell Coyote. Where are we now?

Hastings Park, says Coyote.

That Hastings Park is a big place. Big buildings. Big signs. That big sign says "Livestock Building."

Livestock? All right. So, I ask Coyote, you got any Enemy Alien Horses? That's what I ask. You got any Enemy Alien Horses? I could use a good Enemy Alien Horse.

That Coyote checks that list of Enemy Alien Property. That one checks it again. No, he says, there are no Enemy Alien Horses.

Enemy Alien Cows? I ask Coyote.

No, says Coyote, no Enemy Alien Cows.

Chickens?

No.

Sheep?

No.

Holy, that's all the livestock I can remember. So, I ask that Coyote, what do you keep in that Livestock Building?

Enemy Aliens, says Coyote. That's where we keep the Enemy Aliens.

Boy, that Coyote likes to tell stories. Sometimes he tells stories that smell bad. Sometimes he tells stories that have been stretched. Sometimes he tells stories that bite your toes. Coyote stories.

That's one good Coyote story, I tell Coyote. Enemy Aliens in a Livestock Building.

No, says Coyote. This story is not a good Coyote story. This story is a good Canadian story.

Canadian story. Coyote story. Sometimes it's hard to tell the difference. All those words begin with *c*.

Callous, carnage, catastrophe, chicanery.

Boy, I got to take a breath. There, that's better.

Cold-blooded, complicit, concoct, condemn.

No, we're not done yet.

Condescend, confabulate, confiscate, conflate, connive.

No, not yet.

Conspire, convolute, crazy, crooked, cruel, crush.

Holy, I almost forgot cupidity.

No, no, says Coyote. Those words are the wrong words. The word you're looking for is "legal."

Boy, you're right, I tell Coyote. That legal is a good word. You can do a lot with that one. That's one of those magic words. White magic. Legal. Lots of other White magic words.

Patriotic, Good, Private, Freedom, Dignity, Efficient, Profitable, Truth, Security, National, Integrity, Public, Prosperity, Justice, Property.

Sometimes you can put two magic words together. National Security, Public Good, Private Property.

Stop, stop, says Coyote. All these words are giving me a headache. We only need one word for Enemy Aliens. And that one word is legal.

So Coyote takes me into the Livestock Building and that one shows me the Enemy Aliens.

Boy, I says, you caught a big bunch of them.

You bet, says Coyote.

But what is that smell? I ask Coyote.

Pigs and cows and horses, says Coyote. We had to move the pigs and cows and horses out so we could move the Enemy Aliens in.

That is certainly a strong smell, I says.

It certainly is, says Coyote. We better leave before we get sick.

Maybe the Enemy Aliens would like to leave, too, I tell Coyote. So they don't get sick from the pigs and cows and horses used to live here.

Enemy Aliens don't mind that smell, says Coyote. They're not like you and me.

They look like you and me, I says.

Oh, no, says Coyote, you're mistaken. They look like Enemy Aliens.

So that Coyote shows me all those sights. That one shows me that big building with all that glass. And that one shows me that other big building with all that glass. And then that one shows me that other big building with all that glass.

Boy, I tell Coyote, that's a lot of big buildings with glass.

You want to see another big building with glass? says Coyote.

No, I says, that's enough big buildings with glass for me.

Okay, says Coyote, let's go see that Enemy Alien Property. Maybe we can find you some silverware.

So that Coyote shows me that Enemy Alien Property.

Holy, I tell Coyote. It looks like you confiscated everything.

Yes, says Coyote. The Whitemen have given me a commendation that I can hang on my wall.

Boy, there's another one of those words begins with *c*.

See anything you like? says Coyote. I can give you a really good deal on family heirlooms.

But just as that Coyote is showing me those good deals on those family heirlooms, he gets that phone call. This is before they got those phones you can walk around the house with, and this is before those phones you can carry in your pocket. Call any place you like for thirty cents a minute, plus those roaming charges. This is the time when those phones are nailed on those walls, when those real women place that call for you, when you have to stand right next to them.

No, not the real women.

So that Coyote stands next to that phone and that one nods his head and that one smiles and that one makes happy noises.

Good news, says that Coyote. The Whitemen have given me another job.

Boy, I says, you are one busy Coyote.

Yes, says Coyote, and I have a new slogan. You want to hear it?

You want to hear Coyote's new slogan? No, I don't want to hear it either. But if we say no, we may hurt Coyote's feelings and then that one is going to cry and make a lot of noise and keep everyone awake. Yes, that one will keep the dogs awake, too.

So I tell Coyote, OK, you tell us your new slogan.

OK, says Coyote. Here it is. "Let our slogan be for British Columbia: 'No Japs from the Rockies to the seas.'"

Ho! That's your new slogan?

Ian Alistair Mackenzie, says Coyote. It's Ian Alistair Mackenzie's slogan.

He must be important, I tell Coyote. All Whitemen with three names are important.

He's the Whiteman in charge of making up slogans, says Coyote. But that one is not a good poet. If he was a good poet, he would have said, "Let our slogan for British Columbia be: No Japs from the Rockies to the sea."

Look at that, I says. Now that slogan rhymes.

Be, sea, says that slogan. Be, sea.

Oh, yes, says Coyote, all good slogans rhyme. You want to hear some of Ian Alistair Mackenzie's other slogans?

Is that your new job? I say. Making those Ian Alistair Mackenzie slogans rhyme?

Oh, no, says Coyote, my new job is to Disperse Enemy Aliens.

No, I don't know what "disperse" means. Lots of those words begin with "dis." Disdain, disappear, disaster, disillusioned, disappointed, disingenuous, distrust.

Disperse.

No, I don't think we should ask Coyote. OK, but don't blame me if things get messed up.

Come on, says Coyote, we got to get those Enemy Aliens dispersed.

So Coyote gets all the Women Enemy Aliens and the Children Enemy Aliens out of that Livestock Building smells like horses and cows and sheep, and that one gets those Men Enemy Aliens with those targets painted on their backs from that other place, and that Coyote puts all the Enemy aliens into the back of his pretty good truck says "Okada General Store" on the door.

It's pretty crowded, I can tell you that.

OK, says that Coyote, let's start dispersing.

So that Coyote drives that truck into that valley, and then that one drives that truck into those mountains, and then that one drives that truck onto those prairies, and that one doesn't stop driving until he gets to my place.

My good place. My good place by the river.

Holy, I says, there is my good place.

Yes, says Coyote, this is a good place, all right. Maybe this is a good place to disperse the Enemy Aliens.

Sure, I says, we got lots of room.

So Coyote gets all of the Enemy Aliens out of that truck, and I call my friend Napioa and my friend Billy Frank. Ho, I tell my friends, we got guests.

OK, my friend Napioa and my friend Billy Frank tell me. We'll call that rest of the people. Maybe we'll eat some food. Maybe we'll drink some tea. Maybe we'll sing a welcoming song.

A party? says Coyote. I love parties!

But you know what? Some of those Enemy Aliens look pretty sad. Some of those Enemy Aliens look pretty scared. And some of those Enemy Aliens with the targets on their backs look pretty angry.

Boy, I tell Coyote, those Enemy Aliens don't look too happy.

And after everything I've done for them, says Coyote. And just as that Coyote says this, a big car comes along.

Ho, I says, that is one important-looking car.

Yes, I am, says that important-looking car.

Did you come for the Enemy Alien party? I ask the important-looking car.

No, says the important-looking car, I am looking for Coyote.

Did I get a promotion? says that Coyote. And that one polishes his teeth with his tongue.

Get in, says that important-looking car. We got some secret stuff to talk about.

So Coyote gets in the important-looking car, and I go find the food, and now some of the Enemy Aliens are feeling a little better.

You know, that Billy Frank tells me, this story about the Enemy Aliens have their property taken away by Coyote and the Whitemen and get moved from their homes to someplace else reminds me of another story.

Yes, I tell Billy Frank, me too.

You remember how that story goes, says Billy Frank.

No, I says, but maybe if we think about it, that story will come back.

So we eat some food, and we drink some tea, and Billy Frank and Napioa warm up that drum, and we have a couple of songs.

So pretty soon, that Coyote gets out of that important-looking car. And those RCMPs get out of that important-looking car. And those politician guys get out of that important-looking car, singing O Canada. But they don't sing so good.

Holy, says Billy Frank. We're going to have to get more food.

OK, says Coyote, all the Enemy Aliens back in the truck!

Let's not be too hasty, I tell Coyote. The party is just starting.

No time to party with Enemy Aliens, says Coyote. I got a new job.

Another job! Boy, that Coyote is one busy Coyote.

What is your new job? I ask Coyote.

I got to take the Enemy Aliens to their new homes, says Coyote.

They can stay here, I says. We got lots of room.

Oh, no, says Coyote, that would be too dangerous. We got to take the Enemy Aliens who look sad and the Enemy Aliens who look scared to the Sugar Beet Farms. We going to give them jobs.

OK, I says, working on the Sugar Beet Farms is pretty good money.

We're not going to pay them, says Coyote. Those Enemy Aliens have to work for free, so they can show us that they are loyal citizens.

Boy, I tell Billy Frank, those citizenship tests are tough.

What's a citizen? says Billy Frank.

What about those Enemy Aliens with the targets painted on their backs, who look pretty angry?

Oh, says Coyote, those are the Dangerous Enemy Aliens. Those Dangerous Enemy Aliens are going to Angler, Ontario.

Holy, I says, those Enemy Aliens must be real dangerous to have to go to Ontario. Have any of the Enemy Aliens caused any troubles?

Not yet, says Coyote, but you can't be too careful.

So the Coyote goes to the centre of the party and stands by the drum, and that one holds up his hands.

OK, says Coyote, all the Enemy Aliens back in the truck.

But you know what? Nobody gets in the truck.

Maybe they didn't hear me, says Coyote. And this time he says it really loud. All the Enemy Aliens back in the truck!

But nobody gets in the truck.

OK, says Coyote, we going to have to do this the hard way. And Coyote and the RCMPs grab Billy Frank.

Enemy Alien, says that Coyote and those RCMPs.

Silly Coyote, I says, that's not an Enemy Alien. That's Billy Frank.

Are you sure? says Coyote. He certainly looks like an Enemy Alien.

I'm Billy Frank, says Billy Frank.

So that Coyote and the RCMPs grab another Enemy Alien.

No, I says, that's not an Enemy Alien. That's my friend Napioa.

Nonsense, says Coyote. I know an Enemy Alien when I see one, and Coyote and the RCMPs grab everyone they see. Those politicians stand behind that important-looking car singing O Canada and waving flags.

Enemy Aliens.

No, I says, that's Leroy Jumping Bull's cousin Cecil.

Enemy Alien.

No, I says, that's Martha Redcrow. She's married to Cecil Jumping Bull's nephew, Wilfred.

I wouldn't stand too close to this story if I were you. Coyote and the RCMPs might grab you. Yes, I'd sit in the corner where those ones can't see you.

Enemy Alien.

No, I says, that's Maurice Moses. He's Leroy Jumping Bull's grandson. Leroy's daughter Celeste had twins.

Enemy Alien.

No, I says, that's Arnold Standing Horse. He takes those tourists into those mountains to go hunting.

That silly Coyote even grabs me.

Hey, I says, let me go.

Oops, says Coyote, oops.

You got to stop grabbing everybody, I says.

But Coyote and the RCMPs don't do that. And pretty soon that Coyote has that pretty good truck filled with Enemy Aliens, and that one has that pretty good truck filled with Indians.

I have more Enemy Aliens than when I started, says Coyote. I must be better than I thought.

You got to keep the Indians and the Enemy Aliens straight, I tell Coyote. Otherwise you're going to mess up this story.

And just then the RCMPs grab that Coyote.

Enemy Alien.

No, no, says Coyote. I'm Coyote.

Enemy Alien, shout those RCMPs. Oh Canada, sing those politicians. And everybody drives off in that important-looking car and Coyote's pretty good truck says "Okada General Store" on the door.

And I don't see that Coyote again.

So that Coyote comes by my place. My good place by the river.

Yes, this is still the same story. Yes, that Coyote has been gone a while, but now that one is coming back. Sure, I know where Coyote and the Indians and the Enemy Aliens go. No, they don't go to Florida to play that golf with that alligator. No, they don't go on that cruise to those islands, everybody sits in the sun and drinks out of big nuts. No, they don't give those Enemy Aliens back their Enemy Alien property either.

Hello, says that Coyote. Maybe you have some tea. Maybe you have some food. Maybe you have a newspaper for me to read.

Sure, I says. Sit down. Where's that pretty good truck says "Okada General Store" on the door?

The Whitemen took my pretty good truck, says Coyote. And they took all my Enemy Alien Property. And they took all my Enemy Aliens.

Holy, I says, those Whitemen like to take everything.

Yes, says Coyote, that's true. And that one drinks my tea. And that one eats my food. And that one reads my newspaper.

Hooray, says that Coyote. I have found another job.

Boy, I says, it is dangerous to read newspapers.

This job is better than the other one, says Coyote.

You going to round up more Enemy Aliens? I say.

No, says Coyote. I'm going to that New Mexico. I'm going to that Los Alamos place in New Mexico, help those Whitemen want to make the world safe for freedom.

OK, I says, that sounds pretty good. That New Mexico is mostly that desert and those mountains. Nothing much in that Los Alamos place that Coyote can mess up.

Yes, now Coyote is gone. Yes, now those toes are safe. Yes, that's the end of the story. Well, you should have asked Coyote while he was here. Maybe if you hurry, you can catch him before he gets to that New Mexico.

No, I'm going to stay here. That Coyote will come back. That one always comes back. Somebody's got to be here to make sure he doesn't do something foolish.

I can tell you that.

YVETTE NOLAN

SCATTERING JAKE

ONE

David, Yvette, DM, and Naomi are standing on King and Church, in the yard of St James cathedral.

D: This is so illegal.

N: We haven't done anything yet.

DM: Where is – he?

N: David's purse.

D: It's a man-bag.

N: Purse, man-bag.

DM: At least you didn't call it his—

Y: David's sac.

DM: Jeez!

Y: You don't mind when I call mine my sac.

DM: That's because you— never mind—

D: Don't have one?

DM: *(putting fingers in ears)* La la la la la la

Y: Sac is a perfectly acceptable name for it. Besides, I am saying *sac*, not sack. *Sac*, the French way. *Mon sac a dos*... my backpack.

D: But so much more elegant.

Y: Exactly.

DM: This is not what we should be doing with his body.

N: It's not his body, it's his ashes.

DM: I am probably going to hell for this.

D: More like jail.

DM: Jail?

D: You can't just scatter human ashes anywhere. There are laws.

David takes the box out of his bag and hands it to DM, who takes it and holds it gingerly. He takes a package of cigarettes out of his sac and removes one.

N: I wish you wouldn't smoke.

D: You and my mother.

N: Don't you think it's disrespectful of Jake? Seeing as he—

D: Died of lung cancer?

Y: Technically, he didn't die of lung cancer.

N: Hush.

DM: So light.

Y: He was this light near the end.

N: Hush.

Y: Still, this is no way to finish the journey.

D: The journey? When did you get all-wise Indian?

Y: Always been Indian.

DM: What did his people do?

D: Who were his people?

N: We are his people, people. That's why we are doing this, why he asked for us to do this. 'Cause we are his people.

D: Wow, that's sad.

N: That's not sad, it's an honour.

D: No, there is no way when I died I would want me to be in charge of whatever ceremony or ritual or disposal.

DM: Youch.

D: What? That's what it is…

N: You're not in charge David, you're just—

D: Here for comic relief?

N: No, comic relief is funny.

D: The dispassionate witness?

DM: Dispassionate?

D: Unruffled, cool.

DM: I know what it means, jackass. I just don't think you are dispassionate. I think you're just in denial.

D: Denial? Of what?

DM: Of everything.

N: Alright, that's enough.

D: No, I wanna know what DM means—

N: Well, this is not about you, David.

D: Of course it is. Everything is always about me. How do I fit in this picture? Do I fit in this picture? How did I get in this picture?

Y: Can I have a pair of scissors to cut myself out of this picture?

N: Don't encourage him.

Yvette shrugs.

DM: Strangely, I don't think you are here for the picture, David, I think you are here for the words.

Y: A thousand words maybe.

N: You're the chronicler.

D: Why do I have to be the chronicler? Why can't Yvette be the chronicler? I'll turn it into fiction.

N: Yvette's not the chronicler this time. And she'll turn it into fiction.

Y: Is that a good thing or a bad thing?

D: What are you saying? That I don't make art? That I only document? That my writing is only so much public journaling? Now I think that I will kill myself.

DM: David, for god's sake, stop it! Stop making this about you.

Y: Hush, he's just— we're all just— a little wrought. I think we are all feeling the responsibility, and it's scary.

DM: That's what she's here for.

David goes to speak, Yvette looks at him, he doesn't.

DM: How long?

N: A couple of minutes now.

DM: Maybe we should open the box.

N: Yeah, you're right.

D: You haven't opened the box?

N: No.

D: Well, how are we gonna divvy him up?

DM: What do you mean?

D: Well if we are supposed to put his ashes in four spots, shouldn't we divvy them up first? Or do we just open and shake, like parmesan cheese, and kinda estimate what a quarter of the ashes look like.

N: I don't know.

Y: Well, we better figure it out pretty quickly, because we are coming up on the hour and if we don't do it today, we'll have to come back tomorrow.

D: I can't do tomorrow.

DM: Me neither, I moved everything from today to do this, my tomorrow is completely booked.

Y: I am sure Jake will be fine if he isn't scattered right on the noon bells.

D: You think?

Y: No, I don't think. But I also don't think this is for him. Like I don't think he is hanging around watching us execute his last wishes. If he wanted to hang around, he –

N: Give me something sharp.

DM: Not your tongue.

D: Ha ha

DM: Not your head.

D: Ha fuckin ha. I'm not packing.

DM: Ha

N: Your pen, wiseass, give me your pen.

D: Ah, you metaphor-maniac. Here.

Naomi slices through the tape and opens the box.

N: Oh.

DM: Oh what.

N: More plastic.

DM: Oh.

N: Time?

Y: About 30 seconds by my watch.

D: You'll wreck my pen!

N: I'll get you another.

D: It was a gift.

N: Oh for god's sake.

D: How am I supposed to chronicle if you wreck my pen? Here, give it.

David rips the plastic with his hands. Shakes the bag into the box.

D: Now what?

DM: Yvette?

Y: I think we should all take a handful. And when the bells start to ring, we should scatter the ashes to the four directions.

D: This is so illegal.

Yvette shrugs.

She reaches into the box, takes a handful.

N: You gonna say something?

Y: You want me to?

N nods.

DM: Cops. Cops. Slowing down. Oh shit.

D: Well, don't look guilty.

DM: I can't help it! I'm Black!

David puts his arm around her neck.

D: Look at me. DM. Look at me.

DM does.

D: Look deep into my eyes.

DM looks at him.

D: Deep. Like you mean it.

She does.

DM: Are they gone?

David pulls her towards him and whispers in her ear. DM laughs.

Y: Okay, they're gone.

N: What'd you say?

DM: Secret.

D: The DM whisperer.

Y: Right, everyone take a handful.

David does. DM does, squeamishly. Naomi just stands there.

N: I – I don't know—

Y: It's okay, Naomi. It's all part of it. It's a good thing. This small good thing we are doing.

Yvette goes to her with the box. Takes Naomi's hand, opens it, puts some ashes into it. Closes it.

Y: Our friend Jake loved this city, the dark alleys, the graffiti'd alleys—

DM: The theatres.

D: Especially the theatres.

Y: He loved the bells of this church.

DM: He loved this neighbourhood.

D: Before it got all gentifried, pre-condo, pre-Starbucks.

Y: Our friend Jake wanted to be put back onto the streets of the city he loved, back into the ground and the air and the water of Toronto.

N: He said Toronto saved his life.

Y: And so we put all that is left of Jake back into the city, that he becomes part of the life of—

The bells start to ring. And ring. Yvette faces east and throws ashes. DM faces north and flings. David sprinkles west. Naomi stands. Lifts her fist to her face.

David goes to her, puts his arm around her, takes her hand in his, faces south with her. She opens her hand, turns it over, ashes fall.

N: Pink.

D: Yup.

She cries. He holds her. Yvette puts down something.

DM: Pink.

Yvette nods.

DM: Who knew.

Y: Not me.

DM: What next?

TWO

David, Yvette, DM, and Naomi are standing on the ferry going over to the island. DM is hanging back.

D: This is so illegal.

N: I don't think it is, David.

D: There are rules. You can't just go scattering human remains any old place. Not into Lake Ontario. This is where they get our drinking water.

DM: Yum yum. That's why I don't drink tap water.

Y: Where do you think we go when they bury us in the ground?

D: DM, why don't you join us?

DM: That's okay.

Y: Are you afraid of the water?

DM: No.

Y: Have you ever been on the ferry before?

DM: No.

N: You haven't?

D: DM, come here.

DM: That's okay, there's too much.

N: Too much what?

DM: Nature.

David grabs her, holds her in front of him à la Titanic.

David whispers to her. She laughs.

DM: I'm flying!

N: Maybe we should move further back to do this.

D: They shut the Pirates of the Caribbean Ride in Disneyland because someone scattered someone's ashes in the water in there.

Y: That's dumb.

DM: Who would want to spend eternity in a stupid theme park ride?

D: Either he really liked the ride, or it was revenge on his people.

N: At least he didn't ask for a Viking funeral.

Y: Why would Jake want a Viking funeral? Weren't his people English from way back?

D: And American.

DM: Well, that would explain the Viking thing.

Y: What Viking thing?

DM: Invaders, plunderers—

Y: I thought he *didn't* ask for a Viking funeral.

N: I'm sorry I brought it up.

D: Hey, did you guys ever hear that story about Chocolate's Viking funeral?

DM: They had a funeral for chocolate?

D: For a dog named Chocolate. Put him on a raft and set him on fire and set him afloat, right around here, I think…

Y: That's gotta be urban myth.

DM: I've always wondered how something can be both on fire and on water.

D: No really, someone wrote about it. I read it in – oh, *Geist*, I think.

Y: Bless you.

D: Ha. Anyway, it didn't work. I guess it didn't burn –

DM: See?

D: And a few days later commuters on the ferry were treated to the sight of the hairless bloated corpse of Chocolate bumping up against the jetty.

DM: Gross.

N: David.

D: Sorry. Sorry. Just trying to support you—

N: You're doing a fine job.

D: Don't be sarcastic. That's my job. Or maybe DM's.

DM: I got nothing.

N: Sorry. I— I'm finding this all—

Y: Yeah. *(beat)* You're doing good.

N: I thought it would be easier by now.

DM: Naomi, it's barely been four months. Four months is not very long.

N: But I've been fine. I've been good.

DM: Yeah, you're doing great.

D: *After great pain a formal feeling comes—*
the nerves sit ceremonious like tombs

N: But I feel— I feel—

She touches her chest.

Y: Okay, gang. I think it's time. David?

David reaches into his sac and pulls out the box.

D: Careful now. Don't want him escaping before his time.

N: I forgot about the wind. That it would be windy.

DM: Yikes. Don't want him flying back in my face. No offence, Jake.

They reach carefully into the box and take some ashes. Yvette takes some tobacco from her pocket and adds it to her ashes.

Y: Naomi?

N: No.

Y: David?

David shakes his head.

DM: Our friend Jake lived hard. He died as well as he could. God, we're only human. He was a good friend, a good artist, a good man. He loved life. He hated dying. Don't hold it against him, okay?

DM holds her hand out over the water and opens it.

D: Very Catholic.

DM shrugs.

D: Hey buddy. *(opens his hand)*

Yvette holds hand to sky, then over the water.

They look at Naomi.

Naomi nods. Opens her hand. David puts his arm around her. The other two stand on either side of them, looking at the water.

THREE

David, DM, and Naomi are walking with, variously, a picnic basket, a cooler, a beach bag.

D: At least no one is going to freak out here.

DM: Why's that?

D: 'Cause they're island people, they're already freaky.

N: They are not freaky.

DM: Hey, I'm island people.

D: Not Toronto island people. *(beat)* What island?

DM: Grenada. Do we get cell coverage over here?

N: Ha ha

D: I didn't know that. I thought you were from here. Like, Toronto born and bred.

DM: Nope.

D: Wow. Grenada, eh? Operation Urgent Fury?

DM: Vikings.

D: Ah.

DM: Where is she taking us?

N: To the right place.

DM: Why can't this be the right place? It's got everything. Sand. Shore. Ducks. Those are ducks, right?

N: Ducks.

D: She's doing her faithful Indian guide thing.

DM: It all looks the same to me. Why isn't this spot?

Yvette walks back on. She too carries a basket.

Y: This is good, I think.

DM: See? I knew this was the right place. Blankets?

Y: Yup.

From the bags appear blankets, a tablecloth, and food in Tupperware. They talk as they spread out the feast.

N: Thanks for doing this. All of you.

D: S'nothing.

N: It's a lot. Taking the time to clear your schedules. Trekking around the city with me. All this.

DM: Good reason to play hooky.

N: I didn't know – who to ask – really. Seems like such a weird – quest.

DM: Everything – about death – is weird, isn't it? You so rarely do it, if you're lucky, so when you have to do it… *(beat)* It was good of Jake to leave us such clear directions.

N: Writing the script, choosing the locations, directing us. Even in death.

D: Look at this spread. Chicken, salmon, potato salad, beans, berries—

He reaches to take something from a container, DM smacks his hand.

DM: Uh uh. Feast. Gotta wait.

D: Oh. *(beat)* For what?

DM shrugs, motions to Yvette.

Yvette is collecting a little bit from every container, putting it on a plate.

Y: Plate for the spirits. For Jake.

D: Okay.

Y: Okay. Naomi?

Naomi shakes her head.

Y: David.

D: I don't know how to pray. I don't know what I believe in. I don't have any spiritual – thing.

Y: You don't have to pray. You can just speak.

D: *(beat)* I will arise and go now, for always night and day
I hear lake water lapping with low sounds by the shore;
While I stand on the roadway, or on the pavements grey,
I hear it in the deep heart's core.

Jake was one of my first and best teachers. And here he is four months dead, and still teaching me. I have lived in this city all my life, but today, Jake is showing it to me anew. We live on a lake. We *live* on a *lake*.

I learned a lot from Jake. About art, about words, about passion. I *didn't* learn a lot from him too, though he tried to teach me. About generosity, and humility, and compassion. I know I'm not supposed to say I wish he was here, but I do. I wish he was still here showing me stuff. I would be a better student.

They wait.

D: Sorry. That's it.

N: That was good.

DM: Eat?

Y: Eat.

DM hands them plates.

D: I'm not hungry.

Y: It's a feast. You have to eat.

D: Okay.

Y: Come on, it's my famous roast chicken.

D: The one with the lemons and sundried tomatoes and things—

Y: Yup.

DM: *(piling food on her plate)* Yum yum potatoes, yum yum beans.

Y: It's a feast for Jake, Naomi. We are feasting Jake.

N: I know. Okay, okay.

She begins to put food on her plate.

FOUR

Later that night. There has been a fire, but now it is embers. DM has a mickey of whiskey. She cracks it and pours a bit on the ground, takes a sip, passes it to Naomi.

DM: So what are you gonna do with the rest?

N: Not sure.

D: You could make him into a diamond.

N: What?

D: Sure, there's this company in the States that will turn the ashes of your loved one into a diamond.

N: You're making this up.

D: Nope.

DM: Where do you get this stuff?

D: It's everywhere. On the net, on the television. I'm a playwright. I am a student of the human heart. *(beat)* What?

DM: Sometimes I can't tell if you're quoting one of your poets or if that's actually you speaking.

Y: Wow. I guess people just need to do something – to memorialise – to mark the loving in some way – but that just seems so – wrongheaded – would you wear it?

D: I guess that's the idea.

Y: Seems like the opposite of what we are supposed to do – grieve – mourn – move on – live in the moment – how do you do that with your loved one there around your neck every day?

DM: Or on your finger – like an engagement ring, *stay away stay away, I am spoken for, I am taken.*

N: So the diamond idea is no.

DM: No.

D: Definitely no.

Y: Yeah, no.

N: Well, I guess that leaves eating him.

DM: Eeeyeww

D: Thanks, I am full of feast food.

Y: I'm down with that – DM? Down with? Up with?

DM: Down with, jeeze.

D: You would? You'd eat him?

Y: Sure. Made sense to me in Heinlein.

DM: What's Heinlein?

D: You don't grok Heinlein?

N: Well, we've done concrete, water, sand.

Y: Earth, air, water—

D: I thought it was earth wind and fire.

DM: *Do you remember the 21st night of September?*
Love was changing the minds of pretenders
While chasing the clouds away
C'mon David, *ba de ya de ya de ya*

D: Wow, you know Earth, Wind and Fire?

DM: Of course. C'mon, *ba de ya de ya de ya*

Y: But not Heinlein.

N: Please don't make David sing.

Y: You can't make David sing. Or dance.

N: Or quit smoking.

D: Whoa, are we going back to pick on David? Not that I mind? I'd just like to know, so that I can gird my loins.

DM: Gird your loins? Oooh *(hitting head)* get out! Get out!

Y: You know, you don't have to decide right this instant.

N: Well, I sort of do. He said I would know. St James at noon, the ferry to the island, the island, and then I would know what to do with the rest. Well, here we are. I've done my best, followed instructions, and here we are. Now what? Now the fuck what?!

Silence from the rest.

N: I don't know what to do next. I feel – like all this time – these months – I have just been going forward because that's what Jake expects, he expects me to go on, to keep working, to keep moving. It's what everyone expects, what'd you say? *grieve – mourn – move on.* And I didn't want to grieve too much, too publicly, because—. We die, right? We live, we die, our friends do some rituals, some ceremonies, and life goes on for the rest. To grieve too much or too long is – unseemly. Especially for someone who cared less for his life than I did.

Y: Naomi—

N: He smoked 'til he got lung cancer, which probably only beat cirrhosis by a few years, and then he didn't even have the guts to stick it out 'til the end. He didn't have the guts to fight, he didn't have the desire to stay with me – to stay a few more weeks or months—

I guess I should be grateful he took pills and didn't blow his brains out.

I am not grateful. I am angry. I am angry and I am abandoned.

Nobody knows me the way he knows me. Knew me. I feel unknown now. No one will ever know me like that again.

I feel like something is breaking up in here *(she touches her chest)*, actually breaking—

DM and Y go to her, touching her.

David stands apart. He goes to light a cigarette, then doesn't.

D: *This is the hour of lead*
Remembered if outlived,
As freezing persons recollect the snow—
First chill, then stupor, then the letting go.

N: Yeah. *Yeah.*

Y: See? That's why we brought David, he always has the right quotation.

D: Your own personal Bartlett's.

DM: I can hardly wait to see what he writes from this.

D: Uh uh, pressure.

DM: We have to give you a deadline, or else you'll never write – it. Whatever it is. What is it?

Y: A poem.

D: No, I'm a terrible poet. That's why I memorise so many. Trying to figure out how they do it.

N: A piece for *Geist*?

Y: Bless you.

N: Scattering Jake.

DM: A play?

D: Maybe a play. *Tragedy, comedy, history, pastoral, pastoral-comical, historical-pastoral, tragical-historical, tragical-comical-historical-pastoral, scene individable, or poem unlimited.*

N: Can you write it better?

D: I'll try, Naomi.

N: Okay.

D: Okay.

N: *(looking at her watch)* We should get going, if we want to get the next ferry.

Y: Okay.

DM: Okay.

They start to pack up. David holds the ashes box.

D: Um, what do you want to do with—

N: Oh, put it back in your purse.

D: It's a man-bag.

DM: *(pointing at Yvette)* Don't even think of going there.

Yvette shrugs.

N: I don't have to decide right now.

DM: *(kicking at the fire)* You think this is out enough?

Y: Oh yeah, it's fine.

They pick up the bags and basket and cooler.

N: Oh this is much lighter.

D: That's because I ate an entire chicken and a pound of potato salad.

DM: Oh yeah, this is way better.

Y: Come on, people. We don't want to miss the ferry.

As they exit.

DM: Hey, David. Can I play me? In the play?

D: Sure I guess.

N: I don't wanna play me.

D: Okay.

N: Okay.

The End

RICHARD VAN CAMP

LOVE WALKED IN

The horror show began the exact second I told the truth. This was right after Janette came to town. Single Mom. Body of a stripper.

Kevin was like, "Check out the yummy mummy."

"Yeah," I said.

I always thought women with short hair could only ever be cute. I was wrong. She's white, French. She even sparkled in French. Just listening to her in the Northern line-up warmed The Hammer nicely. The prized ivory of a white woman has put me in the worst kind of heat. Then Wendy's masturbation incident happened, and I lost everything around me.

I saw Janette that aft getting out of her car as I cruised down Candy Lane in my Dad's old truck. She saw me. She was playing hopscotch with her girl and smiled as I drove by for the fiftieth time down her street. God Bless Candy Lane. She stopped to pick something up, and it was the way she bent over that got me. Her shorts were so tight they cupped her ass and I could see her pubic mound. I had to keep on driving, pull over by the airport, turn off and empty myself in gushes onto the high grass. I came squadrons.

The school was still closed until they found a new principal, and this was my life: Jonathan hated me. Nobody waved back; the girls I grew up with ignored me. Fuck them all.

Donna kept calling. She wanted me so badly. She had been cute but that was about it. She had let her hair grow, and that sharpened the curves of her cheeks. Her eyes had gotten darker over the years, like her Mom's, and she was still sort of pretty. And she had those tits. Her ass was a little fat and she was short. I couldn't get her legs over my shoulders if I tried. Funny how she fazed me with those words outside the cafe after the showdown with Jon – "You're a hero" – 'cause I was anything but...

Janette, for some reason, had chosen Doug the Slug Stevens as her bull. I couldn't believe this. The Slug raped his fourteen-year-old babysitter years back. That's how he lost his kids. How the Slug got Janette was beyond me, but I was gonna sink his fuckin' boat just like I sunk the principal's.

Donna was knocking on my window last night at two. Her folks were Cree and let her run wild, I guess, whenever and wherever she wanted. She did three taps, waited and did three more. I waited until she left and stroked one off for Janette.

In the morning, Mom brought me a CD as I was combing out the back stoop of my mullet. Jonathan and I grew them on purpose because we were holdouts for the '80s.

"What's this?" I asked.

"You tell me," she said. It was a CD case: Samantha Fox's *Touch Me*.

"I don't know," I said.

"Well somebody left it for someone here, and I know it wasn't intended for me – and it better not be for your father."

I opened it up and saw that Donna had written her name on the inside sleeve. "I must have dropped it last night."

Mom looked at me, stared at me actually. Her eyebrows rose, then lowered. She swept the back of her hand with her palm and this was a move she used to make when she still smoked. She was nervous. "We need you to clear out that brush in the backyard. Snow's coming soon and it'll block the skidoos."

I figured we were back to business. For a while there, I knew my folks were worried about me. After the social worker came and the RCMP took my statement, I wouldn't leave the house. No one called. The weight of my own clothes on my body made me feel like an old man, and it felt like someone was doing a handstand on my shoulders, pushing me down. I worked out twice a day in the basement, stayed in my room for hours just listening to Van Halen, The Cult, The Outfield. All I did was read *Playboy* and try to plan my future sex life: sex with Janette, break her heart, then move on, find someone younger for sex in an elevator, the Mile High club, sex in the bathtub, sex in the shower, sex outside, sex in the rain, sex in the snow, sex out at the cabin, sex on the trapline!

These days, the only someone who calls is Donna, but at least I'm out and about. The one good thing that happened – and the only reason I'm out and about – is I got a call from Mr. Henderson aka Boss Hog over at Northern Lights Log Homes.

"I heard what you did," he said. I could hear chainsaws in the background. "I need a log peeler who's willing to work hard before the snow comes. After that, we'll see if we can train you on the crane. The money's okay. I can't compete with government, but you'll at least learn how to build your own log home. What do you think?"

Mom and Dad were watching me, and I knew Dad had put the word out that I needed an arrow of light to fly my way.

"Sure," I shrugged. "Why not?"

So I worked all day, peeling logs for Boss Hog. The last thing I wanted to do on coffee break or lunch was ask questions or try to learn about building log homes. The first two days I forgot to bring gloves and shredded my forearms peeling the spruce and pine. After a while I didn't feel it much anymore when the bark bit me. The good news was I was doing push-ups and pull-ups when the boss wasn't around and I got tanned at the same time. To my surprise, that Samantha Fox CD was pretty good. I put it on low and got to work. To my even bigger surprise, Janette drove by in the government truck. I pinched my helmet a few times through my pockets so The Hammer'd swell as she drove by.

I stood up and smiled. I had my shirt off and was sweating something fierce. She smiled back when I flexed the pecs and even turned her head to look directly at me when she came by the second time on her way home from work. Nice.

I ran behind the biggest log pile and jacked off in jets to blast a web of fury and hysteria all over the logs behind the woodpile outside the work site. I surprised myself with how great it felt to come, the relief of it all, but the force and burn didn't fade. It just got better and better. I got quite the tool here that'll last me for life and lead me through a field of women.

⁂

Later, at coffee break, I walked into the office.

"Who's Donna?" Boss Hog asked as he looked up.

"A friend," I said, putting my gloves and hatchet away. "Why?"

"Tell her to quit calling here," he said. "She's called twice today."

"You got it," I said, and blushed in front of the guys.

He paused before getting into his big-ass Duelly. "She wants you to meet her for fries and a Coke after work."

Harold, Boss Hog's oldest son, grinned. "How 'bout fries and a cock after work?" The crew howled like wolves and I looked away. Goddamn him. Fuck he had a big buffalo head. Why didn't he get his front teeth replaced?

And goddamn that Donna...

❧

"Don't call me at work anymore," I said on the phone.

"I want to see you," she said.

I was drip-drying from the shower. The tan was coming along good. I was trimming my muff with Dad's moustache scissors. I wanted to have the perfect V, like what I saw in Mom's *Playgirl.* "Not a good idea," I said.

"Remember when we used to go out?"

"Not really," I said. "Bye."

❧

Janette drove by one more time in the government truck checking the mail for the college. There were four roads to the post office. She chose the road that I was always working next to, which was the slowest. Was I imagining this? No. She looked back, waved and smiled. I waved, stepped out on the road, watched her. She tapped her brake lights twice just to let me know that I wasn't imagining us.

I was gonna fuck her so hard it was gonna be brutal...

I re-read all of my Dad's *Playboys*, couldn't find one Playmate that even remotely looked like Janette. Snuck one of Dad's condoms from the bathroom and came back into rubber.

❧

Donna called during supper, twice. Mom told her to call back after seven.

"Is that Barb's daughter?"

I scooped a chunk of caribou into my mouth and nodded.

"I always wondered what happened to you two."

"Mom," I said, "we were in grade five."

Dad nudged me under the table with his leg. "You know," and I could tell I was gonna get a speech because he pulled out his favourite toothpick and moved to his chair by the woodstove. "I don't know how they do it in Africa, but here in the north, it's the bulls who pick, hey?"

"Here we go," Mom said and rolled her eyes.

I got up and poured Dad a coffee and made one for myself. I even put on water for Mom's tea. "Go on."

Dad put his coffee on the rocks, by the woodstove. "Love only works if it's the man who chooses."

"Hmph," Mom said.

"Now, Norma, hear me out. If a woman picks a man, it never lasts. It has to be the man who chooses. When a man chooses, that's when love lasts."

"Oh baloney," Mom said.

"Think of the caribou, Norma. It's not the cows who pick. It's the bulls. Think of the moose, the bison. That's nature workin'."

"I chose you," Mom said.

Dad stopped and looked at her, and the house fell quiet. My Dad smiled and reached out, "Norma, you just made my day. Son, disregard everything your old man just said."

They laughed and went for a kiss. I saw the eagle feather quiver that Mom made Dad on their wedding day. It was filled with eagle feathers they'd collected together over the years when they went camping. Then the phone rang. They looked at me. Dad got up.

"I'm not here," I said.

"Maybe it's Jonathan," Mom said. "You never know."

"Yeah right," I said.

Dad answered it. "Hello?"

He listened and covered the receiver: "You here?" and motioned by pointing at the receiver and mouthed: "It's her."

"Nope," I ran my fingers through my hair. "Cruisin'."

Candy Lane betrayed me that night. The Slug's Chev was parked outside Janette's house. The only light on at 10:15 couldn't have been her daughter's. Fuckin' guy. I revved my motor outside her house. Nothing. I revved it some more until the neighbour's lights turned on and her neighbour poked his head out. I didn't stop. I kept revving again and an outside light popped on two houses down. Just when I thought the motor was gonna blow through the hood her curtains moved. It was Doug. I peeled out and sped away.

Saw Donna walking down Main Street, swerved down a back road even though we both knew we saw each other. It was true – we did used to go out.

Grade five – she cried at a party and her cousins surrounded me: "You're really mean, you know," they said.

"Mean? Me?"

"You think you're so cool," Dolly said.

"What did I do?"

"Yeah," Jonathan said. "What did he do?"

"Donna likes you, okay?" Dolly said to me. "Are you happy now?"

I knew Donna did. And the whole school did too the day she wrote my initials on her runners where everyone could see. After a week of nagging from all of her cousins, I agreed to go out with her – if she'd just stop crying.

"Okay," I said as we sat on the playground fence. "Here are the rules. If we're going to go out, you can't walk beside me."

"Okay," she said.

"We're not going to hold hands."

"Okay."

I pointed at her. "Ever."

She was smiling, glowing with happiness.

"You can't call my house and you've got to stop crying."

She sniffled. "Okay."

"Okay?"

"Okay."

She tried to touch my hand, but I pulled it away as if burned by water. "I'm not kidding, Donna. That's strike one."

Fuck, I was mean to her. She'd follow me around the playground and I'd shoo her away or ignore her all day. Then she'd cry and I'd have to talk to her. One hug usually made her happy, but then she'd hold on for dear life and I'd be like, "Okay, you can let go. Okay? Okay!" I had to kill it as summer came. Who knew what tourists would be coming for summer vacation bringing their daughters with them?

God, did Donna cry. Her cousins used their bodies to circle and shield her from seeing me. The bell rang and I slunk by. She yelled out to me, "But what was strike two and strike three?"

Her mascara was all over the place. It was too sad to look. I just kept walking. Then the strangest thing happened. She ignored me. Who did she think she was? That summer nobody hot came to Simmer. I'd see Donna in the park and I'd be like "Hi."

And she'd look to her cousin and say, "Did you hear something?"

Dolly popped her gum and was like, "Nah."

The only time she acknowledged me was at the Northern. One time, I was helping Mom shop and I saw Donna with her Mom. While our Moms decided to have a high school reunion in the dairy aisle, I walked up to her. "Hi," I said.

She walked away without saying a word. Her eyes flashed fiercely as she looked away.

"Hey." I followed her but she sped up. I bolted after her and she was trying to hide in the baby food aisle. I had her. And then I said the stupidest line of my life. Right there, across from the Cheez Whiz, I said the stupidest thing I ever could have said and I don't even know why I said it: "Don't walk away mad, okay? Just walk away." I even had my hands out for full effect.

She rolled her eyes and blushed. "Whatever," she said, before walking away.

When I came around the corner, there stood our Moms. I could tell by their eyes that they'd been watching us and were disappointed that I returned alone. How cheap. This had been a set-up.

Donna tapped on my window at three a.m. last night. I was rock hard and tempted. Gotta cool it with The Hammer. Got raw spots where I shimmied that sting when it gasped for air. It would have been a nice night for a walk with her, to talk and stuff, but I thought it was best not to lead her on.

I couldn't believe she walked all the way across town to stalk me. That was a lot of pussy power making her do that. I always wondered what it was like for a woman to feel horny with nothing to get hard with but their pink erasers. Maybe the pull I felt for Janette was the same pull Donna felt for me?

Goddamn that Janette. Stopped cruising down my street at work. I was desperate all day. Went behind the log pile and measured The Hammer with a tape measure: a little over seven and a half. Not growing, not shrinking, just was.

Then – then! I slammed my frickin' thumb with the back of the hatchet by accident. God, the pain! It throbbed with agony that did not let up.

"She'll turn black," Boss Hog said at the first-aid station, "and fall off pretty quick."

Harold handed me an ice pack and shook his walrus head. "You should have a new thumbnail by the time grade twelve starts."

I looked out the window and winced as a new wave of throbbing came for my thumb. At least Donna had quit calling work.

⁂

Just as I thought all was lost, I cruised down Candy Lane and Janette's car wasn't there. I raced across the potato field and sped down Main. Sure enough, her car was outside. The Slug's. There. In the car. They were sitting and yelling at each other. The Slug looked like he was barking at her, he was yelling so loud. I cruised by, but she didn't see me. Things were looking up.

⁂

"Dad," I yelled as we cleared the last of the deadfall. "Tell me about Doug Stevens."

Dad turned off his chain saw. "The Slug?"

"Yeah."

"Bad dude. Nasty temper. I told you what he did to his babysitter."

"Yeah."

"He gets a lot of women, that guy."

"But how? Is he rich, or what?"

"No more than the rest of us."

"So why do women go after him?"

"Funny how that works. Women just can't seem to get enough of a mean man. Isn't he seeing that new woman? What is she – French?"

Dad already knew. He and his pallies got together every night at Stan's house and had a couple cold ones. They listened to Waylon, shot some stick. I couldn't wait until the day they invited me to join them for a drink. They knew, I was sure, all about Janette and the word was out, you could bet, that I had it for her something fierce.

"What's it take, Dad," I asked, "to break a woman's grip on a man?"

Dad stopped and looked at me. He looked at my build and read my eyes. "A good fight can settle things pretty quick. Women respect that. But you're a little young for her, don't you think? Why not go for the one who's calling the house?"

I wrinkled my nose. "Too young."

He nodded and said nothing before starting the chainsaw back on and getting to work. Doug was a dirty fighter, mean. I was worried. I knew I couldn't beat him. Fuck, I was only seventeen.

Last night there was no tapping on my window. As I waited to hear her footsteps on our gravel driveway, I remembered us going out. I'd known Donna since kindergarten. Before we became strangers, she told me she used to wash her hair twice a day. She also washed her socks with bleach so they always looked new. You could smell it. She had always liked me. I couldn't remember her ever having a boyfriend. She left town for a couple years. Her Dad made some great money in Fort McMurray as a carpenter, but I guess they missed Simmer.

❧

The day Jonathan and I had it out, Donna was working at the Coffee Shop. I went there to talk to Jonathan but I knew the second I walked in the whole place was brewing for him and me to fight. He hadn't cut his hair so that was a good sign.

"Way to go, winner," Jonathan said and pushed me.

"What's up?"

"What do you mean – what's up? I'm not going to Disneyland is what's up. All because of you."

A small group of girls raced from their seats and surrounded us. "Fight! Fight!" they were yelling. The rest of the girls ran outside.

Uh oh, I thought. Once the girls ran outside, there was no turning back. Jonathan shook his head at me because we both knew the girls would lock their arms into the shape of an octagon like in UFC.

"Fuck sakes anyways," he said. "Now we gotta fight."

"Way to go," I said. They'd probably want us to whip our shirts off and fluff out our mullets now. That's the classic in this town. I looked around. Even the adults and the Chinese owners knew there was no turning back.

"All right," Valerie announced as she walked in. "Let's get it on!"

Jonathan stood and we walked out into the bright sunlight and practically half the town was there. The girls had joined arms and they were all grinning. "Fight! Fight! Fight!" Adults even stood outside the post office while trucks slowed down and pulled into the Terminal parking lot. I'd have to fight Jonathan now, and I didn't want to. He had a bad knee from basketball but that was off limits. Maybe his face bone or his bony ribs. The circle of woman power opened to receive us. The girls all started to cheer and stomp their feet. How cheap. I just couldn't even believe this was my life right now.

Jonathan led me right to the centre before spinning around. "Come on, fucker!" he yelled. He whipped off his shirt and fluffed out his mullet! The girls cheered to hysteria and I could tell by his eyes he was really into this now. I couldn't believe he'd turn this into an academy award performance. He tucked his shirt around his belt. I let out my breath and felt ninety years old. "Take your shirt off, Gerald!" one of the girls yelled. And then they all started cheering. "Shirt! Shirt! Shirt!"

I wasn't going to do it.

"Come on, Gerald!" Debbie yelled. "Take that frickin' shirt off and show us what you got!"

The circle quieted for a second. Debbie's brother committed suicide last summer in their basement so even Jonathan looked at me like I'd better.

He lowered his fists. "Come on, Gerald."

Well, geez, I thought. I took off my shirt and all the girls cheered even louder. Even Debbie. They cheered so loud the back stoop of my mullet practically blew sideways. I tucked my shirt into my belt and smiled. This wasn't so bad. I understood why our Dads did this. It was a Simmer mating ritual and our culture all rolled up in one!

"Fluff the mullet! Fluff the mullet! Fluff the mullet!" they started to chant and I shook my head. God, the women of this town were so bossy.

Jonathan motioned that I had to, so I did. I took my time and leaned back like Dog the Bounty Hunter all slow and luxurious. I flicked my back hair out like I was a party on two legs waiting to happen. The girls went crazy and I wondered if this was what it felt like to be one of the Beatles in their prime. The girls were stomping their feet and going bananas over our hair and I caught Jonathan smiling at me. He loved this. Holy cow, his nipples were the colour of Monday morning hickeys. Then his face hardened so I made mine, too.

"I'm gonna down you!" he yelled and there was more cheering. The fight was on now.

But I stood my ground. I planted my feet on the pavement and raised my hands into fists. "Okay, Jonathan. How long have you known me?"

"Too long," he said and spit by my shoe. He gauged the crowd. The electricity was building. Even the bar stars had made their way around us. And they'd want an all-out brawl with bannock slaps and drop kicks.

"Down him!" someone yelled.

"Yeah," another jeered. "Think you're good, Gerald?"

Jonathan was tough, but he wasn't that tough. He raised his fists and started hopping back and forth, just like in grade seven when I had to teach him how to dance. We stood so close I could see the sweat beads he got on his nostrils in gym class. I started reading his eyes to see how far he was going to take this when a girl kicked me hard towards him. I looked back. All I could see were hands and eyes, hair and purses.

"Listen to me," I yelled to the crowd. "The second that fuckin' principal left town is the second he admitted he did it."

"Bullshit! He's embarrassed," someone yelled back.

"So embarrassed that he stole all your money?" I looked to the crowd. "All of yours? Think about it. This guy's an adult, and he left town in the middle of the night—"

"He's our principal," Jolene yelled. "He wouldn't do anything like that!"

"Yeah!" the crowd yelled. "You're just jealous 'cause you didn't fundraise."

"You lazy Dogrib!"

"Frickin' loser!"

Someone spit on my face and I could smell tobacco and coffee and something like fries and gravy in it. Gah! Jonathan and I looked together to see who it was. Whoever it was was hidden behind the wall of people circling us, kicking us together so hard that Jonathan and I had to hold each other up.

"We're not friends anymore," he said. "I thought I knew you, but it's true. You didn't fundraise. You were jealous 'cause we were gonna go to Disneyland and you weren't."

"Punch the back of his head through the front of his face!" a voice yelled and the circle grew quiet.

It was Torchy and his brother Sfen. I didn't even know how they got where they were but they had their leather jackets off and we could see their tattoos and muscles. They were hardened criminals and their eyes were warlike and fierce. How cheap. They were Dogribs, like me, Kevin Garner, and Wendy.

"Come on," Torchy said. "Is this a fuckin' fight, or what?"

Fuck, he looked rough with his crooked smile. I looked and, sure enough, they had their cowboy boots on. Dad told me they stuffed their cowboy boots with lead so they could kick you in the eyes when they got you down. Also, they only looped their belts at the 3 and 9 position so they could whip them out in a knife fight. They had Tonka-sized belt buckles, which they sharpened, to aim for your teeth and face.

Once the whole crowd realized Torchy and Sfen were there, everyone broke up and stood still. I saw fear in Jonathan's eyes as he kicked himself back into the crowd, turned, and pushed his way out of the horde.

"Awwww," the crowd yelled. "Fight him, Jon!"

But even that sounded weak.

Torchy started rolling a smoke and Sfen watched me, to see what I would do. It was like he could melt steel with his eyes he was so tough. I felt the cold gob of spit roll to my neck. I turned and walked away. I used my shirt to wipe the saliva off. It was just slimy and I'd probably get TB now. Gross! I was listening for someone to run behind me and try a cheap shot, but then Donna came running beside me.

"Gerald! Wait!"

I didn't stop walking. She held a hot J-cloth to my face and wiped the spit off me. She had to hop up 'cause she's so short.

"Hold still," she said, and I smelled dishwashing soap and vinegar.

"Go away," I said.

"You're a hero," she said.

I rolled my shirt on. "Leave me alone."

"No," she said. "I love you."

My eyes bugged as I walked away. "Take it easy," I said.

❧

Janette never cruised by work that day, so I went for a little cruise myself. Told the boss I had something in the mail and there, before my eyes, walked Janette and The Slug holding hands, downtown, together. I drove by, looked back and she looked away. I double tapped the brakes so the rear lights would flare and Doug saw that. Fuck. I seen him turn to her and I knew he knew. Fuck.

❧

Cruised all day with the sun hot on my arms listening to The Cult's "She Sells Sanctuary" and Van Halen. Didn't know what to do. Janette was in his grip and my dog balls were so loaded for her.

I finally admitted it: goddamn this Beaver Fever. I was so fucking lonely and one woman had to be like any other, right? I cruised by Donna's with the Madness feeling me up. The air was sweet with the aroma of leaves freshly burned in the front yards all over town.

Sure enough, there was a pile of smouldering leaves off to the side of their property and two rakes propped against their porch. Donna was sitting out on her deck with her folks. She saw me and sat up. I stopped, waved her over. She looked at her folks and they checked me out. Her Mom wanted to wave but looked at her hubby. Donna's Dad – Ronny? Donny? – I could never remember his name – looked back down at his paper and Mom put her spatula down. They looked at their daughter, but Donna was already on her way over. She was smiling and blushing. I saw those big knockers of hers sway together as she made her way to my truck, and I saw she was wearing moccasins.

"Hi."

"Hi."

"Nice moccasins."

She looked down and I checked her out. "Thank you. My Mom and I made them." I started to harden, just thinking about it. I got brave. "I missed you last night."

She smiled the sexiest smile and looked left. "I didn't think you ever heard me."

I looked away. "I'm playing hard to get."

She laughed and whispered, "You always have. Did you get my CD?"

I nodded. "She's pretty good."

"What's your favourite song?" she asked, and I could tell she was testing me, reading the wind ahead of us.

I thought about it. "That one that goes, 'Baby I'm lost for words.'"

Her eyes brightened. "That's mine too."

"Can I see you tonight?"

I saw a flush at the base of her neck. She had a little fire in her. "Sure."

"Where and when?"

"Meet me at the park at eleven."

She looked at her folks and looked back at me. "Okay."

"Dress sexy," I said, and I was surprised I said it. Both of us were shocked with my hunger. Her mouth parted and she nodded before looking away. She was blushing. So was I. I drove away feeling like Rocky.

The other good thing that happened occurred on Day Two of being blacklisted: Pops knocked on my door.

"Come in," I said and sat up.

He saw his stack of *Playboy* and smiled. "Good reading, hey?"

I nodded. "I'm learning."

He chuckled. "I know the Posties think we're swingers, but we renew our subscriptions each Christmas. I can't remember how it started, but I couldn't imagine this house without 'em."

I smiled. "Me either."

"You know, son," he said, and there was his toothpick. "I want you to know I am proud of you, and we stand by you. I think you calling social services took courage, and this is a time that will show you who your true friends are. Your mother and I, well..." He put his hand on mine. "You're a man now." He pulled out the keys to his truck and handed them to me.

Surprised, I asked, "What's this?"

"She's yours now. Take good care of her."

I sat up on the bed. Dad's truck – mine?

"She's got four months left on insurance. After that, it'll be in your name. You're in charge of putting gas in her, and she could use an oil change before the snow comes."

I was speechless.

He held out his hand. "Deal?"

I could not believe it. I took his hand. "Deal."

He hugged me and said, "Love you, son."

I felt the tears well up and had to wait a bit. "Love you too."

"Take her for a cruise," he said. "Your Mom's worried sick, and it'll do her good to know you're getting out."

It was ten at night. "You sure?"

He patted my shoulder. "Sure."

Best ride of my life. I put on one of my Dad's tapes: The Outfield's "Taking My Chances." I cranked it as I cruised. Got out. Saw the townies. Rode by Jonathan's. Saw his light on but didn't honk. I bet he was practicing his guitar and listening to The Cult. I bet he was getting his hair cut to betray me even more. We were supposed to grow it out until we graduated from PWS. Cheap.

I missed the way we could just call each other up to call each other down.

"Hello?"

"Hey. I heard you got a big one."

"Uh huh. That's right. How's you doin'?"

"Got a sore cock and a full belly."

"Same, baby. Same."

I thought about how we used to go snowshoeing out by the highway and one of us – usually Jon – would always say, "They say the grandfathers always take care of you when you're on the land."

Then we'd pretend to be Cree and go, "Tapwe. Tapwe."

I drove by the church and shook my head. The truth never set me free. Doubled back and went down the figure-eight loop to the airport and, despite my nervousness, drove down the clutch-my-sack (Raven talk for cul-de-sac) to where the principal lives.

The lone streetlight caught the hood of the truck, and I could see the dents my father couldn't – or didn't mention – from the afternoon Jonathan and I practised being the Dukes of Hazzard, rolling across the hood of the truck in imaginary getaways.

"I'm Luke!" Jonathan slid across the hood.

I did too. "I'm puke!"

We fell on our knees and held our hands out to the spruce trees. "We're the Dukes, and we're gonna plug you through your panties!"

God, we were like eleven years old. Man that was fun. That was the day we tried Red Man chew like old timers, and threw up in the potato field on the way home for supper.

I got out of the truck, pissed on the principal's lawn, gave him the finger. "That's haunted ground now, fucker," I said. "I hope you burn in hell for what you did."

Just as I hopped in my truck and pulled away, the lights caught something and I slammed on the brakes. There. By the picture window. Someone had touched the house with bloody hands. Wendy?

"Fuck," I whispered.

It was the spookiest thing: a single red handprint on the front of the white house.

"Fuck," I said again and drove away.

I swerved to Jonathan's part of town and stopped outside his house, "And fuck you, Jonathan, for not backing me up!" before smoking the tires and racing away.

I saw his bedroom light turn on in the rearview, but nobody ran out of his house. And that was when I saw another handprint in front of Baxter's house. From what I read in the paper, he was charged with molesting kids at his son's sleepovers. He put something in the food. The kids were never really asleep; they were almost unconscious when he played with their bodies. What the fuck was going on?

Eleven o'clock. On the road. Picked Donna up, and she never looked finer: jean jacket, hair long, tight jeans and new shoes. Perfume in the cab and she couldn't look at me as we cruised down the highway. Was she a virgin? I didn't have the balls to ask. I was thinking about Janette and the Slug. No cars at her house. Or his. Maybe they would accidentally surprise us in their vehicle as they searched for a place to make out.

We drove down the highway to the towers. I pulled up, turned off the truck but kept the tunes running. I'd brought Samantha Fox and I could tell she loved this. I stared straight ahead and felt her huge eyes on me.

"Strip," I said and looked right at her. "Show off for me."

And she did. Right down to her bra and panties. Donna took her socks off and hissed. "The floor's cold."

I winced when I thought about how I should have cleaned the truck out.

"Okay," she said. "Your turn."

I pulled my shirt over my head, unzipped my pants, took them off and kept my Calvin K's on. She was looking at The Hammer straining to get out. People thought I'd banged my share, but I hadn't. Fooled around. Got a sloppy lick from a Hay River girl with carrot shredder teeth, but no pelt.

"I love your lips," she said.

"Take off your bra," I said.

She looked into my eyes. "I always have, Gerald."

I smiled because I felt that and it felt sweet.

"Turn up the heat," she said.

I did and she reached behind to reveal the most beautiful knockers in town: slopers that supported their own weight with a little bit of side swell. Lovely nipples as long as bullets and cookies as big as loonies. "Damn," I said.

She covered her chest. "What?"

"When did you get that body of yours?"

She was horrified. "Why?"

"'Cause you are hot."

She was still frozen but looked down. She cleared her throat. "Since grade ten."

I couldn't believe what a treasure I'd found. I started sudsing up when she asked, "Bring any condoms?"

"No," I said. "You?"

"No," she said. "I thought you—"

Too late. I was so horny I was shivering and started to kiss her. I pulled her panties off and I could feel her skin against mine. She tasted good, smelled great. Before she knew it, I spread her legs and she leaned back.

"If you love me and my lips," I said, "you're going to love this."

I pull my gonch off and there, fully exposed, rose my hot tusk rising – The Hammer.

"God," she said. She couldn't catch her breath.

I smiled. "Yeah."

"You better not give me the dose, Gerald," she said and pointed at me.

"You too," I said and pointed back.

And we burst out laughing. I was surprised at how good she looked naked. I looked at her fur. She was quiet for a bit before she said, "Don't knock me up."

I scooted towards her trying to aim. "I won't."

She gripped me with her hand and squeezed. "No hickeys or doing your business inside of me, okay?"

"Okay."

She guided me into her and I melted with how hot she was inside. Even my toes started to shiver. And I was shameless. I squeezed her tits and ass and burned my mouth through her neck. I gave her monkey bites all over. I scared myself with how ferocious I was and the whole time she loved everything I gave her. I thought she was gonna blow my eardrums she was so loud.

I could not believe what a great body she had.

So this is how it is? I thought as I glided inside her. This isn't so hard. There was a wet burning heat inside of her and every thrust only got us hotter. I thought I was gonna lose it. I was worried I couldn't come but then I thought about Janette. She tightened and tried to kick away. "No! Not yet. Not inside me."

But I only came harder. It came searing out of me so perfectly I even surprised myself by crying out, grabbing her shoulders and biting her neck.

"Fuck sakes," she said and pushed me hard.

"Sorry."

"What the fuck were you thinking? I told you not to!"

"I wasn't – Sorry! Take it easy."

"Take it easy? I'm not on the pill, Gerald."

I looked at her, made sure no one was coming down the road. No romance here.

She got dressed. I got dressed. We argued back to town. I told her I was sorry a hundred times in the longest twelve minutes of my life that it took to get her home.

"I'm not going home like this," she said. "Take me to the gas station. I need to wash up. My Mom'll be waiting for me at the house."

Fuck sakes. I did. I pulled up and she got out before I could say anything. I bought her an Orange Crush and I grabbed a Coke. When the cooler door opened, I caught a whiff of myself and I smelled us together. Sex!

Lisa Snow was working the counter. Her eyes followed Donna, and I just knew she couldn't wait for me to leave so she could call her friends.

"Hey," I said as I put the drinks on the counter.

She nodded, rang it up and looked out the window. "Two-fifty."

I gave her a loonie and a toonie. "Keep it," when she tried to hand me back my change. She still didn't look at me. Well, now that I know what to do, I could fuck her next, if I wanted to.

"Loser," she whispered as I walked away.

"No cock for you," I said loud enough for her to hear as I opened the door.

❧

Donna washed up, came out smelling great with that perfume of hers.

"Sorry," I said.

"I can't believe this," she said and slammed the door. She was really mad. I'd never seen her mad before and it scared me.

"We'll cruise, okay?"

We cruised to the airport, and I felt bad. She didn't deserve that. I put Van Halen on and "When Love Walks In" came on. We were quiet for a bit, both wishing for something neither of us could have.

After a while I said, "Come on now. Don't be like that."

"Do you do this to all your girlfriends?" she asked and looked out her window. She didn't open her Orange Crush.

I didn't want to go for the sympathy vote, but I told her. "That was my first time."

She looked at me. "What?"

I told her again. "Honest. You're my first."

"Stop the truck!" she yelled.

I pulled over and she was hugging me and kissing me all over my face. "Oh thank you thank you thank you," she said. "Thank you, Gerald."

She was happy and I was relieved. "I'm sorry I was rough," I said. "I was just nervous, I guess."

"Be as rough as you want," she said, "I just don't want a baby yet."

She rubbed her tummy when she said that and that scared me. "Me too," I peeped.

"Let's cruise," she said and she was smiling. "First time, huh?"

I blushed. "Yes."

"Honest?"

"Honest," I said. "Don't tell anyone."

"I won't."

I gave her a mean look. "Do not tell your cousins."

She crossed her arms. "I won't."

"You better not." I said, "especially Bonny."

She reached out and touched my dimple, and for some reason we burst out laughing. I felt great. I felt really good.

By then it was midnight. I thought, if I'm going to get it when I get home, I might as well get it good. We cruised around. Did the figure-eight route between Kid City and the airport and we drove by the principal's turn-off.

"Stop," she said.

"No," I said.

She touched my wrist. "Please."

I stopped, backed up, and turned into the clutch-my-sack facing the house. There was that red handprint again. My heart raced wild and I finished my Coke. I pointed to the handprint and she leaned forward. "What is that?"

I shrugged and flashed my brights on it. "Don't know."

"What happened to your thumb?" she asked. "And your wrists. What are they – those marks?"

"Huh?"

She peeled back my sleeves to reveal the spruce gum stains and scrapes from bark bite. "Suicide," I said and she covered her mouth. I burst out laughing. "No. I'm sorry. That wasn't funny."

Her eyes were huge.

"From work," I said. "The bark of the trees slices me up when I pull it off."

"Why are the marks so black?"

"Spruce gum."

She punched my arm. "Don't joke about suicide!"

"Hey," I pulled away. "Sorry. You really make me nervous, you know."

She pulled away from me. "Well so do you."

"Hey," I said softly.

"Hey what?"

I held out my arm and she looked at me. What was that in her eyes – disappointment? She scooted over and I put my arm around her, and it hit me that we were sitting in my truck like every couple in Simmer does when they make it official. My back started to burn. She had clawed me up!

"You did the right thing," she said.

I tried to figure out which room had been Wendy's. "You figure?"

She nodded and leaned into me. "Can I ask you something?"

I shrugged. "Go ahead."

"How did you know?"

I took a big breath. My folks hadn't even asked me this yet. I knew they were biding their time and giving me mine.

"It's okay if you don't want to talk about it," she said.

Her hair smelled nice. "If you give me a sip of your Orange Crush, I'll tell you, but don't tell anyone, okay?"

"Okay."

I took three mouthfuls and handed it back. I couldn't look at her.

"It was Wendy."

"What about her?"

"Well, you know she was slow, hey?"

She nodded.

"Did you know she was Dogrib?"

"No."

"She is. Same as me. In fact, we're probably related. We were at track practise. This was when Jonathan was still my friend. Well, there we were, getting ready for the high jump when Wendy laid down, took off her clothes and started playing with herself."

Donna cleared her throat and put her hand on my leg. I looked at the principal's house and wondered, which room didn't you rape her in?

"But how did you know?"

I looked at those trees. "This may sound sick, but she had a hot body. The boys knew it. We all knew it. The way she was playing with herself..."

She was quiet for a bit before she answered, "Okay."

"Well, she was doing this for show. She was looking at all of us and licking her lips. I don't know where the fuck she got it, but, somehow, she'd smeared lipstick on her lips and was trying to be all sexy, and I could tell this was rehearsed. Like she was trained, you know? And then I saw her toenails."

"What about them?"

I sat up and flashed my brights on that handprint. "They were painted red. Like that."

"So?"

"A sexy, deep red. The kind women wear."

Donna was quiet, giving me the space I needed.

"Did you ever see his wife?" I asked.

"I keep thinking I did, but now I don't know."

"You couldn't miss her. She was two hundred and forty pounds. She didn't wear nail polish like that. She was a Bible thumper, remember?"

"Go on."

"Wendy didn't put that nail polish on herself, and I know the principal's wife wouldn't. He did."

I could tell this scared her and that was why I was telling her the PG-13 version. She sat up and checked to see if the door was locked. "So what happened?"

"I knew, in that second, that he was molesting her. Think about it: they never took her anywhere. They got a big ol' house. When I called social services, the worker came and took my statement. I didn't tell the coach. I didn't tell Jonathan, but a cop car and a social services vehicle in my driveway pretty much alerted the town it was me who had something to do with his little midnight run."

I pointed to the living room window. They left the drapes closed. You could never see into this house, even on a sunny day. "Look at this house. It's like a wolverine den. He can see everyone who's coming down the road, but you can't see in."

I pointed to the fence. "That fucker put fence all round his property, high walls, barricading himself in. He doesn't have any neighbours, so he could be as loud as he wanted. Whatever went on in that house was so horrible, my Dad told me the sergeant walked out and vomited when they did the raid."

"God," she said. She made a motion like the sign of the cross but stopped herself.

"The sad thing is his wife knew. You didn't see her out in public much, did you?"

"No." She took another sip and leaned over and kissed my cheek before resting her head on my shoulder. "You should be a cop."

I pulled her closer and could smell her shampoo and perfume. That felt nice. "That fucker called the moving company the night I told and paid cash to Bully's to pack and move his entire house in the middle of the night."

"I can't believe his wife stuck with him."

"Stupid white bitch. They were gone before the cops knew what happened."

"At least social services got Wendy before they left."

"Yeah."

The R-rated version was that it was Kevin Garner, Simmer's Dogrib drug dealer, who pointed out the obvious clue: she was shaved bald.

"You better call social services," he said.

"What? Why not you?"

He looked at her and turned away. "You and I both know she couldn't do that to herself. I'm a dealer, Gerald. You call. They'll believe you."

And he walked.

"He stole our money," Donna said quietly.

"Huh?"

"You know how he was going to take all of the students who fundraised to Disneyland?"

"Yeah."

"We raised over eight thousand dollars."

"Were you a part of that? How much did you raise?"

She looked up "Three hundred and twenty-four dollars. My Mom and I baked pies."

"Really? What else?"

"Cookies and cakes."

I smiled, thinking about this. "You bake?"

She smiled. "Of course."

"You a good cook?"

"Maybe."

I got hard again, thinking of her baking with her Mom, maybe listening to country and western and laughing with her ma as her pops read the paper, smiling in the living room. "What's your best dish?"

"Um??? Pork chops, gravy, mashed potatoes—"

I flew upon her something fierce. Right then and there across from the house. In the truck. Across from the principal's, I had her undressed with me on top in seconds.

"Don't do your business," she kept saying. "Don't you do it."

"I won't, baby," I said.

She gripped my shoulders and pulled me deep into her with her thighs. "I love you, Gerald," she said suddenly.

"Me too," I said, surprised.

"Oh," she shivered as she swallowed me between her legs. "We fit so perfect."

I didn't do my business. Couldn't. But she did. And how. She took all of me. To the hilt.

Afterwards, we shivered together.

"Wow," she said. "What happened?"

I got embarrassed. "You turned me on, okay?"

"By talking about cooking?"

"Yeah," I said. "Sorry."

She laughed and kissed my forehead. "Well, if that's all it takes, we'll be great."

I kissed her back. This time I kissed her and no one else. I mean it.

We cruised around and she asked, "You lost a lot by telling, hey?"

I nodded. "Jonathan doesn't talk to me anymore. They just can't shake the fact they're not going to Disneyland."

"Think about what he might have done to the students who went," she said.

I looked at her. That's exactly what the social worker said when she came to the house to take my statement and do follow-up. "Thank you for saying that."

She kissed me and touched the side of my face gently. "You are a hero. You saved that girl from more rape. The cops'll get him."

We pulled up to her place. "Hope so."

"Call me, okay?" She looked around. "I've lost my sock."

"I will. Sorry I did my business."

"Where's my sock?"

I looked around. "Maybe you dropped it when we were in the gas station."

"Maybe. Just don't knock me up, and thanks for your cherry."

I laughed out of shock and when I looked up I had tears in my eyes. She kissed my neck and then, in the sign of the cross: forehead, chin, cheek, cheek. We ended by kissing and she walked away. I went home without cruising down Candy Lane. Can't disrespect my woman, hey.

I wondered: Why didn't we do this years ago?

I went to sleep part of the de-virginized club without washing up. In fact, before I fell asleep, I reached down and used my fingers to smell her all over again.

And the smell was animal. I loved it. I sniffed my fingers and smiled before rolling over. Donna Donna Donna, you finally got me. I thought of Wendy, how I used to pass her in the halls without ever looking at her. The only special needs in high school and she had to be Dogrib. The Crees, Chipewyan, Gwich'in, Slavey and whites just loved that. She made me ashamed to be Tlicho, but I was glad I helped her. I hoped she was safe, wherever she was.

Woke up smiling. Thank you, God, and thank you, Donna. Felt the weight of telling and being banished leave me as I washed myself clean.

Came out of the bathroom and Mom was standing there holding up a sock. "What's this?" she asked. It was Donna's sock. Bleached white but scuffed from the truck's floormats. The one she left behind.

"I went swimming last night," I said. "Gave a friend a ride home."

"I bet," she said and looked at me. "You make an honest woman out of whoever it is you're seeing. Do this right and with respect."

"I just gave her a ride home, Mom."

I was out the door to work before she could ask when I'd be home for supper.

Worked all day wincing. Donna's claw marks on my back stung the more I worked up a sweat. Janette drove by twice. The second time she cruised by, I walked out to the road and blocked her. She pulled up beside me and rolled down her window.

"Hi," I said.

"Hello," she said.

"I'm Gerald."

Her eyes sparkled. "Hello, Gerald."

"You're Janette. How's Doug?"'

"Fine. Why do you ask?"

"He's mean," I said. Her eyes changed. They narrowed and she stared straight ahead. "What do you want?"

"You."

This got her. She looked back at me. "Can I ask how young you are?"

"Going into grade twelve this September," I said.

She was checking out my chest and arms. "So young," she said. "She yours?" she asked and pointed with her chin to Donna walking down the road towards us.

I glanced at Donna quick. I had maybe two minutes to do this. "Nope. Can I ask you something?"

"Better hurry before your lady gets here."

"She's not my lady." I took a big breath. "I got eight inches. How much does Doug got?"

She looked straight ahead again. Why couldn't she be seventeen? I saw the wrinkles on her face, around her eyes, at the edges of her mouth. She looked weathered. The sag of her neck and the back of her hands gave her age away: "He's got a lot more than that, since you're asking." She lit a smoke, squinted, motioned with her chin, "Look, your little honey's waving at you."

I turned. Donna was waving away. There was a wild panic in her eyes. Shit! "She's a friend." I had to hurry before Donna arrived. "Doug raped his babysitter, you know."

"I've been told this by everyone I meet here."

"We're a Block Parent community."

"They couldn't prove anything."

"No? Then how come his old lady left him? How come he never sees his daughter?"

"Can we change the subject?"

"Can I see you sometime?"

"No."

"Please?'

She looked at me. "This is crazy."

"I'm a great guy," I said, realizing I was burning across my face.

"I can see that," she said. "She's getting closer."

I looked. Donna was running towards us, her little fists and legs just pumping.

"I have to go," she said.

"Call me at my house," I said. "2999."

She looked away, and I shut the door. She drove away. No double tap on the brakes this time. I couldn't believe how old she looked up close and wondered if The Slug thought of her being seventeen again when he was plums deep...

Donna walked up to me, panting. Her cheeks were a scorched red, like how they always were in gym class after running laps. "Who was that? She has a boyfriend, you know."

"I know," I said. "She's just saying hi."

"Well stop it," she said. "You're taken."

"Says who?"

"Me."

I looked away. I blew it!

"Did you like last night?"

"Sure," I shrugged and blushed. I couldn't believe I'd just made a move on a forty-year-old. "It was fun."

"I think it was more than fun. God, I'm sore and covered in hickeys."

How will I ever get out of this? Boss Hog came out of the office and motioned for me to peel more logs.

"I gotta go," I said.

"Can I help?"

I looked at her and was genuinely touched. Here she was wearing a nice white BUM Equipment pullover and I was covered in spruce gum and she was ready to work with me. "No thanks." I looked at her and knew in a second that she was ready to marry me, cook for me, clean the house, have a few kids.

"Can we go for fries and a Coke after work?" she asked.

I thought about this. I at least owed her that. "I can be there at five."

When I met her, all five of her cousins were there as witnesses. I could totally tell she told them I'd be there. Donna took her T-shirt off under her pullover. The entire restaurant could see the monkey bites I gave her, and the word was out: Gerald tagged Donna. Film at eleven. Shit. I was a hostage. Janette, save me! Dolly watched me throughout the entire half-hour episode. Suspicious eyes asked, "How long before you hurt her again?"

When I cruised home, there were police outside Janette's house. Cherries were going and everything. Two social services cars were on the lawn. Man, this was serious. I would've pulled over but the road was too skinny. Half the town drove by to get a good filthy look and I had to keep moving or block traffic. I pulled into my driveway and considered walking back to Janette's to find out what was going on. I was trying to think about what to do when Dad pulled up and wanted me to pluck ducks with him.

"Hear the news?" he asked.

I shook my head.

"See the cops outside that new teacher's house?"

"Yeah."

"The Slug strikes again."

"What?"

"Apparently Doug was starting to abuse that French woman's daughter."

Mom hissed when she took her breath in.

"What?"

"Yeah. Apparently he tried something but her girl told on him."

"Where is he?"

"Jail."

"What about her?"

"She packed up and left with her girl."

"What!"

"She's gone, son."

The breath left my body and it was like I was watching TV for the next four hours but staring straight ahead. I went in my room and lay on the floor, looking up. I was suddenly so very tired and I dozed off. When I woke, Mom and Dad were gone with a note.

> *Gone shopping for grub.*
> *Surprise supper at seven.*
> *Love, Mom.*

I looked at the clock on the stove. I had an hour. I grabbed my coat and cruised to Janette's house. I parked down the street and walked back in the grass. No one was around. I went around back and kicked in the door and it was true. All that was left was the furniture.

Upstairs, downstairs, they left traceless. They were gone. Just as I came out of the house, I surprised two kids who went tearing towards the bush.

"Hey!" I yelled and sprinted after them.

They were wearing hoodies and giving 'er, but I kicked the legs out from under one of them and pushed the other one as he ran so he went face first into the willows. Both boys were down and one was crying. I saw blood on their hands. "What the fuck are you guys doing?"

The first boy looked at me and stared hard. "A rape happened here, right? We left the mark." He pointed back to the house and there were red, bloody handprints all around the house.

"Jesus," I said.

I looked at the other boy who I realized was a girl with sheared hair. She was holding her leg and leaving red marks on her pants. "Did you cut yourselves?" I asked.

The boy and girl shook their heads. The boy pointed behind me. Then I saw the open bucket of paint. I got goose pimples and remembered the handprints I'd seen around town. "You kids go home. You shouldn't be around a place like this."

"Were you raped too?" the girl asked.

"What?"

"Were you leaving your mark in the house?"

"No—"

"'Cause you're supposed to leave it on the outside or else they won't see."

"Who – the cops?"

"Torchy and his brother."

I helped them both up. "Wait. I don't understand. I'm seeing handprints around town. Are they behind this?"

"We're behind this," the boy said. "All of us. Cops won't do nothing. Parents don't do nothing. Torchy and Sfen are going to do something about it."

"Like what?" I asked.

"Wait and see," the boy said.

I shook my head and remembered Janette and her daughter. "I gotta go, but you kids go home, okay?"

They looked at each other and nodded. I felt spooky, like I'd interrupted something wicked and holy – I didn't know. I left, hopped in the truck and got back to patrolling.

The cop shop was busy: two cruisers with their cherries off and CBC North were parked outside as I sped by. I was tempted to just hit the highway, but I wouldn't even have known where to go, and she had a good four-hour head start on me, and what the hell would I even have said?

"Damn," I said and punched the dash. "Goddamn this town!"

I cruised and cruised with a death grip on the wheel. I looked at the clock on the dash and headed for home.

❧

When I walked in, Donna was at the house. She was helping Mom in the kitchen. Surprisingly, Dad was upstairs watching TV. Mom looked at Donna who was wiping the counter.

"You never told me Donna was the one who was calling."

I looked at Donna. She was blushing and reading my eyes carefully. "I stopped by," she said, "to give you this."

I looked. There was a small bowl covered in Saran Wrap.

"It's yarrow," she said, "for your arms."

"Now that's sweet," Mom said.

I'm stunned. What the hell was going on here?

"You can put it on after supper," Donna said. "It's pretty strong."

I had to look away.

"What do you say, son?" Dad called from the loft.

"Thank you, Donna," I repeated and dipped my head. This was almost great, but Janette was gone. She was gone.

"Well," Mom said, "Supper's ready. We made your favourite." She looked at me. "Steak, mashed potatoes and niblets with lots of onions."

"That's a lot of food," I said, "for four."

"Oh, we've invited Donna's folks over. It's been years since Barb and I had a good visit."

Whoah, I thought. Wait—

"Is your Dad still a quiet dude?" Dad asked.

"Yes," Donna smiled. "Still quiet."

"He was always like that," Mom said and put water on for tea. "Even when we were in school. I guess he only needs your Mom to talk to, hey?"

Donna was looking at me. Her eyes sparkled. "That's what my cousins say."

I looked at Donna and my folks. This could work, I thought. Sweetness like hers. Kind eyes. And that simple question: "Can I help?" really got me. I suddenly got this feeling like we could do anything together. She had wanted me for a while and now she had me. She was my first and she could take all of me.

I caught Mom staring at me. She swept the back of her hand with her palm and her eyes asked: is this what you want? I looked at Donna who smiled back and wiped her hands on the dishtowel. This could be my life.

"I remember our first supper," Mom said, "we were just starting out."

"You tricked me," Dad called out from the loft, "and now look at us."

"Yes, look at you," Mom said, "a happy, grateful Dogrib man. Now get down here and set the table."

Donna's folks pulled into the driveway. I saw her Mom in the cab, putting on some lipstick, while her father took off his sunglasses. I could tell he wanted to be somewhere else. They were dressed up real snazzy. Her dad wore a buttoned up cowboy shirt and it looked freshly ironed. Donna's mom had a suit top on and probably slacks cause she worked for the government. I looked at Donna. She blushed, looking at me, waiting for me to say something. Maybe we can do this, I thought.

"I'll get the door," I said to Donna. "Your folks are here."

"Wait." She put the dishtowel down and walked across the room. She was smiling, looking into my eyes. She brushed by me, took my hand and faced the door. "We should do this together."

And we did.

FLOYD FAVEL

GOVERNOR OF THE DEW

A MEMORIAL TO NOSTALGIA AND DESIRE

This drama was workshopped at the Takwakin Performance Workshop and the Playwright's Workshop Montréal in 1997. It premiered at the Globe Theatre in 1999, and had its most fully realized incarnation under the direction of Floyd Favel when presented at the National Arts Centre in September 2002.

CHARACTERS

NARRATOR

MOTHER

ROSE

BEAVER

YOUNG BEAVER

OLD BEAVER

NARRATOR

The story goes something like this.
It's been so long since I heard it,
it's from another time, another place,
before I became a man
in the whorehouse of the world.

This is a story my mother told me.
She did not leave much when she left this world,
no money or possessions
just words, stories, like this one.

nikâwiy, your smile brightened the world,
and you will live forever through your words.

MOTHER

Once upon a time, an old woman,
Rose Billy, was at home.
The afternoon was still and quiet,
when all we could hear is the wind rushing through the trees.

ROSE

"Grandmother's Song"

niya ôma nôcikwesiw	*[I am the old woman*
Rose Billy kâ-isiyihkâsot	*who is called Rose Billy*
ôta niwkin	*This where I live*
e-peyakoyân	*I am alone*
e-kaskeyihtamân	*filled with loneliness*
ekwa mina e-kitimâkisiyân	*and I am so pitiful*
ekwa mina e-kitimâkisiyân.	*and I am so pitiful.]*

Musical interlude.

niya ôma nôcikwesiw	*[I am the old woman*
Rose Billy kâ-isiyihkâsot	*who is called Rose Billy*
ôta niwkin	*This where I live*
e-peyakoyân	*I am alone*
e-kaskeyihtamân	*filled with loneliness*
ekwa mina e-kitimâkisiyân	*and I am so pitiful*
ekwa mina e-kitimâkisiyân.	*and I am so pitiful.]*

Chant.

ROSE

I was at home
I hear these steps on the porch, Ma!
and a scratching sound at the door.
awina etikwe? [Who can it be?]
Could it be my grandson
who has gone away to school?
Or an old sweetheart
coming to warm these old bones?

So I open the door,
and standing there is this old beaver!
wahwâ, mitori nimâmaskâten [I was incredibly astounded
e-manâhtâwahk! It was a holy event!]

ahm mosôm, tawâw. [Grandfather, you are welcome.]

MOTHER

The beaver entered,
and sat beside the table,
the room was silent

and filled with power.
The beaver hung his head
and tears poured down his face.
His body heaved with his broken heart.

BEAVER

I have lived my life in shame,
and please, *nôsisim* don't judge me.

ROSE

mosôm, you know as well as I
that it is not us who can judge.

BEAVER

tâpwe nôsisim, kitâpwân. [That is true, grandchild,
you are right.
kimiyopikiskwân You speak well.]
You speak truthfully and with kindness
which I do not deserve.

ROSE

I gave him some tea, lifted it to his mouth,
and he drank.
I wiped the tears from his eyes
and caressed his head.

ahm âcimo! [Come on, tell your
story!]

BEAVER

iyaw, kâya nânitaw iteyimin [Don't think bad of me,
ôma kâ-wî-âcimoyân. about what I am going
to tell.]

This story happened over there at the shallows
where the wagons used to cross.
This story is about the time I fell in love.
Yes, I was in love once, to look at me
you would find that hard to believe, *cî*?

ROSE

No, *mosôm*, you are still handsome.
Your visit blesses me!

BEAVER

Yes, I was in love once.
It is difficult to speak about it.
ahm nôsisim, give me some more tea. [Come on, grandchild]
It happened like this.

YOUNG BEAVER

One morning, I was up earlier than usual
and I sat on the bank of the creek.
I looked at the willows that lined the banks
and listened to the birds
rousing us to wakefulness and vigilance.

This is my home, *nitaskiy ôma!* [this is my land!]
Someday, I will be the Governor of my tribe,
and this is our land.
I lifted my hand, and turned a half circle
then lifted the other hand, and turned in the other direction
and said a little prayer;
wishing for a long life and the health of our tribe,
for the unborn who come crying over the next horizon.

BEAVER

How naïve our prayers can be.
We never know what life will bring tomorrow.
I laugh now at my prayers
for they showed the naïveté
and ignorance of my understanding.

mâka, I believed in my prayers.
was that not enough, I ask you!

MOTHER

The room was heavy with his question
and Rose Billy could not answer him.

BEAVER

But I believe in my heart
that I have been blessed in this life.
When I think back to that morning,
I at least knew the taste of Faith,
however brief, Praise the Creator!

YOUNG BEAVER

I went on my stomach and slid down the mudslide
and splashed in the cool clear water.
Frightening a school of jack fish in front of me.

MOTHER

He made his way downstream
to the narrows where the shade is cool.
Where members of his tribe
gather in the heat of the brief summer,
to settle tribal disputes and have their ceremonies
under the light of the full moon.

Here the horses use to come to drink at dawn,
silently, warily, like outlaws.
Led by the dappled stallion
who stood off to the side, keeping watch
nose testing the air for danger.
New to this land,
they had been accepted by the various animal nations
and given their space and freedom.

A distant solitude is in their nature.
Perhaps it is memories of their past suffering
in the far south and across the Big Water
that have made it difficult for them to trust.

Here they have found Peace.
It is not true that Peace
is what we all seek?

YOUNG BEAVER

I emerged and saw some humans on the shore.
They were different from the ones I knew.
They had with them some horses, dark with sweat
and carrying bundles on their backs.
Slowly and silently I watched them.
The bearded men called to each other
in a language I had never heard before.

mitoni, e-miyohtâkosicik. [They sounded nice.]

One man sat in the shade
playing a musical instrument he held under his chin.
The instrument made a high beautiful sound
that I felt deep in my soul.

I drifted closer, seduced and curious.

And then, I saw her.
This young woman, sitting on a rock by the creek.
How strange, her skin so smooth and bronzed,
her hair so long, black and wavy.

WOMAN

Regretter

Regretter, c'est combattre le temps	[To regret is to battle time
et tout au fond des entrailles	against all that is important
un chant d'oiseau a midi	such as the bird's song at midday
si tu pouvais goûter mon coeur	if you could taste my heart
tu reconnaitres le goût	you would know the taste
de la cruelle nostalgie	of cruel nostalgia
là, solitude des *grand-mama*	the deep solitude of the grandmother
de la mure fraîche de l'été	the taste of the ripe summer berry
de l'amant et de l'aimée	the shadow between the loved and the lover]

Ton nom remue d'inconsolable désire	[My land, your name stirs inconsolable desire
là, dans tu sombre forêt	for the dark mysterious forest
sous un flou soleil d'hiver	the prairie under the winter sun

cheveaus venant s'abreve alaube
dans l'ombre de la clairiere
le lieu où les guerriers prient.

for the place where the horses used to drink
in the shade of the clearing
where ancient warriors once prayed.]

Si tu pouvjais goûter mon coeur
tu reconnaitres le goût
de la cruelle nostalgie
là, solitude des grand-mama
de la mure fraîche de l'été
de l'amant et de l'aimée
si tu pouvjais goûter mon coeur
si tu pouvjais goûter mon coeur!

[My love, if you could taste my heart
you would know the taste
of cruel nostalgia
the deep solitude of the grandmother
the taste of the ripe summer berry
the shadow between the loved and the lover
if you could taste my heart
if you could taste my heart!]

BEAVER

Her eyes found mine
and I was never so aware of myself.
I knew shame, and I knew desire.
Nothing in all of my life had prepared me for this.
Our warriors had faced death many times
and we had been taught to face it bravely.
But against this great force, desire
I had not been taught what to do.

I returned her gaze.
Could she love me?
What would my tribe say if I brought her home?

OLD BEAVER

Namôya konita mâna
kehte-ayak e-kî-itwecik,
eh âyiman ôma pimâtisiwin.
e-pâpam moskôtehiyahk
e-pôni-mâtoyahk
ekosi, e-pôni pimâtisyahk.

[It is not for nothing that
the elders say,
Life is hard.
We go around with crying hearts
we stop crying
then, we die.]

YOUNG BEAVER

There I stood, wondering
if she would accept me.
âstam, ki-nôhte pe-wîcewin?
e-nitaweyihtamân ka-pe-wîcewiyan.

[Come, do you want to come with me?
I want you to come join me.]

She came; she waded into the water
against the cries of her countrymen.
I reached out my hand.
The roar of their thundersticks was loud in my ears.
The smell of gunpowder harsh to my nose.
The thud of their bullets around my body
only made me laugh.
There was no turning back
and I abandoned my body to death.
Nothing lasts forever.

I took her hand
and swung her to my back.
Hold on tight! hold on tight! hold on tight!
And we dove.

Her people will have a great story to tell about me!

We swam along the moss-covered rocks
at the bottom of the creek.
We met some of my relatives
who were running for safety.
Away from the sounds of War.

We swam through the doorway into our world,
and came bursting into the sunlight.
She was weak and collapsed in my arms.
She was even more beautiful.

MOTHER

They say we came from the land of the sun.
There, where the land, sky and water meet.
It is there where it all began.
This is where the muskrat brought up land
from the depths of the water.
The little piece of Earth was clutched in his little hands
as he emerged dead from his efforts.
From this we learn that
all earthly actions are accomplished with a sacrifice.

kistesinaw, Our Elder Brother, the Son of the Creator,
was floating on a raft, destroyed by grief.
He delicately opened the hands of the muskrat

and retrieved the little piece of earth
that had cost the muskrat his life.
Our Elder Brother placed the earth into his hands,
blowing upon it all the while.
The land began to grow and grow,
and soon it made a little island,
then a larger island, *ôma ministik.* [This island.]
This land that we now live upon.

YOUNG BEAVER

My love, *mon amour, nisâkhâkan*
ôta ôma e-wikiyân. [This is where I live.
ôta ôma e-ki-pe-ohpikhhikawiyân. This is where I was raised.
ôta k"sta ka-wikin. This is where you will live also.]

This is where you will live also.

The End

ROBERT ARTHUR ALEXIE

excerpt from

THE PALE INDIAN

John and Tina woke early on Christmas Day and gave Abraham and Sarah their gifts. There was another church service at eleven that morning, which Sarah and Tina attended; John and Abraham didn't. John was trying to think of what to say to Eva about their parents. He also had to tell his family that he was engaged. He looked at photos while Abraham told him of his family history and how most of them were related in one way or another. John realized that he and Tina might be related on her mother's and his father's sides of the family. They may be fourth or fifth cousins, once or twice removed. It was so far removed, though, he was sure their kids wouldn't be sitting on a porch swing picking on a banjo. "What do you know?" he asked.

Abraham wondered if John knew. He had been young when he'd left. "What do you know?" he asked.

"Tina told me they died up the river and my uncle found them."

"That's about it. Nothin' much I can add. They were drinkin' an' must 'a passed out an' froze. That's when Edward found them."

"What can you tell me about my uncle?"

"What you know about him?"

"Nothing. I didn't even know I had an uncle."

"Don' know when he was born, but he join the army when he was young."

"When?"

"Sixty-one. He wasn't even twenty."

"When did he come back?"

"After you lef'. Seventy-three, I think. Yeah, seventy-three, 'cause he found your parents the year after."

"What happened to him? Up at the cabin, I mean."

"He said he found them. Never said much after that. He brought them back to town all dressed up, ready to bury."

"Why'd he go quiet?"

"Nobody knows. He was always quiet, slow."

"Slow?"

"Yeah, he wasn' retarded, jus' slow. He use to take care of himself, but after he foun' your parents, he just seem to go inside. Know what I mean?"

"Yeah, I think so. Anyone go see him?"

"Eunice an' Olive went out once, but they said he just sat there an' didn' say a thing. He didn' even know them."

John wondered what made his uncle go silent. And how could his parents freeze? They were Indians. But they were drunken Indians. Drunken Indians and the cold do not mix.

Later that afternoon, Sarah and Tina began preparing Christmas dinner. "You call your sister?" Tina asked.

"Not yet."

"Will you?"

"Have to."

"They're gonna wonder why you haven't called yet."

"Yeah, guess you're right," he said, and then took the phone into the bedroom. Eva answered. "Merry Christmas," he said.

"Merry Christmas to you. Why didn't you call earlier? We were worried."

"Busy morning."

"Whatcha do?"

"Went visiting an' talked with her grandfather."

"They nice?"

"Yeah."

And then she asked, "You see them?"

'No," he said. "I've got some bad news."

Somehow he wasn't surprised when she said, "They're dead." It wasn't a question; it was more of a statement.

"Yeah, they died ten years ago."

"How?"

"They froze upriver at their cabin according to what I've heard."

"That's too bad."

"You don't feel bad?"

"I don't remember them," she said. "Anything else I should know about?"

"We have two aunts, one uncle an' a few relatives."

"Yeah?"

"Remember I told you about Chief James? His son is now the Chief an' his wife is our aunt. Her name's Eunice."

"She's our mom's sister?"

"No, our father's."

"She nice?"

"Yes. We also have another aunt who lives in Whitehorse, but she's here for the holidays. Her name's Olive."

"What about the uncle?"

He's nuts, he thought. "He's in Edmonton. In an institution or someplace like that."

"What? Why?"

"No idea."

"Is he nuts?"

"Tina's grandfather told me he was quiet and couldn't take care of himself, so they sent him there."

"Wow. Anything else?"

"That's it."

"How are you?" she asked.

"Okay. You?"

"Great. How many people there?"

"Six or seven hundred."

"Really?"

"Yeah, lots of changes. Not the same as I remember. Different an' not all good."

"Why?"

"Drugs, alcohol, violence, same ol', same ol'."

They talked for a few more minutes, and then he talked to his parents and his other sisters and wished them all a Merry Christmas. "You got a number we can reach you at?" his mom asked.

He gave it to her, then hung up and took the phone back into the living room. "What they say?" Tina asked.

"Nothing. They jus' asked a few questions."

"Maybe they don't want you to marry someone from here."

He grinned sheepishly. "I forgot to tell them."

He redialed the number and Eva answered again.

"I'm getting' married," he said, then hung up and handed the phone to Tina.

A few seconds later, it rang. "You answer it," she said.

He only grinned, so she picked up the phone. "Hello?"

"Tina?" Eva asked.

"Yeah?"

"Is it true?"

"Yes, it's true, but I'm having second thoughts," she said, and then laughed.

"Congratulations!"

"Thanks, but it's all happening so fast."

"When's the big day?"

"Haven't set it yet, but sometime in the spring, or nex' fall."

"Why so long?"

"He's gotta get back to work an' so do I. And I have to save up for college nex' fall."

"Where are you going?"

"Calgary, I hope."

They talked for a few minutes, and Tina met his parents on the phone. "They're nice," she said as she hung up.

"They are. You'll like them."

"I'm sure I will."

The next day, for whatever reason, John found himself standing in the cemetery that was next to the church and covered with at least two feet of snow. There was a large spruce tree, probably a few hundred years old, decorated with Christmas lights. At least a hundred granite, marble, and wooden crosses poked through the snow. He checked the graves near the church and eventually found his parents'. Their wooden crosses were painted white and had their names on them. They'd died in February 1974, two years after he and Eva had left. They'd been in their early thirties; they'd been young. He looked at the hills and the mountains and wondered why he felt no anger or sympathy. Over the last decade, he'd thought about returning to kill his dad for all the abuse he'd put them and his mom through. But now, today, the day after Christmas, he felt absolutely nothing. He turned and walked away, and wondered what his uncle, Edward Brian, had seen. He shook off the thought and tried to get into the holiday spirit.

He returned to Abraham and Sarah's and helped them cut up caribou meat for the feast, then decided to take a nap. A few hours later, Tina woke him and they took the meat down to the community hall where the feast and dance was to be held. John was surprised to see so many people. One of the elders said an opening prayer in the language and the feast began. It was traditional and there was a lot to eat. He had caribou soup, boiled meat and bannock. After everyone had eaten, the local minister said a prayer, and then Chief Alfred spoke in the language and John had no idea what he was talking about. "What's he sayin'?" he asked Tina.

"He's thanking the people an' hopes they had a good Christmas."

After Chief Alfred finished, his father, Chief James, spoke in the language and looked at John, and then mentioned his name.

"He's telling them about you," Tina said. "Stand up."

He did and everyone applauded, and then he sat back down and Chief James continued speaking.

"He's telling them about your hunt with my grandfather. He's saying you left when you were young, so you never had the chance to go hunting, to get your first caribou. But now, you've returned an' you've got your first caribou an' you're sharing it with the people."

The people looked at him, nodded their approval and applauded.

Chief Alfred spoke again and this time they applauded louder. Tina looked as if she wished she could disappear. He assumed correctly that Chief Alfred had told them about their upcoming marriage. "An' don't forget dance tonight!" Chief Alfred said in English. Start at nine!"

As they walked back to the house, John recalled the dances. He remembered the fiddle and guitars, and the square dances, waltzes and jigging. "We gonna go to the dance?" he asked.

"You wanna?"

"Not really. I'm tired."

"Me too," she said, and then whispered, "We'll be home alone."

"I'm not that tired."

"Good," she said, smiling.

That night, after they had made love, Tina asked, "You wanna head back tomorrow?"

"Yeah," he said. "This is a little too much too fast for me."

And then John had a thought, a flashback if you will. He remembered the tradition of walking around on New Year's Day. This meant meeting at the Chief's house early in the morning and walking from house to house wishing everyone a Happy New Year. "Do they still walk around on New Year's Day?" he asked.

"Yeah, they still do that."

He remembered the last time they'd come to his house and found his parents both passed out. The Chief said nothing and led the men out while John and Eva watched through one of the many holes in the attic floor. They had been cold, hungry, and dirty. He shook the memory off and tried to think of better times; warmer times, summer. But even in the summer, they had still been hungry and dirty.

⁂

The leaves were green, almost luminescent. It had been a long time since he'd seen them this green. He looked at the hills and the mountains and wondered why they were blue. The last time he went up into the hills, they were green and grey, not blue. He wondered why the river was silver, and not brown. Things were not what they seemed.

"Hi, Edward."

He glanced up.

He grinned. "Hi."

She was a beautiful girl, barely twenty, with long, black hair and an infectious smile. She was dressed in a pair of black slacks with black running shoes and a pale yellow blouse over which she wore a blue cardigan. She sat beside him on the bench. "Whatcha doin?"

"Nothin'," he said. "Jus' lookin'."

He remembered she liked walking along the shore, picking up stones and throwing them into the river. He wanted to take her in his arms and tell her he loved her like he seen them do in the movies. He'd told Elizabeth he was in love with Margaret and wanted to marry her. He wanted to live in one of those towns in the south where nobody knew who he was. He wanted to go to a place where they didn't call him stupid or slow. He wondered if she'd marry him, even if he was stupid. They were almost the same age, but he dropped out of grade nine when it became too difficult for him. He didn't like being called slow and he hated being called stupid. He did like the hostel, though. At least there they made rules he could follow and not get into trouble.

"Did you really join the army?" she asked.

"Yeah." He had joined a few days earlier when the soldier had come to town. Floyd asked him to join. He said he'd take care of him. *They'll make men out of us,* he'd said. *We'll make good money too.* It was then he thought maybe she'd marry him if he became a man and made money.

When you're leavin'?" she asked.

"Couple 'a weeks."

"Me too. Back to school."

A week later he was outside their house talking to her father, Abraham. Over the last few years he'd helped Abraham and Sarah by cutting wood and getting water from the creek, or ice from the river. He was trying to show them he was a good man and a hard worker. He also did that to get close to her, but something was wrong. Over the last few days he'd hardly seen her. He'd gone to her house a few times, but she stayed inside and never came out. Maybe she was mad at him. Maybe she didn't like him because he was slow. Maybe they were right, maybe he *was* stupid.

"When are you leaving?" Abraham asked in the language.

"Tomorrow," he answered in the language, then switched to English. "Me and Floyd."

"How long?"

"Don't know. Two, three months."

"And then?"

"Don' know."

Abraham smiled and put an arm on his shoulder. "You'll be okay."

She came out carrying a galvanized tub full of clothes, walked by without looking at him and began hanging clothes on the clothesline.

"Margaret, you forgot this," Sarah said in the language, holding up a bag of clothespins.

Margaret walked to her mom, her arms folded across her as if she had a stomach ache, took the bag of clothespins and then walked back to the clothesline, her gaze never once leaving the ground.

"She's going back to Helena for school," Abraham said.

"Oh."

Being in the army was like being in mission school: he lined up, they shaved off his hair, they gave him the same clothes as everyone else, he slept in a big dorm, he ate in a dining room, and he did what they told him to do and he did it without asking. Whatever he couldn't understand, Floyd helped him with. He wondered if Margaret was still mad at him. He wondered what he had done to make her mad. He wished he could write to her, but he didn't know what street she lived on and his letter might get lost. He wished he were smart, like Floyd and the rest.

"You comin'?" Floyd asked.

"Where you goin'?"

"Edmonton for the weekend. Gonna have some fun."

"Okay," he said, even though he didn't like to go to the bars. Maybe he could go to the place they have those rides. He had fun there. Everyone acted like kids there.

Later that night, or early the next morning, they tried to get a taxi to take them back to the base but Floyd was drunk and had no money. He had some, but even so, each time they tried the driver would look at them and drive off.

"Fuck it," Floyd said. "Let's walk. It's only thirty miles. We can do 'at in our sleep."

Three hours later they were on the highway walking back to the base when he heard the big truck and stepped off to the side of the highway. He turned just in time to see Floyd put his arm up in a futile effort to stop the big truck. It was futility, but it was instinctive.

And just like that, Floyd was gone, and so was the truck. He couldn't remember how far he had to run before he finally found Floyd. It had to be Floyd. He was wearing Floyd's clothes, but his face was gone and his arm and legs were twisted and bent out of shape. He tried to fix them, but they were broken. He tried to wake him, but he knew Floyd had disappeared into the night and had gone back to the Old People up in the Blue Mountains. He didn't know how long he waited, but after a long, long time, he saw the lights. They were far away, but they grew brighter and then blinded him.

After a long while, the lights disappeared and someone asked, "Private Brian, are you okay?"

"Yes, sir."

"What happened to Private Chinke?"

"Truck, sir. Big truck."

"Where is it?"

"It's gone, sir."

"Did you get the licence number?"

"No, sir."

They kept him in the hospital for a long time and a doctor came in each day and checked his heart, then looked for his soul with a bright light. They had another doctor come in and ask him questions, and they even made him write some tests. He kept looking for Floyd to help him, but Floyd was AWOL again.

After what seemed like forever, the sergeant told him he was going home. "Private Brian?"

"Yes, sir."

"We're sending you home."

"Home, sir?"

"Yes, you're being discharged for medical reasons."

He didn't know what that meant, so he just said, "Yes, sir."

The doctor tried one last time to look for his soul, but he couldn't find it. "I don't know how he made it this far without anyone noticing," he said to the sergeant.

"Me neither, but he was a good soldier."

DANIEL DAVID MOSES

The Witch Of Niagara

A Confabulation in One Act

This world was already complete
even without white people.
There was everything
including witchery.

Ceremony
Leslie Marmon Silko

This drama premiered at the Robert Gill Theatre from 9-12 December 1998, produced by the Centre for Indigenous Theatre, and was directed by Carole Greyeyes.

CHARACTERS

The GIRL

The BOY, the Girl's cousin through her Father

The Chief, the Girl's FATHER

The Girl's UNCLE through her Mother, a War Chief

The OLD MAN

The Girl's GRANDmother through her Mother,
a Clan Mother

The Girl's MOTHER

The Girl's AUNT through her Father

The Thunderer, the God of Rain

The God's Helper

The Snake

SETTING

The action occurs in a village, in the fields, and on the paths through the forest along the river and gorge in the vicinity of Niagara Falls, the residence of the Thunderer, the Iroquois god of Rain.

SCENE 1

The new moon looms over Niagara Falls. The GIRL lies in her grandmother's lodge in the village. She opens her eyes.

GIRL

In the story— The story? In the dream! In the dream, I'm alone. Alone in the village. Alone in the longhouse. Alone in my bed. In the dream, everything's quiet. No kids. No dogs. No birds. No wind. I can't even hear the falls. The sun's shining.

Then this shadow's there standing in the doorway. It's a man, a stranger, but in the dream I'm not afraid because he's so beautiful. I can't see his face but I know he's beautiful. He speaks to me. His voice is soft, whispering. He sounds far away, even though he's right here beside me. I don't know the words he uses, it's another language, but I understand him all right. I want to ask him who he is, what's going on, where everyone is, but he puts a finger to my lips, puts a finger to my lips – and then kisses me. In the dream, he kisses me. No man has ever ever kissed me before.

Then he's gone and I'm awake. And my belly is big and tight as a drum. And Mama and Grandma, they're standing over me, mumbling and shaking their heads. Shaking their heads. And then this pain like a blade down there makes me look, this tickling and trickling between my legs. We all look under my dress. There's this flood, this flood of little baby snakes squirming out of me. I can't breathe, I can't breathe, my Mama, my Grandma, they're the ones, they're the ones in the dream who scream. And this flood, this flood of little baby snakes, it crawls back – back inside me.

She closes her eyes. Thunder. The moon sets.

SCENE 2

Dawn. The hunting camp. The BOY tends the fire; the Girl's FATHER and UNCLE sleep in the lean-to. The OLD MAN enters from the path from the woods.

OLD MAN

Hello? Hello! Anybody there?

BOY

Uncle, cousin, wake up.

FATHER

What is it?

OLD MAN

How are you this morning?

UNCLE

Who's that?

FATHER

I recognise him. Long time, no see, Grey Hair!

UNCLE

Oh no. The Trader.

BOY

That's him?

OLD MAN

Long time, no see, Chief. Can I bother you for some tea?

FATHER

Sure. Sit, sit.

BOY

Here you go.

OLD MAN

You've been hunting?

FATHER

Down river, far as the lake.

OLD MAN

No luck?

FATHER

As you see, empty hands.

OLD MAN

Hard times, hard times everywhere.

FATHER

We'll be fine.

OLD MAN

Going home now? I'll walk with you then.

UNCLE

You haven't visited us since when?

OLD MAN

The spring. It's so sad for me, coming home now.

UNCLE

You've been where?

OLD MAN

East and west. The salt lake and the dirty river. I've got shells and copper and seed corn.

FATHER

The women will be glad to see you.

OLD MAN

I'll be glad to see them. I've got herbs for them, some medicines.

BOY

You travel alone?

OLD MAN

Who would go with me?

BOY

Don't you get lonely?

FATHER

Don't be rude. I'm sorry, Grey Hair. He's not used to strangers.

OLD MAN

Your sister's boy? Just out of the house, is he?

FATHER

I'm afraid so.

OLD MAN

He'll learn how to treat his elders someday.

BOY

What's he mean by that?

UNCLE

Sh! Let your uncle do the talking.

FATHER

And you?

OLD MAN

Could be worse. I do get lonely sometimes. I'm thinking about getting me a wife.

BOY

Who would marry him?

UNCLE

Sh!

OLD MAN

Someone will marry me, little boy. I'm a catch!

FATHER

I'm sorry, Grey Hair. Boy, pack up! Go on! Get your stuff and go.

BOY

What? Why?

UNCLE

Go! We'll catch up at the midday camp. Go on. You remember where? Then light a fire. We'll cook some meat for a change.

The BOY grabs his bedroll, his bow and another pack and walks off.

FATHER

I'm sorry about my nephew. He's a child with a big mouth.

OLD MAN

Too big for his own good! No, no, I like him.

FATHER

Forgive him.

OLD MAN

Don't worry, Chief. What do I care about children? There are more important things in the world.

UNCLE

I'll start packing too.

OLD MAN

Fresh meat for lunch! You're so generous.

UNCLE

You're our guest.

OLD MAN

Still, I won't let my wife have children. She'll have enough to carry.

FATHER

More tea before I dump it?

OLD MAN

So Chief. These times we're living in. Stories of war, of cannibals.

UNCLE

Cannibals?

FATHER

Where do you hear this?

OLD MAN

Upriver. At the west end of the lake. So tell me. How are things at home?

FATHER

What do you mean?

OLD MAN

I could cry, thinking about it. Every time I come home. The same old story.

FATHER

Can't this wait? The day's half over.

OLD MAN

I'm sorry. Help me. I don't want to hurt anyone's feelings by mentioning names I shouldn't. I know how I felt when, I suppose, my own mother was the first...

UNCLE

Since the spring?

FATHER

We shouldn't have to talk about this.

UNCLE

Since the spring my wife, my child have died.

FATHER

My father too.

OLD MAN

That's all?

UNCLE

It's enough.

OLD MAN

It's too much.

FATHER

Come on. It's a long day to get home.

UNCLE

Can I carry something for you?

OLD MAN

Would you? I hope I can keep up.

Exeunt.

SCENE 3

Mid-morning. The GIRL meets her GRANDmother, carrying a load of sticks along a path through the woods.

GIRL

Grandma!

GRAND

Sleepy head!

GIRL

Let me help you.

GRAND

Careful. It's heavy.

GIRL

You didn't wake me up?

GRAND

You need your rest.

GIRL

I'm tired of resting!

GRAND

I'm tired of working. Time for a breather. You should rest while you can. You were awake in the middle of the night.

GIRL

I had a dream.

GRAND

Everyone's having a hard time sleeping.

GIRL

The dream woke me up.

GRAND

Even Mother Earth. There was an earthquake.

GIRL

An earthquake?

GRAND

Like the beat of a heart. You woke right up. Squeaked like a little bird! I was awake anyway.

GIRL

I was scared.

GRAND

Scared?

GIRL

When I woke up. This morning. There was nobody around.

GRAND

We all have work to do.

GIRL

Mama usually wakes me up.

GRAND

I made her let you sleep.

GIRL

They in the cornfield?

GRAND

Don't tire yourself out now. We don't want to have to lug you home again. Your father's still out in the woods.

GIRL

I'll be careful.

GRAND

I'll be back out there soon as I stack this.

GIRL

Grandma, why don't they live together, Mama and my father?

GRAND

He wouldn't do what he was told, so I sent him back to his sister.

GIRL

Because of me?

GRAND

What?

GIRL

Because I'm sick all the time?

GRAND

Yes, that must be the reason. And why he always helps us out when he can.

GIRL

But it doesn't make sense.

GRAND

It doesn't. Come here.

The Girl's GRANDmother hugs her.

GRAND

Now go on. There's work to do.

Exeunt separately.

SCENE 4

The midday camp. The OLD MAN is snoring. The BOY and the Girl's FATHER and UNCLE wait.

UNCLE

What a noise!

BOY

Sounds like someone dying.

FATHER

Be quiet.

BOY

It'll be dark by the time we get home. I'm going.

FATHER

We'll all go soon as he wakes up.

BOY

Let's wake him.

FATHER

He's an old man. Don't offend him.

BOY

He offends me.

UNCLE

You're downwind.

FATHER

Go ahead then. I'll wait for him.

UNCLE

You sure?

BOY

We'll be upwind!

FATHER

I'll say you saw game or something, maybe there'll be really fresh meat for him when we get home.

BOY

The way he chews!

UNCLE

Three teeth maybe. Come on.

BOY

Why don't we just leave?

FATHER

He's an old man.

UNCLE

He's our guest. Here. You carry his pack. We'll go fishing. We can get fish for sure.

BOY

Not fish!

The BOY and the Girl's UNCLE exit. The Girl's FATHER pours himself more tea. The OLD MAN sits up.

OLD MAN

I need to talk with you, Chief.

FATHER

You're awake!

OLD MAN

They think old ears are deaf!

FATHER

That boy, I'm sorry about—

OLD MAN

Never mind. He's a child. They both are. I don't mind either of them. I need to talk to a grown-up alone. This is so embarrassing.

FATHER

Tea?

OLD MAN

It's— The sickness in the village.

FATHER

What about it?

OLD MAN

I know what to do about it. That's why I'm coming home now.

FATHER

You have a cure?

OLD MAN

I have a cure. I wasn't sure before.

FATHER

How do you know this?

OLD MAN

Do you really want me to say? Whisper the story in your ear? Something like this happened out west. It seems there was this witch around—

FATHER

I won't listen to gossip. Some things shouldn't be said out loud.

OLD MAN

But you believe me?

FATHER

We'll try anything once.

OLD MAN

Good. But then there's this embarrassing part.

FATHER

What?

OLD MAN

Embarrassing for you. I want to make a trade.

FATHER

A trade.

OLD MAN

We're the same age, but I'm an old man. Remember when we were that boy's age?

FATHER

What do you want?

OLD MAN

I need a wife. Who would marry me? I'll tell you. I'll cure the village, but you, you'll give me your daughter.

FATHER

You're crazy.

OLD MAN

I know she's sickly. No loss to you, giving her to me. And I might make her better too. I'll find the medicine for it. Good for her.

FATHER

She's not mine to give. My daughter's mother, her grandmother—

OLD MAN

Even to save the village?

FATHER

I don't know.

OLD MAN
How embarrassing for you, Chief.

SCENE 5

Dusk. A bucket under a tree at the edge of the corn field. The GIRL and her GRANDmother enter.

GRAND

It's thirsty work, pulling weeds. Hand me that ladle. Oh that's good.

GIRL

That's the last. Should I go get more?

GRAND

No. Sit back. We're almost done. See?

The Girl's MOTHER enters.

MOTHER

You look like a couple of old women.

GRAND

We're tired enough for maybe four.

MOTHER

The water?

GRAND

I just drank it up.

MOTHER

Gone! I give you one job to do all day and you can't even—

GIRL

I'll go to the spring now.

GRAND

No, wait. We're done for the day. What's the point now?

GIRL

I'm sorry, Mama.

MOTHER

Don't whine.

GRAND

I told her she could wait.

MOTHER

Stop covering up for her.

GRAND

I'm not covering up—

MOTHER

Stop it. I know how useless she is.

The GIRL exits with the bucket.

GRAND

What's the matter with you?

MOTHER

Nothing. A girl who's good for nothing.

GRAND

Look at me. I said look at me.

MOTHER

I'm tired.

GRAND

Did I teach you to act like this? Did I ever treat you like that? No wonder her father left you.

The Girl's AUNT enters.

AUNT

Water! I'm dying here.

GRAND

The girl's gone to the spring.

MOTHER

I didn't sleep last night.

AUNT

I'll go help her.

MOTHER

No, wait.

AUNT

What's wrong?

MOTHER

Someone saw lights travelling along the creek last night. To the spring.

GRAND

Lights?

AUNT

Witch lights?

GRAND

Who? Who saw them?

MOTHER

I did.

GRAND

Up wandering around in the middle of the night! Serves you right.

AUNT

You all right?

GRAND

Why did you say "someone"?

AUNT

Something bad going on?

GRAND

You really saw lights?

MOTHER

She really saw lights.

GRAND

Can you make sure the girl gets back before dark?

AUNT

Don't worry.

The Girl's AUNT exits in the direction the Girl went.

GRAND

Come on. Let's go home.

Exeunt toward the village.

SCENE 6

The Girl's UNCLE, bow at the ready on the creek bank, watches for fish. The BOY enters.

BOY

Let's go.

UNCLE

Not yet.

BOY

I'm hungry.

UNCLE

Eat it raw.

BOY

I'm tired of fish.

UNCLE

Be quiet.

BOY

They'll be home before us at this rate.

UNCLE

Fine with me.

BOY

You don't like that old man any more than I do.

UNCLE

I saw him looking you over. Did he pinch your bum?

BOY

Shut up. Why do you treat him so good?

UNCLE

You going to be quiet?

BOY

He's not from here.

UNCLE

He used to be. We treat our elders with respect.

BOY

But he doesn't live here now.

UNCLE

He just lives over on the island.

BOY

Above the falls? But that island's haunted.

UNCLE

Ah!

BOY

What? You see one?

UNCLE

You scared it off.

BOY

Sorry.

UNCLE

The women, they say he has medicine.

BOY

You said he's a trader.

UNCLE

Maybe that's how he gets his medicine.

BOY

Medicine. I'd kill him if...

UNCLE

Maybe he's just an ugly old man.

BOY

My father's with him.

UNCLE

He's safe. Doesn't have a big mouth.

BOY

Don't laugh at me.

UNCLE

I'm not laughing at you. Sometimes you almost make sense. You should speak up in council. Be quiet now.

A moment of silence. Then the GIRL, with bucket, enters from the woods.

GIRL

Uncle! Welcome back.

UNCLE

I give up!

BOY

Hello, cousin.

GIRL

Cousin. Water?

BOY

Sure.

UNCLE

How's your mother?

GIRL

Working hard.

BOY

It tastes fishy.

GIRL

It's from the spring. Uncle, it's going to be dark soon.

UNCLE

I'm going back the long way.

GIRL

All right.

UNCLE

Your father should be home by now.

The Girl's UNCLE exits.

BOY

Come on.

GIRL

My father went straight home?

BOY

We met this old trader.

GIRL

A trader!

BOY

The Grey Hair.

The Girl's AUNT enters.

AUNT

Pumpkin!

BOY

Ma!

AUNT

I'm just glad to see you. I'm your mother. How'd you do? You'll do better next time. Was that your uncle?

BOY

No, hers.

AUNT

Where's he off to?

GIRL

That path.

AUNT

Past the platforms. Oh, the poor guy.

GIRL

He'll want to be alone anyway.

BOY

Can we go? I'm hungry.

GIRL

My father's got some trader with him.

AUNT

He might have fresh herbs?

BOY

He said he had medicines.

Exeunt.

SCENE 7

The Girl's GRANDmother and MOTHER are in their lodge.

MOTHER

It's late, isn't it?

GRAND

Just sunset.

MOTHER

Where are they?

GRAND

Sit down, rest.

MOTHER

She's the one who rests. What good is she to us?

GRAND

Sit down. What were you doing, wandering around in the dark?

MOTHER

You were awake too.

GRAND

Who sleeps these days?

MOTHER

Who will take care of them if I die? You're too old.

The Girl's FATHER and the OLD MAN enter.

FATHER

Can we talk with you? I've brought the trader with me.

OLD MAN

Long time, no see, grandmother.

GRAND

You're welcome. Both of you. Have a seat, Grey Hair.

MOTHER

What do you want here?

GRAND

Forgive her. She's tired.

OLD MAN

Hard times, hard times everywhere.

MOTHER

You want to help me?

OLD MAN

I want to help you, child.

FATHER

He wants to help all of us.

GRAND

What is it?

FATHER

It's hard to say this.

MOTHER

You know what's going on here, don't you?

OLD MAN

I know enough of the story.

MOTHER

What do you know?

GRAND

Be patient.

FATHER

He knows what to do now. Against the sickness.

GRAND

What do you know?

FATHER

He says it's witchery.

MOTHER

Witches!

GRAND

Is this true?

OLD MAN

It's hard to explain it. They're watching us.

MOTHER

I knew it. I knew it.

GRAND

Nobody's seen strangers.

OLD MAN

They've been watching all along. They're all around the village.

GRAND

What do you want? What's he want?

OLD MAN

To make a trade.

GRAND

A trade?

FATHER

We're here to ask your permission for my daughter to marry Grey Hair.

OLD MAN

Your daughter's so lovely.

MOTHER

Who would want a wife so sickly?

OLD MAN

I do. I'll take her.

GRAND

You're old. And you're no hunter. Why would she want to marry you?

OLD MAN

If she marries me, I'll put a stop to the dying.

MOTHER

You'll stop the dying! How?

FATHER

You said it yourself, clan mother. His medicine's powerful.

OLD MAN

Convince her. You'll all be saved. If only I'd known how before my own mother died.

FATHER

My daughter will save us all.

OLD MAN

So lovely, that girl.

MOTHER

Let him have her.

OLD MAN

Oh thank you, thank you.

GRAND

You can't fight witches you can't see.

OLD MAN

I will fight them. For her, I will fight them.

GIRL

(with bucket, entering) Grandma, my uncle and cousin, at the creek, said my father—

FATHER

Here I am, girl. Come here.

GRAND

No. Over here.

GIRL

What is it, Grandma?

GRAND

Come. Sit by me.

FATHER

Sit with your Grandma.

GIRL

What's wrong? You guys fighting again?

MOTHER

Be quiet.

FATHER

This is the trader.

OLD MAN

Hello, Girl.

FATHER

Listen to your Grandma. She has something to ask.

GIRL

What is it, Mama?

MOTHER

Listen to her.

GRAND

This man?

GIRL

Why's he looking at me?

GRAND

He's brought us some medicines.

FATHER

He might make you better.

OLD MAN

I'll try.

FATHER

He says he's going to stop the dying.

GIRL

Stop the dying?

GRAND

He needs help. Will you help him?

GIRL

Me? How?

GRAND

Will you marry him—?

FATHER

Marry him—

MOTHER

Marry him!

GRAND

Will you be his wife—?

MOTHER

His wife—

FATHER

His wife!

GRAND

Look at me. What's the matter?

GIRL

A pain. Like a blade.

MOTHER

Good for nothing.

UNCLE

(O.S.) Mother? Mother, are you there?

The Girl's UNCLE, a scrap of blanket in hand, enters, followed by her AUNT and the BOY.

GRAND

What is it, son?

UNCLE

Look at this. Look.

MOTHER

What's wrong, brother?

UNCLE

This is the blanket. This is all that's left.

BOY

It reeks!

UNCLE

The platform's a mess.

GRAND

What are you talking about? This is what blanket?

UNCLE

Where we put my wife and child. It's gone.

FATHER

The platform's gone?

UNCLE

Their bodies are gone.

OLD MAN

This is witchcraft.

UNCLE

Witchcraft?

OLD MAN

This is the witchcraft for sure. Witches use dead bodies in their tricks.

GRAND

What's going on...?

OLD MAN

What else could it be? I hate to think what those witches will do to that poor little baby's body.

UNCLE

I'll kill them! Show me how!

MOTHER

Don't cry, brother.

UNCLE

I'll kill them.

OLD MAN

Will you give her to me now? I promise I'll kill them. I'll stop the dying.

MOTHER

We can fix things now.

GRAND

I feel like crying.

MOTHER

Grey Hair knows how.

OLD MAN

Give her to me!

GRAND

Go on. Go to him.

GIRL

Mama? Papa?

GRAND

Go to Grey Hair. Take his hand.

GIRL

Grandma, no.

FATHER

You'll do as you're told—

MOTHER

Do as you're told!

GRAND

You'll marry him in the morning.

OLD MAN

I'll treat you good. I'll make you better.

GIRL

No!

The GIRL exits at a run.

SCENE 8

The new moon hangs over Niagara Falls. The BOY sits in his mother's lodge in the village. The moon grows full during the BOY's monologue and dawn comes at the monologue's end.

BOY

Who knew she could run like that? But that old man, hey, you'd run away from him too.

They chased her – we chased her, out of the village. Down the street, through the gate, into the dark. Mostly it was her father, her uncle and me chasing, us and the dogs. Everybody looked at us like we were crazy. Maybe we were. The dogs barking, thinking it was all a game.

Out the gate into the dark and once around the fields, like she used to playing tag. I could have caught her, I saw what she was up to then, circling back, but— Later on my mom says, You know, pumpkin; yeah, like I'm still her pumpkin— You know, I used to think maybe you and her would get together someday. I mean I'd never thought of it before that but I think I probably thought so too, yeah, otherwise why'd I let her get away like that? I thought about it later a lot, because I thought I'd let her go die.

Yeah, she runs out along the path, along the creek past the springs and gets to the river and gets cornered there out on the point. I don't think she's ever been that far from the village before.

I catch up to the men in time to see her climbing into a canoe.

What it's doing there, who knows, but it's white like the moon, like the birch bark ones the Ojibwa use, so afterwards her mother says that proves it was just more witchery. It's strange to see, the way it moves out over the river, over the rapids, like a bit of light on the surface, and her not needing to paddle it at all. We call after her to come back. Her grandmother and the other women are there too by now, calling her, saying she don't have to marry the trader after all. He's standing there, just standing there grinning all three teeth, watching it all.

All too late. The canoe rides out to the brink of the falls, out toward the thunderhead of mist, rides out and goes, just like that. No one else sees it. I ask. There's a rainbow, yeah, the ghost of a rainbow there in the dark, just where she's disappeared.

We can't find her, or the canoe. Or the old man – he just isn't there the next morning. We keep on looking for her though, her grandmother's so sad, right until freeze up. Her grandmother starts to get old. Her uncle too. Her father and mother can't even look at each other anymore on the street. My ma and me, we try to help—

And then one day, in the spring, walking back in through the gate and up the street, there she is, big as life— Big with life, mutters my ma, dogs and kids following her, following her past her grandmother's house, her father's house, straight into the meeting, the meeting of the council.

SCENE 9

Day. The Girl's MOTHER, GRANDmother and AUNT sit on one side of the council house, her FATHER, UNCLE and the BOY sit on the other, the GIRL stands in the space in the centre near the fire. They stare at her.

BOY

She looked around.

GIRL

They were just staring!

BOY

Then her grandmother—

GRAND

Are you alive?

GIRL

I'm alive, Grandma!

BOY

Then the rest of us, we got brave enough to touch her too. Her story was—

GIRL

I've been in the caves. The caves under the falls? With the God of Cloud and Rain. The Thunderer. His helpers saved me. When that witch canoe—

MOTHER

It was a witch!

GIRL

When it carried me away over the falls—

GRAND

I wanted to cry!

GIRL

—the God's Helper caught me in a rainbow blanket. He took me into their lodge and gave me rainwater and made me well.

Sunset. Moonrise.

GRAND

We were so sad.

AUNT

We missed you, didn't we, son?

MOTHER

What about the witch?

GIRL

The God's Helper, he told me the witch is still there. On the island in the river.

FATHER

The Grey Hair!

GIRL

Watching for his chance at the rest of us.

GIRL

The Grey Hair's been trading with a giant snake, it lives underground, dreaming of the meat from dead bodies. The Grey Hair's been trading our dead for power.

UNCLE

A snake that big must get hungry—

GIRL

So that old man's been poisoning our springs.

GRAND

So we die before our time. It isn't fair.

Moonset. Sunrise.

BOY

So the very next day—

FATHER

—we moved the village across the river, away from the snake and the poison.

AUNT

We weren't there four days before there's this rumbling coming louder than the falls.

BOY

Worse than the ice at break up.

UNCLE

That snake must have been hungry!

AUNT

It crawled out right in broad daylight.

MOTHER

It's following us! If it gets across the river—

AUNT

Nobody could miss it. The earth was shaking and quaking!

UNCLE

Look at the size of that thing!

BOY

Thick as an oak.

AUNT

Where's it going?

MOTHER

It's heading for the river!

UNCLE

Look at that thunderhead!

GRAND

It's walking off the river.

BOY

The Thunderer! It's the Thunderer!

MOTHER

He's chasing that snake.

FATHER

He's throwing rocks at it.

AUNT

They're turning into bolts of lightning.

UNCLE

Lightning bolts!

BOY

The snake's trying to bite at them but they're too bright!

FATHER

Too loud!

UNCLE

Too many forks!

GIRL

And sharper than it's own tongue. The snake's dead.

Sunset.

BOY

The body falls into the river and floats down stream.

MOTHER

That body floated by—

FATHER

—and by—

UNCLE

—and by...

AUNT

Lullaby?

Moonrise.

BOY

Then the body gets stuck—

FATHER

—stuck on the rocks—

UNCLE

—at the brink of the Falls.

MOTHER

Under all that weight—

GRAND

—the rocks there finally give way.

AUNT

Crash!

FATHER

Boom!

BOY

Bang!

AUNT

What a mess!

BOY

Which is why those falls don't go straight across today.

GIRL

That crash wrecks the God's cave, so he and his Helper pick up and move out west somewhere. I never saw him again.

AUNT

Typical!

The sun and moon both rise over Niagara Falls.

MOTHER

Later, she whispers to her mother about the God's Helper.

GIRL

I'm not afraid because he's so beautiful. I can't see his face but I know he's beautiful. He speaks to me. His voice is soft, like falling rain far away on leaves, even though he's right here beside me. The words he uses, it's strange, but I understand him all right. He puts a finger to my lips and kisses me.

MOTHER

Later, she makes her mother a grandmother.

BOY

Later, we— We have other children, but when her oldest child grows to be a man, he almost kills me with a lightning ball.

GIRL

So I send him west.

BOY

To live in his father's new house.

GRAND

She lives to be as old as her grandmother.

BOY

The witch disappears from the island and is also never seen again.

GRAND

For which we give thanks.

GIRL

We give thanks to our Mother, the Earth, for sustaining us.

BOY

We thank the rivers and streams for giving us water.

MOTHER

We give thanks to all herbs who furnish medicines for the cure of our sicknesses.

GRAND

We thank the Corn, and her sisters, the Beans and Squashes, who give us life.

UNCLE

We give thanks to the bushes and trees for their fruit.

AUNT

We thank the wind who banishes sicknesses.

FATHER

We give thanks to the moon and stars who give us their light when the sun is gone.

GIRL

We thank our grandfather, the Thunderer, for protecting his grandchildren from witches and serpents, and for giving us his rain.

BOY

We give thanks to the sun for looking upon the earth with a beneficent eye.

GRAND

Finally, we thank the Giver of Life, who embodies all goodness and who directs all things for the good of his children.

The sun and moon both set over Niagara Falls.

The End

KATHARINA VERMETTE

WHAT NDNS DO

i walk home with rita just after midnight. we had left the bar after only three beer. a week night and i promised i wouldn't keep her out too late.

the night is brisk, too cold for first snow. we are walking fast, puffing on smokes, and swimming in the shallow waters of only three beer. we are so weary. weary from our work weeks, weary of our sadnesses. she is seeing a white guy she isn't really into. i am suffering from my most recent broken wing, the first guy i've been excited about in a long, long

such a long time.

i had made a wish this past summer - i wanted so badly to be excited about someone. only, i forgot to order that he should be excited about me too.

"it wasn't right for him to treat you like that," rita spits out cigarette smoke and ill will. "i think i might've lost all respect for him." she pauses her speech to inhale, then flicks her butt down the sidewalk without losing a pinch of stride. "i hope you know that, lou. i hope you know that that is how rude he was."

"i did my fair share of fuckery, reet" i defend.

"naw i don't believe that," she shakes her head, combs her long bare fingers through her messy black hair. "i think it would have turned out the same no matter what you did."

i shrug in the new cold knowing rejection stings like the first bite of winter, a shock you will get used to in a few days. adapt to.

"it was so... deliberate, his shtick, his..." she made a fishing motion with her cold, red hands - the universal sign of casting out and reeling in.

"but i was the one who asked him out!" still defending.

"that just told him you were up for it, babe."

"really?" i ask.

"yes" rita says definitively. "really!"

"that's sad." i say and mean it.

"tell me about it" she looks aside at me.

i think i see pity.

i am happy she loves me enough to feel protective, and i didn't entirely disagree with her. but still, if i was being truthful, i am also happy to have had his attention, if only

for a little while.

i saw you like i see everything, like it is poetry. your story, your narrative arc was just a path to me, a path meandering off into the distant landscape. so many of us are so distracted by the twists, the turns, the journey. but me, no, i didn't care much about all that. i was bent at the side of your road, distracted by a simple pretty little flower growing wild and unnoticed. i wanted to know its pedals, its stem and leaves. had no interest in your story, what has been, said, so many times before, the typicals, the ego. i was only hung up on those little bits, those tiny gems, flowers, those minute rays of light that shone out through the briefest cracks of your thick, iron clad, armour.

rita thinks i am too forgiving; i think she isn't paying attention.

she assures me that he is just a good example of what arrogant ndns do. and i can only nod, not knowing what to say about this.

i don't understand arrogance. never have. that blatant lack of humility, or more often, the indignant lack of self awareness. a thinly veiled attempt to ward off the merest trace of vulnerability.

maybe?

this latest misstep all started a few months ago. too long ago. not long at all. rita and i and a warm late spring patio night, patio season is so very short and oh so beloved. we sat nestled into oversized windows drinking tall pints in narrow glasses. smoking too many cigarettes.

i was recovering from the reality of my first one night stand since i was 19. it was relatively painless. considering. rita was looking forward to summer.

"hey, that guy you like is single now you know?" she said with a smirk over her half empty glass.

"what guy?" i grinned, sipping draft coyly knowing exactly who she was talking about even before she laughed her knowing laugh and lit another smoke.

i met you like a clap of thunder out of a near clear summer sky. you were a noise that demanded attention. and i remember you vivid, walking toward me with your beautiful bulk and latent cynicism. you shook my hand with a polite smile and all the things i wanted to do to your body flooded through my brain like prairie rain, solid, smooth, constant, heavy.

you said, nice to meet you.

i think my exact response was, uh duh duh.

then you introduced your girlfriend.

"so?" i smirked at rita.

and we laughed, rita and i, into the new light night. we laughed because we knew it was all good and nothing mattered and everything is so beautiful in june.

"i might just have to ask that boy out then" i said like i was that tough, that brave.

"do it!" she encouraged because she was that tough, that brave.

"should i?"

"definitely"

"really?"

"do it!"

"maybe i just will then"

"well then," she polished off her beer with a gesture of finality. "better hurry though" at this we both nodded our knowing little nods, knowing that these ndn men treat us like cigarettes, like beer bottles, craved, savoured, enjoyed, and tossed aside. at best, we'd get a relationship, for awhile, something intense and quick, most likely volatile, but still, in relationships, we were little more than trampolines, something good for fun, a quick boost, but eventually the nausea sets in and he is forced to make a painless though graceless dismount.

and there was me, happy in june, drinking too much and so fucking excited at the prospect of being jumped on,

just asking for it.

"got another smoke?" rita asks into the long walk night. i pull my bare hands out of my pockets for her, dig into my bag for my pack, then my lighter. of course i will do this for her.

she thinks i am a hero ëcause, a year and a half ago, i finally kicked out the baby daddy who was running around on me. i think she is a hero because she has learned how to sleep with people without letting her feelings get in the way. of course they are there, and sometime they are cumbersome, but she just doesn't let them get in the way.

this year, she is trying to teach me how to do this.

it's not going very well.

i am thankful for her patience. she thinks i should pay better attention.

it was a perfect little date. you're good at first dates, aren't you? we were both so talkative and smiley. the kind of date where opinions dance around with nervous gestures to the cloudy song of newly pumping blood.

my thunder calmed to a brisk heart beat.

and there was no move, no illicit remark, respect was our chaperone and by the time i got home, a cute little email message was waiting for me. a perfect first date.

then i called and said, fuck it come over.

of course you did.

but then you never called

only texted occasionally, sometime between midnight and three a.m, nearly every other saturday, saturdays after we had drank beer with other people, after our opinions danced with other people's opinions, only then would you text, or i would. an exciting idea that quickly gets routine, a beautiful gesture that gets old fast.

my mistake.

you never intended for it to be beautiful.

earlier at the bar, rita was telling me how she could never imagine getting married, couldn't see the white dress, the veil, the husband.

she said the word like it was foreign, german maybe. hus - ban - d.

i said i had the whole thing planned already, a beach, at sunset, and i will walk down to my love in a simple white dress, the beat of the big drum thumping my delicate steps in the sand. our families will all intermingle in the fading crimson sunshine, all smiling. my sons will walk with me, one on each side, all the way up to my faceless love, and my firstborn will put my shaking little hand into my forever love's big strong brown one. and i will cry. and i will feel as if i have arrived,

"do you, louisa may, take this man?"

of course i do.

i don't tell rita all of this though. just bits, not even the particularly cheezy bits, but still her eyes roll, her clear seeing eyes. mine blur, i know this. i know i see things in hazy pink hues, the edges smudged, the insults softened, the obvious obscured.

i would love to see the world the way rita does. the harsh brittle brutal reality of it all. the darkened grey concrete of it all. to her, it is never the picturesque romantic path in a merry little springtime. it is a dirty muck trodden gum littered downtown street that stinks like beer and piss at 3 am with few choices and oh so many needs.

and your eyes may be blurry but that doesn't make it beautiful.

"never works out for me either" rita's breath in the cold air. "when i ask a guy out. always gives off the wrong impression somehow"

"then why the hell did you tell me to go for it?" my hands out in the wind, exposed.

"oh c'mon, lou" she scoffs. "'s not like you were thinking about talking to the guy!"

she makes a point. it's just not entirely true.

i did think about talking to him. i do fantasize about quick wit and spry intellectuo matches where words joust in thick air between two bodies that move like they want to fuse together. and i dream of fights that end with kisses. conversations that have to continue even after clothes are off. questions that pull me out of sleep, questions i have to ask the person lying next to me because i know he is waiting, in sleep, to answer.

but i also want to be called the next day, the morning after, or in the evening, for a quiet bedtime phone call that i can curl up to, in bed, with his voice to my ear. when i can turn out the light, and we can whisper nonsensical details about our individual days, feeling like teenagers, feeling wanted.

i am not interested in your little boy games. passive aggressive is so last year. i am not impressed by your remarkable ability to wield power over little girls. i feel bad for them. for me. for that white girl who once believed you loved her. that white girl now so wrecked and confused.

didn't think i knew that did you? my cousin told me. how your ex came to town, how you guys were still "friends," how she showed up at the bar looking so good for you. and how you and your friends laughed at her when her back was turned, and fed her beer and tequila when she faced you. got her drunk for fun until she spewed, first her hurt, heartbroken words that made no sense and held no weight, and then her projectile vomit all over that sticky old carpet in that slimy old bar. humiliated. for what? for loving you? for being confused by you? hell! i've had one hundredth of the you she has had and i'm confused. but i'm not humiliated. thank creator for small graces.

that's all i have over that poor white girl.

other than that we're still both rejected and bruised.

"don't worry too much about it, doll," rita says huddled in her jacket lighting another smoke, she emerges and says, "there are plenty of people to judge you, no need to do it yourself." she says this with a cigarette dangling off her chapped lips and the harsh north wind whipping up her thick black hair.

i smile, shrug again, feeling quiet, tired, midweek. then i stop to light another smoke for myself. i lean into a storefront window to block the wind, the neons lights are out. they sell candy bars and chinese specialty items in large bulk bins.

her words bounce around in my head, "really?" i ask.

she nods. gives me a look that is the equivalent of rolling her eyes or shaking her head, only kinder.

we are pessimistic at the best of times.

or at least i strive to be. i imagine it would be easier than living in this perpetual hope that consistently gets beaten down. i am a salmon swimming frantically upstream with a stupid look of glee on my plump, wet face even though i keep hitting rocks,

kissing frogs,

laying down with dogs.

"oh lou my girl, don't be like that. you can still see him you know. don't be ashamed. just know what it is!"

but i know i can't do that.

i know i am too far gone.

always have been.

"c'mon lou, you're dating now. you've got to realize it's just a game. and really, if this guy wanted you, and turned around and said, i want to be with you, i love you, i love you, have my babies. well, then you'd be all, fuck that! challenge done! chase over! and you'd be so bored. its the hunt, doll, its the game. it's what we want. it's what we do."

i nod yes like this is stoic wisdom passed down through seven generations. and flick my half smoked smoke into the street, watch it get run over by a big noisy truck. we step in unison, off another curb, around another corner, like we know exactly where we are going and we're walking so fast like we can outrun the cold. we don't want to admit that it will be winter soon. how much we all dread the winter.

but she is right. in a way. this is what we convince ourselves. that it's a game and we're playing too. like we're privy to the rules and a part of the equation.

not just ambling by, stumbling on, getting rejected over and over through no obvious fault of our own.

it's true, i don't want to admit it. admit that i want nothing more that to hold and be held, to have a man that i love bring me beer and flowers. to make popcorn, for him, on the stove, old fashioned-like, and lie on our sides with our feet intertwined under my ratty crocheted blanket, and fall asleep in front of a boring movie just rented for the excuse to lie around, together, doing nothing.

to feel your breath on my hair,

no! better to believe i just can't stop myself, think i won't ever be satisfied, better to over analyze his every move, gesture, to find meaning in his cruelty, and an answer more substantial than ëhe is just not that into me.' i can do that, i can mull and twist together all my thoughts and then i won't have to let him go. not yet. not just yet.

i can ramble through the way his hands held his beer and picked at the label like he was nervous too.

the pensive way he hugged me goodbye that first time, as we stood on the grass just off the bridge when i silently dared him to kiss me. but he didn't.

i can stretch, out, these, moments, and keep them as worthy as memories that have only to warm, me, for, awhile, and then, fade,

rita wants me to be angry. maybe i will be. one day. maybe i will shout and punch and kick my way into the next ne'er do well heart i find. maybe i won't. maybe i will be alone ëtil i die and scream old lady anger out at the world behind me. and i think i will say,

damn it you're all the fucking same aren't you? y'all with your cheap ass air of "the stoic ndn" cologne, thinking you can have anyone anytime all the time. don't you know that however many numbers you rack up, you're still going to be so fucking alone. in here. ëcause you're all too fucking arrogant to man up and just be good fucking people. faithful partners. damn you all. damn your blazing fucking arrogance thrown on like fancy clothes barely covering up your pitiful, bottomless insecurity. yeah, that's right i can see it. we all can. that's why we want you. that's why we put up with you. try to take care of you ëcause y'all have that crazy kind of insecurity inside you that brings out the mamas in us. the kind of insecurity that can only come from unhappy ndn childhoods and the predictable dysfunctional family bullshit that comes with it. shit. we fall for it everytime. we give and we give and still you're all the kind of fuckers freud would have a field day with, you and all your oedipal garbage forever treating women like disposal objects all ëcause you thought your mamas didn't love you good enough. i feel so goddamn sorry for your mamas ëcause if i ever found out my boys were treating women like y'all do i would beat them with a stick until they learned right. damn it, we are not beer bottles. we are not cigarettes. we are queens, muthafuckers and if you are in it for anything less pure and abject adoration then you should leave us the fuck alone before you get your dicks into places they really have no business going.

yeah! that's what i'd say, don't let your dick write a cheque your heart can't cash, buddy. that, or, i could just say no. but that's not likely. i'm too...optimistic. shit. everytime. a certain grin, a certain twist of a lovely hairless forearm, crap, i forget my name, nevermind my past heartaches, headaches, tribulations, trepidations.

"why does it have to be like that? i mean fuck, i feel so...compartmentalized" i shrug, defeated, cold.

"that's just how it is. it's how they think. you sleep with them - you go in that box. you don't sleep with them - you stay in the other one," she says this with hands out, smoke burning. i can visualize the boxes in the air.

"that's stupid" i say

"tell me about it"

i wasn't concerned with the plot, maybe i should've been, but it was the image that intrigued me. that loose, lackadaisical character who unravelled slowly like a smooth concise read on the back jacket of a real good looking book. only all the pages inside were blank.

its alright, i really didn't want the story anyway. i just wanted the flower. i mean, i knew it was red, but what? a gardenia? a blossom? what shape are your pedals? what shade is your hue? are there buds in the foliage just waiting for the right tilt of sun to open? these are the things i wanted to know. they are the things you didn't tell me. but those were the things i wanted to know.

"but i thought all ndn men u-haul it from one date to the next?"

"some do" rita nods to the night. "some are just dogs, lou, they just want to fuck anything they can."

i sigh out loud. these things i thought i knew.

and she adds, "others date white women, then they play by white people rules"

fuck.

this is complicated.

i think i should be taking notes.

rita thinks i'll get it one day. i really don't think i even want to.

don't worry. i will keep your secrets. the one that you are not really such a nice guy or a sincere person. the one that you probably drink too much. and the one that you are really a pretty smart guy, only cover it up with predictable tattoos and crude slang. i will keep it all, don't worry. i will even keep the one where you really want to care about the world but just don't have the time after caring about yourself so damn much. and i will especially keep close to me the secret that you are such a cuddly sleeper, how you always reached out for me with only half awake hands and held me tight enough for our skins to sink into each other, all night. and right here, i will keep the secret that you were so beautiful in the dark, when you thought no one was watching and all you had to do was rise above me with your broadly stretched body, loosened hair, and brief shine, and you couldn't help it, couldn't help but look at me with a question, unsure but you had to ask anyway, because even you, arrogant boy, even you don't always have all the answers.

"do you know any?" i ask as we get near her house.

"what? ndns who aren't arrogant?" rita snorts.

"and single?"

"single or married – no." she didn't even think about this.

"no?"

"no!"

"thats sad"

"tell me about it"

i feel sorry for us. shivering down her street, not long past midnight, midweek, midlife, cinderellas with both shoes on. hands tucked deep in our jackets, shoulders bracing against the wind, forever strong and bracing against, of all the people we knew between us, not a single worthwhile Aboriginal man, not one prince for us to look after, one who knew enough not to trust his own bullshit, one who wouldn't be afraid to ask out loud, or answer, or follow through,

damn it was cold, barely october and time to haul it in. face another long hibernation, alone, again, under my ratty crocheted blanket, falling asleep in front of a boring movie rented just because there is nothing else to do.

but i walked my friend to her gate and give her a long warm hug under the almost full moon.

i love her that she has accepted all of this. she loves me that i haven't.

"but i thought all ndn men u-haul it from one date to the next?"

"some do" rita nods to the night. "some are just dogs, lou, they just want to fuck anything they can."

i sigh out loud. these things i thought i knew.

and she adds, "others date white women, then they play by white people rules"

fuck.

this is complicated.

i think should be taking notes.

rita thinks i'll get it one day. i really don't think i even want to.

don't worry. i will keep your secrets. the one that you are not really such a nice guy or a sincere person. the one that you probably drink too much. and the one that you are really a pretty smart guy, only cover it up with predictable tattoos and crude slang. i will keep it all, don't worry. i will even keep the one where you really want to care about the world but just don't have the time after caring about yourself so damn much. and i will especially keep close to me the secret that you are such a cuddly sleeper, how you always reached out for me with only half awake hands and held me tight enough for our skins to sink into each other, all night. and right here, i will keep the secret that you were so beautiful in the dark, when you thought no one was watching and all you had to do was rise above me with your broadly stretched body, loosened hair, and brief shine, and you couldn't help it, couldn't help but look at me with a question, unsure but you had to ask anyway, because even you, arrogant boy, even you don't always have all the answers.

"do you know any?" i ask as we get near her house.

"what? ndns who aren't arrogant?" rita snorts.

"and single?"

"single or married – no." she didn't even think about this.

"no?"

"no!"

"thats sad"

"tell me about it"

i feel sorry for us. shivering down her street, not long past midnight, midweek, midlife, cinderellas with both shoes on. hands tucked deep in our jackets, shoulders bracing against the wind, forever strong and bracing against,

of all the people we knew between us, not a single worthwhile Aboriginal man, not one prince for us to look after, one who knew enough not to trust his own bullshit, one who wouldn't be afraid to ask out loud, or answer, or follow through,

damn it was cold, barely october and time to haul it in. face another long hibernation, alone, again, under my ratty crocheted blanket, falling asleep in front of a boring movie rented just because there is nothing else to do.

but i walked my friend to her gate and give her a long warm hug under the almost full moon.

i love her that she has accepted all of this. she loves me that i haven't.

EDEN ROBINSON

Queen of the North

FROG SONG

Whenever I see abandoned buildings, I think of our old house in the village, a rickety shack by the swamp where the frogs used to live. It's gone now. The council covered the whole area with rocks and gravel.

In my memory, the sun is setting and the frogs begin to sing. As the light shifts from yellow to orange to red, I walk down the path to the beach. The wind blows in from the channel, making the grass hiss and shiver around my legs. The tide is low and there's a strong rotting smell from the beach. Tree stumps that have been washed down the channel from the logged areas loom ahead – black, twisted silhouettes against the darkening sky.

The seiner coming down the channel is the *Queen of the North*, pale yellow with blue trim, Uncle Josh's boat. I wait on the beach. The water laps my ankles. The sound of the old diesel engine grows louder as the boat gets closer.

Usually I can will myself to move, but sometimes I'm frozen where I stand, waiting for the crew to come ashore.

The only thing my cousin Ronny didn't own was a Barbie doll speedboat. She had the swimming pool, she had the Barbie-Goes-to-Paris carrying case, but she didn't have the boat. There was one left in Northern Drugs, nestling between the puzzles and the stuffed Garfields, but it cost sixty bucks and we were broke. I knew Ronny was going to get it. She'd already saved twenty bucks out of her allowance. Anyway, she always got everything she wanted because she was an only child and both her parents worked at the aluminum smelter. Mom knew how much I wanted it, but she said it was a toss-up between school supplies and paying bills, or wasting our money on something I'd get sick of in a few weeks.

We had a small Christmas tree. I got socks and underwear and forced a cry of surprise when I opened the package. Uncle Josh came in just as Mom was carving the turkey. He pushed a big box in my direction.

"Go on," Mom said, smiling. "It's for you."

Uncle Josh looked like a young Elvis. He had the soulful brown eyes and the thick black hair. He dressed his long, thin body in clothes with expensive labels – no Sears or Kmart for him. He smiled at me with his perfect pouty lips and bleached white teeth.

"Here you go, sweetheart," Uncle Josh said.

I didn't want it. Whatever it was, I didn't want it. He put it down in front of me. Mom must have wrapped it. She was never good at wrapping presents. You'd think with two kids and a million Christmases behind her she'd know how to wrap a present.

"Come on, open it," Mom said.

I unwrapped it slowly, my skin crawling. Yes, it was the Barbie Doll speedboat.

My mouth smiled. We all had dinner and I pulled the wishbone with my little sister, Alice. I got the bigger piece and made a wish. Uncle Josh kissed me. Alice sulked. Uncle Josh never got her anything, and later that afternoon she screamed about it. I put the boat in my closet and didn't touch it for days.

Until Ronny came over to play. She was showing off her new set of Barbie-in-the-Ice-Capades clothes. Then I pulled out the speedboat and the look on her face was almost worth it.

My sister hated me for weeks. When I was off at soccer practise, Alice took the boat and threw it in the river. To this day, Alice doesn't know how grateful I was.

There's a dream I have sometimes. Ronny comes to visit. We go down the hallway to my room. She goes in first. I point to the closet and she eagerly opens the door. She thinks I've been lying, that I don't really have a boat. She wants proof.

When she turns to me, she looks horrified, pale and shocked. I laugh, triumphant. I reach in and stop, seeing Uncle Josh's head, arms, and legs squashed inside, severed from the rest of his body. My clothes are soaked dark red with his blood.

"Well, what do you know," I say. "Wishes do come true."

Me and five chug buddies are in the Tamitik arena, in the girls' locker room under the bleachers. The hockey game is in the third period and the score is tied. The yells and shouting of the fans drown out the girl's swearing. There are four of us against her. It doesn't take long before she's on the floor trying to crawl away. I want to say I'm not part of it, but that's my foot hooking her ankle and tripping her while Ronny takes her down with a blow to the temple. She grunts. Her head makes a hollow sound when it bounces off the sink. The lights make us all look green. A cheer explodes from inside the arena. Our team has scored. The girl's now curled up under the sink and I punch her and kick her and smash her face into the floor.

My cuz Ronny had great connections. She could get hold of almost any drug you wanted. This was during her biker chick phase, when she wore tight leather skirts, teeny-weeny tops, and many silver bracelets, rings, and studs. Her parents started coming down really hard on her then. I went over to her house to get high. It was okay to do it there, as long as we sprayed the living room with Lysol and opened the windows before her parents came home.

We toked up and decided to go back to my house to get some munchies. Ronny tagged along when I went up to my bedroom to get the bottle of Visine. There was an envelope on my dresser. Even before I opened it I knew it would be money. I knew who it was from.

I pulled the bills out. Ronny squealed.

"Holy sheep shit, how much is there?"

I spread the fifties out on the dresser. Two hundred and fifty dollars. I could get some flashy clothes or nice earrings with that money, if I could bring myself to touch it. Anything I bought would remind me of him.

"You want to have a party?" I said to Ronny.

"Are you serious?" she said, going bug-eyed.

I gave her the money and said make it happen. She asked who it came from, but she didn't really care. She was already making phone calls.

That weekend we had a house party in town. The house belonged to one of Ronny's biker buddies and was filled with people I knew by sight from school. As the night wore on, they came up and told me what a generous person I was. Yeah, that's me, I thought, Saint Karaoke of Good Times.

I took Ronny aside when she was drunk enough. "Ronny, I got to tell you something."

"What?" she said, blinking too fast, like she had something in her eye.

"You know where I got the money?"

She shook her head, lost her balance, blearily put her hand on my shoulder, and barfed out the window.

As I listened to her heave out her guts, I decided I didn't want to tell her after all. What was the point? She had a big mouth, and anything I told her I might as well stand on a street corner and shout to the world. What I really wanted was to have a good time and forget about the money, and after beating everyone hands down at tequila shots, that's exactly what I did.

"Moooo." I copy the two aliens on *Sesame Street* mooing to a telephone. Me and Uncle Josh are watching television together. He smells faintly of the halibut he cooked for dinner. Uncle Josh undoes his pants. "Moo." I keep my eyes on the TV and say nothing as he moves toward me. I'm not a baby like Alice, who runs to Mommy about everything. When it's over he'll have treats for me. It's like when the dentist gives me extra suckers for not crying, not even when it really hurts.

I could have got my scorpion tattoo at The Body Hole, where my friends went. A perfectly groomed beautician would sit me in a black leather dentist's chair and the tattoo artist would show me the tiny diagram on tracing paper. We'd choose the exact spot on my neck where the scorpion would go, just below the hairline where my hair comes to a point. Techno, maybe some funky remix of Abba, would blare through the speakers as he whirred the tattoo needle's motor.

But Ronny had done her own tattoo, casually standing in front of the bathroom mirror with a short needle and permanent blue ink from a pen. She simply poked the needle in and out, added the ink, and that was that. No fuss, no muss.

So I asked her to do it for me. After all, I thought, if she could brand six marks of Satan on her own breast, she could certainly do my scorpion.

Ronny led me into the kitchen and cleared off a chair. I twisted my hair up into a bun and held it in place. She showed me the needle, then dropped it into a pot of boiling water. She was wearing a crop top and I could see her navel ring, glowing bright gold in the slanting light of the setting sun. She was prone to lifting her shirt in front of complete strangers and telling them she'd pierced herself.

Ronny emptied the water into the sink and lifted the needle in gloved hands. I bent my head and looked down at the floor as she traced the drawing on my skin.

The needle was hot. It hurt more than I expected, a deep ache, a throbbing. I breathed through my mouth. I fought not to cry. I concentrated fiercely on not crying in front of her, and when she finished I lay very still.

"See?" Ronny said. "Nothing to it, you big baby."

When I opened my eyes and raised my head, she held one small mirror to my face and another behind me so I could see her work. I frowned at my reflection. The scorpion looked like a smear.

"It'll look better when the swelling goes down," she said, handing me the two mirrors.

As Ronny went to start the kettle for tea, she looked out the window over the sink. "Star light, star bright, first star—"

I glanced out the window. "That's Venus."

"Like you'd know the difference."

I didn't want to argue. The skin on the back of my neck ached like it was sunburned.

I am singing Janis Joplin songs, my arms wrapped around the karaoke machine. I fend people off with a stolen switchblade. No one can get near until some kid from school has the bright idea of giving me drinks until I pass out.

Someone else videotapes me so my one night as a rock star is recorded forever. She tries to send it to *America's Funniest Home Videos*, but they reject it as unsuitable for family viewing. I remember nothing else about that night after I got my first hit of acid. My real name is Adelaine, but the next day a girl from school sees me coming and yells, "Hey, look, it's Karaoke!"

The morning after my sixteenth birthday I woke up looking down into Jimmy Hill's face. We were squashed together in the backseat of a car and I thought, God, I didn't.

I crawled around and found my shirt and then spent the next half hour vomiting beside the car. I vaguely remembered the night before, leaving the party with Jimmy. I remembered being afraid of bears.

Jimmy stayed passed out in the backseat, naked except for his socks. We were somewhere up in the mountains, just off a logging road. The sky was misty and gray. As I stood up and stretched, the car headlights went out.

Dead battery. That's just fucking perfect, I thought.

I checked the trunk and found an emergency kit. I got out one of those blankets that look like a large sheet of aluminum and wrapped it around myself. I searched the car until I found my jeans. I threw Jimmy's shirt over him. His jeans were hanging off the car's antenna. When I took them down, the antenna wouldn't straighten up.

I sat in the front seat. I had just slept with Jimmy Hill. Christ, he was practically a Boy Scout. I saw his picture in the local newspaper all the time, with those medals for swimming.

Other than that, I never really noticed him. We went to different parties.

About midmorning, the sun broke through the mist and streamed to the ground in fingers of light, just like in the movies when God is talking to someone. The sun hit my face and I closed my eyes.

I heard the seat shift and turned. Jimmy smiled at me and I knew why I'd slept with him. He leaned forward and we kissed. His lips were soft and the kiss was gentle. He put his hand on the back of my neck. "You're beautiful."

I thought it was just a line, the polite thing to say after a one-night stand, so I didn't answer.

"Did you get any?" Jimmy said.

"What?" I said.

"Blueberries." He grinned. "Don't you remember?"

I stared at him.

His grin faded. "Do you remember anything?"

I shrugged.

"Well. We left the party, I dunno, around two, I guess. You said you wanted blueberries. We came out here—" He cleared his throat.

"Then we fucked, passed out, and now we're stranded." I finished the sentence. The sun was getting uncomfortable. I took off the emergency blanket. I had no idea what to say next. "Battery's dead."

He swore and leaned over me to try the ignition.

I got out of his way by stepping out of the car. Hastily he put his shirt on, not looking up at me. He had a nice chest, buff and tan. He blushed and I wondered if he had done this before.

"You cool with this?" I said.

He immediately became macho. "Yeah."

I felt really shitty then. God, I thought, he's going to be a bragger.

I went and sat on the hood. It was hot. I was thirsty and had a killer headache. Jimmy got out and sat beside me.

"You know where we are?" Jimmy said.

"Not a fucking clue."

He looked at me and we both started laughing.

"You were navigating last night," he said, nudging me.

"You always listen to pissed women?"

"Yeah," he said, looking sheepish. "Well. You hungry?"

I shook my head. "Thirsty."

Jimmy hopped off the car and came back with a warm Coke from under the driver's seat. We drank it in silence.

"You in any rush to get back?" he asked.

We started laughing again and then went hunting for blueberries. Jimmy found a patch not far from the car and we picked the bushes clean. I'd forgotten how tart wild blueberries are. They're smaller than store-bought berries, but their flavour is much more intense.

"My sister's the wilderness freak," Jimmy said. "She'd be able to get us out of this. Or at least she'd know where we are."

We were perched on a log. "You gotta promise me something," I said.

"What?"

"If I pop off before you, you aren't going to eat me."

"What?"

"I'm serious," I said. "And I'm not eating any bugs."

"If you don't try them, you'll never know what you're missing." Jimmy looked at the road. "You want to pick a direction?"

The thought of trekking down the dusty logging road in the wrong direction held no appeal to me. I must have made a face because Jimmy said, "Me neither."

After the sun set, Jimmy made a fire in front of the car. We put the aluminum blanket under us and lay down. Jimmy pointed at the sky. "That's the Big Dipper."

"Ursa Major," I said. "Mother of all bears. There's Ursa Minor, Cassiopeia… " I stopped.

"I didn't know you liked astronomy."

"It's pretty nerdy."

He kissed me. "Only if you think it is." He put his arm around me and I put my head on his chest and listened to his heart. It was a nice way to fall asleep.

Jimmy shook me awake. "Car's coming." He pulled me to my feet. "It's my sister."

"Mmm." Blurrily I focused on the road. I could hear birds and, in the distance, the rumble of an engine.

"My sister could find me in hell," he said.

When they dropped me off at home, my mom went ballistic. "Where the hell were you?"

"Out." I stopped at the door. I hadn't expected her to be there when I came in.

Her chest was heaving. I thought she'd start yelling, but she said very calmly, "You've been gone for two days."

You noticed? I didn't say it. I felt ill and I didn't want a fight. "Sorry. Should've called."

I pushed past her, kicked off my shoes, and went upstairs.

Still wearing my smelly jeans and shirt, I lay down on the bed. Mom followed me to my room and shook my shoulder.

"Tell me where you've been."

"At Ronny's."

"Don't lie to me. What is wrong with you?"

God. Just get lost. I wondered what she'd do if I came out and said what we both knew. Probably have a heart attack. Or call me a liar.

"You figure it out," I said. "I'm going to sleep." I expected her to give me a lecture or something, but she just left.

Sometimes, when friends were over, she'd point to Alice and say, "This is my good kid." Then she'd point to me and say, "This is my rotten kid, nothing but trouble. She steals, she lies, she sleeps around. She's just no damn good."

Alice knocked on my door later.

"Fuck off," I said.

"You've got a phone call."

"Take a message. I'm sleeping."

Alice opened the door and poked her head in. "You want me to tell Jimmy anything else?"

I scrambled down the hallway and grabbed the receiver. I took a couple of deep breaths so it wouldn't sound like I'd rushed to the phone. "Hi."

"Hi," Jimmy said. "We just replaced the battery on the car. You want to go for a ride?"

"Aren't you grounded?"

He laughed. "So?"

I thought he just wanted to get lucky again, and then I thought, What the hell, at least this time I'll remember it.

"Pick me up in five minutes."

I'm getting my ass kicked by two sisters. They're really good. They hit solidly and back off quickly. I don't even see them coming anymore. I get mad enough to kick out. By sheer luck, the kick connects. One of the sisters shrieks and goes down. She's on the ground, her leg at an odd angle. The other one loses it and swings. The bouncer steps in and the crowd around us boos.

"My cousins'll be at a biker party. You want to go?"

Jimmy looked at me like he wasn't sure if I was serious.

"I'll be good," I said, crossing my heart then holding up my fingers in a scout salute.

"What fun would that be?" he said, revving the car's engine.

I gave him directions. The car roared away from our house, skidding a bit. Jimmy didn't say anything. I found it unnerving. He looked over at me, smiled, then turned back to face the road. I was used to yappy guys, but this was nice. I leaned my head back into the seat. The leather creaked.

Ronny's newest party house didn't look too bad, which could have meant it was going to be dead in there. It's hard to get down and dirty when you're worried you'll stain the carpet. You couldn't hear anything until someone opened the door and the music throbbed out. They did a good job with the sound-proofing. We went up the steps just as my cousin Frank came out with some bar buddies.

Jimmy stopped when he saw Frank and I guess I could see why. Frank is on the large side, six-foot-four and scarred up from his days as a hard-core Bruce Lee fan, when he felt compelled to fight Evil in street bars. He looked down at Jimmy.

"Hey, Jimbo," Frank said. "Hear you quit the swim team."

"You betcha," Jimmy said.

"Fucking right!" Frank body-slammed him. He tended to be more enthusiastic than most people could handle, but Jimmy looked okay with it. "More time to party," he said. Now they were going to gossip forever so I went inside.

The place was half empty. I recognized some people and nodded. They nodded back. The music was too loud for conversation.

"You want a drink?" Frank yelled, touching my arm.

I jumped. He quickly took his hand back. "Where's Jimmy?"

"Ronny gave him a hoot and now he's hacking up his lungs out back." Frank took off his jacket, closed his eyes, and shuffled back and forth. All he knew was the reservation two-step and I wasn't in the mood. I moved toward the porch but Frank grabbed my hand. "You two doing the wild thing?"

"He's all yours," I said.

"Fuck you," Frank called after me.

Jimmy was leaning against the railing, his back towards me, his hands jammed into his pockets. I watched him. His hair was dark and shiny, brushing his shoulders. I liked the way he moved, easily, like he was in no hurry to get anywhere. His eyes were light brown with gold flecks. I knew that in a moment he would turn and smile at me and it would be like stepping into sunlight.

In my dream Jimmy's casting a fishing rod. I'm afraid of getting hooked, so I sit at the bow of the skiff. The ocean is mildly choppy, the sky is hard blue, the air is cool. Jimmy reaches over to kiss me, but now he is soaking wet. His hands and lips are cold, his eyes are sunken and dull. Something moves in his mouth. It isn't his tongue. When I pull away, a crab drops from his lips and Jimmy laughs. "Miss me?"

I feel a scream in my throat but nothing comes out.

"What's the matter?" Jimmy tilts his head. Water runs off his hair and drips into the boat. "Crab got your tongue?"

This one's outside Hanky Panky's. The woman is so totally bigger than me it isn't funny. Still, she doesn't like getting hurt. She's afraid of the pain but can't back down because she started it. She's grabbing my hair, yanking it hard. I pull hers. We get stuck there, bent over, trying to kick each other, neither of us willing to let go. My friends are laughing their heads off. I'm pissed at that but I'm too sloshed to let go. In the morning my scalp will throb and be so tender I won't be able to comb my hair. At that moment, a bouncer comes over and splits us apart. The woman tries to kick me but kicks him instead and he knocks her down. My friends grab my arm and steer me to the bus stop.

Jimmy and I lay down together on a sleeping bag in a field of fireweed. The forest fire the year before had razed the place and the weeds had only sprouted back up about a month earlier. With the spring sun and just the right sprinkling of rain, they were as tall as sunflowers, as dark pink as prize roses, swaying around us in the night breeze.

Jimmy popped open a bottle of Baby Duck. "May I?" he said, reaching down to untie my sneaker.

"You may," I said.

He carefully lifted the sneaker and poured in some Baby Duck. Then he raised it to my lips and I drank. We lay down, flattening fireweed and knocking over the bottle. Jimmy nibbled my ear. I drew circles in the bend of his arm. Headlights came up fast, then disappeared down the highway. We watched the fireweed shimmer and wave in the wind.

"You're quiet tonight," Jimmy said. "What're you thinking?"

I almost told him then. I wanted to tell him. I wanted someone else to know and not have it locked inside me. I kept starting and then chickening out. What was the point? He'd probably pull away from me in horror, disgusted, revolted.

"I want to ask you something," Jimmy whispered. I closed my eyes, feeling my chest tighten. "You hungry? I've got a monster craving for chicken wings."

BLOODY VANCOUVER

When I got to Aunt Erma's the light in the hallway was going spastic, flickering like a strobe, little bright flashes then darkness so deep I had to feel my way along the wall. I stopped in front of the door, sweating, smelling myself through the thick layer of deodorant. I felt my stomach go queasy and wondered if I was going to throw up after all. I hadn't eaten and was still bleeding heavily.

Aunt Erma lived in East Van in a low-income government-housing unit. Light showed under the door. I knocked. I could hear the familiar opening of *Star Trek*, the old version, with the trumpets blaring. I knocked again.

The door swung open and a girl with a purple mohawk and Cleopatra eyeliner thrust money at me.

"Shit," she said. She looked me up and down, pulling the money back. "Where's the pizza?"

"I'm sorry," I said. "I think I have the wrong house."

"Pizza, pizza, pizza!" teenaged voices inside screamed. Someone was banging the floor in time to the chant.

"You with Cola?" she asked me.

I shook my head. "No. I'm here to see Erma Williamson. Is she in?"

"In? I guess. Mom?" she screamed. "Mom? It's for you!"

A whoop rose up. "Erma and Marley sittin' in a tree, k-i-s-s-i-n-g. First comes lust—"

"Shut up, you social rejects!"

"—then comes humping, then comes a baby after all that bumping!"

"How many times did they boink last night?" a single voice yelled over the laughter.

"Ten!" the voices chorused enthusiastically. "Twenty! Thirty! Forty!"

"Hey! Who's buying the pizza, eh? No respect! I get no respect!"

Aunt Erma came to the door. She didn't look much different from her pictures, except she wasn't wearing her cat-eye glasses.

She stared at me, puzzled. Then she spread open her arms.

"Adelaine, baby! I wasn't expecting you! Hey, come on in and say hi to your cousins. Pepsi! Cola! Look who came by your birthday!"

She gave me a tight bear hug and I wanted to cry.

Two girls stood at the entrance to the living room, identical right down to their lip rings. They had different coloured mohawks though – one pink, one purple.

"Erica?" I said, peering. I vaguely remembered them as having pigtails and making fun of Mr. Rogers. "Heather?"

"It's Pepsi," the purple mohawk said. "Not, n-o-t, Erica."

"Oh," I said.

"Cola," the pink-mohawked girl said, turning around and ignoring me to watch TV.

"What'd you bring us?" Pepsi said matter-of-factly.

"Excuse the fruit of my loins," Aunt Erma said, leading me into the living room and sitting me between two guys who were glued to the TV. "They've temporarily lost their manners. I'm putting it down to hormones and hoping the birth control pills turn them back into normal human beings."

Aunt Erma introduced me to everyone in the room, but their names went in one ear and out the other. I was so relieved just to be there and out of the clinic I couldn't concentrate on much else.

"How is he, Bones?" the guy on my right said, exactly in synch with Captain Kirk on TV. Kirk was standing over McCoy and a prone security guard with large purple circles all over his face.

"He's dead, Jim," the guy on my left said.

"I wanna watch something else," Pepsi said. "This sucks."

She was booed.

"Hey, it's my birthday. I can watch what I want."

"Siddown," Cola said. "You're out-voted."

"You guys have no taste at all. This is crap. I just can't believe you guys are watching this – this cultural pabulum. I—"

A pair of panties hit her in the face. The doorbell rang and the pink-haired girl held the pizza boxes over her head and yelled, "Dinner's ready!"

"Eat in the kitchen," Aunt Erma said. "All of youse. I ain't scraping your cheese out of my carpet."

Everyone left except me and Pepsi. She grabbed the remote control and flipped through a bunch of channels until we arrived at one where an announcer for the World Wrestling Federation screamed that the ref was blind.

"Now this," Pepsi said, "is entertainment."

By the time the party ended, I was snoring on the couch. Pepsi shook my shoulder. She and Cola were watching Bugs Bunny and Tweety.

"If we're bothering you," Cola said, "you can go crash in my room."

"Thanks," I said. I rolled off the couch, grabbed my backpack, and found the bathroom on the second floor. I made it just in time to throw up in the sink. The cramps didn't come back as badly as on the bus, but I took three Extra-Strength Tylenols anyway. My pad had soaked right through and leaked all over my underwear. I put on clean clothes and crashed in one of the beds. I wanted a black hole to open up and suck me out of the universe.

When I woke, I discovered I should have put on a diaper. It looked like something had been hideously murdered on the mattress.

"God," I said as Pepsi walked in. I snatched up the blanket and tried to cover the mess.

"Man," Pepsi said. "Who are you? Carrie?"

"Freaky," Cola said, coming in behind her. "You okay?"

I nodded. I wished I'd never been born.

Pepsi hit my hand when I touched the sheets. "You're not the only one with killer periods." She pushed me out of the bedroom. In the bathroom she started water going in the tub for me, poured some Mr. Bubble in, and left without saying anything. I stripped off my blood-soaked underwear and hid them in the bottom of the garbage. There would be no saving them. I lay back. The bubbles popped and gradually the water became cool. I was smelly and gross. I scrubbed hard but the smell wouldn't go away.

"You still alive in there?" Pepsi said, opening the door.

I jumped up and whisked the shower curtain shut.

"Jesus, don't you knock?"

"Well, excuuuse me. I brought you a bathrobe. Good thing you finally crawled out of bed. Mom told us to make you eat something before we left. We got Ichiban, Kraft, or hot dogs. You want anything else, you gotta make it yourself. What do you want?"

"Privacy."

"We got Ichiban, Kraft, or hot dogs. What do you want?"

"The noodles," I said, more to get her out than because I was hungry.

She left and I tried to lock the door. It wouldn't lock so I scrubbed myself off quickly. I stopped when I saw the bathwater. It was dark pink with blood.

I crashed on the couch and woke when I heard sirens. I hobbled to the front window in time to see an ambulance pull into the parking lot. The attendants wheeled a man bound to a stretcher across the lot. He was screaming about the eyes in the walls that were watching him, waiting for him to fall asleep so they could come peel his skin from his body.

Aunt Erma, the twins and I drove to the powwow at the Trout Lake community centre in East Vancouver. I was still bleeding a little and felt pretty lousy, but Aunt Erma was doing fundraising for the Helping Hands Society and had asked me to work her bannock booth. I wanted to help her out.

Pepsi had come along just to meet guys, dressed up in her flashiest bracelets and most conservatively ripped jeans. Aunt Erma enlisted her too, when she found out that none of her other volunteers had showed up. Pepsi was disgusted.

Cola got out of working at the booth because she was one of the jingle dancers. Aunt Erma had made her outfit, a form-fitting red dress with silver jingles that flashed and twinkled as she walked. Cola wore a bobbed wig to cover her pink mohawk. Pepsi bugged her about it, but Cola airily waved goodbye and said, "Have fun."

I hadn't made fry bread in a long time. The first three batches were already mixed. I just added water and kneaded them into shapes roughly the size of a large doughnut, then threw them in the electric frying pan. The oil spattered and crackled and steamed because I'd turned the heat up too high. Pepsi wasn't much better. She burned her first batch and then had to leave so she could watch Cola dance.

"Be right back," she said. She gave me a thumbs-up sign and disappeared into the crowd.

The heat from the frying pan and the sun was fierce. I wished I'd thought to bring an umbrella. One of the organizers gave me her baseball cap. Someone else brought me a glass of water. I wondered how much longer Pepsi was going to be. My arms were starting to hurt.

I flattened six more pieces of bread into shape and threw them in the pan, beyond caring anymore that none of them were symmetrical. I could feel the sun sizzling my forearms, my hands, my neck, my legs. A headache throbbed at the base of my skull.

The people came in swarms, buzzing groups of tourists, conventioneers on a break, families, and assorted browsers. Six women wearing HI! MY NAME IS tags stopped and bought all the fry bread I had. Another hoard came and a line started at my end of the table.

"Last batch!" I shouted to the cashiers. They waved at me.

"What are you making?" someone asked.

I looked up. A middle-aged redheaded man in a business suit stared at me. At the beginning, when we were still feeling spunky, Pepsi and I had had fun with that question. We said, Oh, this is fish-head bread. Or fried beer foam. But bullshitting took energy.

"Fry bread," I said. "This is my last batch."

"Is it good?"

"I don't think you'll find out," I said. "It's all gone."

The man looked at my tray. "There seems to be more than enough. Do I buy it from you?"

"No, the cashier, but you're out of luck, it's all sold." I pointed to the line of people.

"Do you do this for a living?" the man said.

"Volunteer work. Raising money for the Helping Hands," I said.

"Are you Indian then?"

A hundred stupid answers came to my head but like I said, bullshit is work. "Haisla. And you?"

He blinked. "Is that a tribe?"

"Excuse me," I said, taking the fry bread out of the pan and passing it down to the cashier.

The man slapped a twenty-dollar bill on the table. "Make another batch."

"I'm tired," I said.

He put down another twenty.

"You don't understand. I've been doing this since this morning. You could put a million bucks on the table and I wouldn't change my mind."

He put three more twenty-dollar bills on the table.

It was all for the Helping Hands, I figured, and he wasn't going to budge. I emptied the flour bag into the bowl. I measured out a handful of baking powder, a few fingers of salt, a thumb of lard. Sweat dribbled over my face, down the tip of my nose and into the mix as I kneaded the dough until it was very soft but hard to shape. For a hundred bucks I made sure the pieces of fry bread were roughly the same shape.

"You have strong hands," the man said.

"I'm selling fry bread."

"Of course."

I could feel him watching me, was suddenly aware of how far my shirt dipped and how short my cutoffs were. In the heat, they were necessary. I was sweating too much to wear anything more.

"My name is Arnold," he said.

"Pleased to meet you, Arnold," I said. "'Scuse me if I don't shake hands. You with the convention?"

"No. I'm here on vacation."

He had teeth so perfect that I wondered if they were dentures. No, probably caps. I bet he took exquisite care of his teeth.

We said nothing more until I'd fried the last piece of bread. I handed him the plate and bowed. I expected him to leave then, but he bowed back and said, "Thank you."

"No," I said. "Thank you. The money's going to a good cause. It'll—"

"How should I eat these?" he interrupted me.

With your mouth, asshole. "Put some syrup on them, or jam, or honey. Anything you want."

"Anything?" he said, staring deep into my eyes.

Oh, barf. "Whatever."

I wiped sweat off my forehead with the back of my hand, reached down and unplugged the frying pan. I began to clean up, knowing that he was still standing there, watching.

"What's your name?" he said.

"Suzy," I lied.

"Why're you so pale?"

I didn't answer. He blushed suddenly and cleared his throat. "Would you do me a favour?"

"Depends."

"Would you—" he blushed harder, "shake your hair out of that baseball cap?"

I shrugged, pulled the cap off, and let my hair loose. It hung limply down to my waist. My scalp felt like it was oozing enough oil to cause environmental damage.

"You should keep it down at all times," he said.

"Good-bye, Arnold," I said, picking up the money and starting toward the cashiers. He said something else but I kept on walking until I reached Pepsi.

I heard the buzz of an electric razor. Aunt Erma hated it when Pepsi shaved her head in the bedroom. She came out of her room, crossed the landing, and banged on the door. "In the bathroom!" she shouted. "You want to get hair all over the rug?"

The razor stopped. Pepsi ripped the door open and stomped down the hall. She kicked the bathroom door shut and the buzz started again.

I went into the kitchen and popped myself another Jolt. Sweat trickled down my pits, down my back, ran along my jaw and dripped off my chin.

"Karaoke?" Pepsi said. Then louder. "Hey! Are you deaf?"

"What?" I said.

"Get me my cell phone."

"Why don't you get it?"

"I'm on the can."

"So?" Personally, I hate it when you're talking on the phone with someone and then you hear the toilet flush.

Pepsi banged about in the bathroom and came out with her freshly coiffed mohawk and her backpack slung over her shoulder. "What's up your butt?" she said.

"Do you want me to leave? Is that it?"

"Do what you want. This place is like an oven," Pepsi said. "Who can deal with this bullshit?" She slammed the front door behind her.

The apartment was quiet now, except for the chirpy weatherman on the TV promising another week of record highs. I moved out to the balcony. The headlights from the traffic cut into my eyes, bright and painful. Cola and Aunt Erma bumped around upstairs, then their bedroom doors squeaked shut and I was alone. I had a severe caffeine buzz. Shaky hands, fluttery heart, mild headache. It was still warm outside, heat rising from the concrete, stored up during the last four weeks of weather straight from hell. I could feel my eyes itching. This was the third night I was having trouble getting to sleep.

Tired and wired. I used to be able to party for days and days. You start to hallucinate badly after the fifth day without sleep. I don't know why, but I used to see leprechauns. These waist-high men would come and sit beside me, smiling with their brown wrinkled faces, brown eyes, brown teeth. When I tried to shoo them away, they'd leap straight up into the air, ten or twelve feet, their green clothes and long red hair flapping around them.

A low, grey haze hung over Vancouver, fuzzing the streetlights. Air-quality bulletins on the TV were warning the elderly and those with breathing problems to stay indoors. There were mostly semis on the roads this late. Their engines rumbled down the street, creating minor earthquakes. Pictures trembled on the wall. I took a sip of warm, flat Jolt, let it slide over my tongue, sweet and harsh. It had a metallic twang, which meant I'd drunk too much, my stomach wanted to heave.

I went back inside and started to pack.

HOME AGAIN, HOME AGAIN, JIGGITY JIG

Jimmy and I lay in the graveyard, on one of my cousin's graves. We should have been creeped out, but we were both tipsy.

"I'm never going to leave the village," Jimmy said. His voice buzzed in my ears.

"Mmm."

"Did you hear me?" Jimmy said.

"Mmm."

"Don't you care?" Jimmy said, sounding like I should.

"This is what we've got, and it's not that bad."

He closed his eyes. "No, it's not bad."

I poured myself some cereal. Mom turned the radio up. She glared at me as if it were my fault the Rice Crispies were loud. I opened my mouth and kept chewing.

The radio announcer had a thick Nsga's accent. Most of the news was about the latest soccer tournament. I thought, That's northern native broadcasting: sports or bingo.

"Who's this?" I said to Mom. I'd been rummaging through the drawer, hunting for spare change.

"What?"

It was the first thing she'd said to me since I'd come back. I'd heard that she'd cried to practically everyone in the village, saying I'd gone to Vancouver to become a hooker.

I held up a picture of a priest with his hand on a little boy's shoulder. The boy looked happy.

"Oh, that," Mom said. "I forgot I had it. He was Uncle Josh's teacher."

I turned it over. *Dear Joshua*, it read. *How are you? I miss you terribly. Please write. Your friend in Christ, Archibald.*

"Looks like he taught him more than just prayers."

"What are you talking about? Your Uncle Josh was a bright student. They were fond of each other."

"I bet," I said, vaguely remembering that famous priest who got eleven years in jail. He'd molested twenty-three boys while they were in residential school.

Uncle Josh was home from fishing for only two more days. As he was opening my bedroom door, I said, "Father Archibald?"

He stopped. I couldn't see his face because of the way the light was shining through the door. He stayed there a long time.

"I've said my prayers," I said.

He backed away and closed the door.

In the kitchen the next morning he wouldn't look at me. I felt light and giddy, not believing it could end so easily. Before I ate breakfast I closed my eyes and said grace out loud. I had hardly begun when I heard Uncle Josh's chair scrape the floor as he pushed it back.

I opened my eyes. Mom was staring at me. From her expression I knew that she knew. I thought she'd say something then, but we ate breakfast in silence.

"Don't forget your lunch," she said.

She handed me my lunch bag and went up to her bedroom.

I use a recent picture of Uncle Josh that I raided from Mom's album. I paste his face onto the body of Father Archibald and my face onto the boy. The montage looks real enough. Uncle Josh is smiling down at a younger version of me.

My period is vicious this month. I've got clots the size and texture of liver. I put one of them in a Ziploc bag. I put the picture and the bag in a hatbox. I tie it up with a bright red ribbon. I place it on the kitchen table and go upstairs to get a jacket. I think nothing of leaving it there because there's no one else at home. The note inside the box reads, "It was yours so I killed it."

"Yowtz!" Jimmy called out as he opened the front door. He came to my house while I was upstairs getting my jacket. He was going to surprise me and take me to the hot springs. I stopped at the top of the landing. Jimmy was sitting at the kitchen table with the present that I'd meant for Uncle Josh, looking at the note. Without seeing me, he closed the box, neatly folded the note, and walked out the door.

He wouldn't take my calls. After two days, I went over to Jimmy's house, my heart hammering so hard I could feel it in my temples. Michelle answered the door.

"Karaoke!" she said, smiling. Then she frowned. "He's not here. Didn't he tell you?"

"Tell me what?"

"He got the job."

My relief was so strong I almost passed out. "A job."

"I know. I couldn't believe it either. It's hard to believe he's going fishing, he's so spoiled. I think he'll last a week. Thanks for putting in a good word, anyways." She kept talking, kept saying things about the boat.

My tongue stuck in my mouth. My feet felt like two slabs of stone. "So he's on *Queen of the North*?"

Of course, silly," Michelle said. "We know you pulled strings. How else could Jimmy get on with your uncle?"

The lunchtime buzzer rings as I smash this girl's face. Her front teeth crack. She screams, holding her mouth as blood spurts from her split lips. The other two twist my arms back and hold me still while the fourth one starts smacking my face, girl hits, movie hits. I aim a kick at her crotch. The kids around us cheer enthusiastically. She rams into me and I go down as someone else boots me in the kidneys.

I hide in the bushes near the docks and wait all night. Near sunrise, the crew starts to make their way to the boat. Uncle Josh arrives first, throwing his gear onto the deck, then dragging it inside the cabin. I see Jimmy carrying two heavy bags. As he walks down the gangplank, his footsteps make hollow thumping noises that echo off the mountains. The docks creak, seagulls circle overhead in the soft morning light, and the smell of the beach at low tide is carried on the breeze that ruffles the water. When the seiner's engines start, Jimmy passes his bags to Uncle Josh, then unties the rope and casts off. Uncle Josh holds out his hand, Jimmy takes it and is pulled on board. The boat chugs out of the bay and rounds the point. I come out of the bushes and stand on the dock, watching the *Queen of the North* disappear.

Notes on the Authors

ALEXIE, ROBERT ARTHUR (b. 1956) was born and raised in Fort McPherson in Canada's Northwest Territories. He became the chief of the Tetlit Gwich'in of Fort McPherson, served two terms as vice president of the Gwich'in Tribal Council and helped obtain a land claim agreement for the Gwich'in of the Northwest Territories. He now lives in Inuvik. He has published *Porcupines and China Dolls* (2002), and *The Pale Indian* (2005).

BOYDEN, JOSEPH (b. 1966) is of Irish, Scottish and Métis heritage. He writes about the First Nations voice, heritage and culture. He teaches Canadian literature and creative writing at the University of New Orleans and splits his time between Louisiana and Canada. The novel *Three-Day Road* won the Giller Prize in 2008, and he has published the short-story collection *Born with a Tooth* (2001), *Through Black Spruce* (2009), and *Extrardinary Canadians Louis Riel and Gabriel Dumont* (2010).

DANDURAND, JOSEPH A. (b. 1964). Kwantlen First Nation, BC. His published works are *Upside Down Raven* (1992), *I Touched the Coyote's Tongue* (1993), *Crackers and Soup* (1994), *No Totem for My Story* (1995), *Where Two Rivers Meet* (1995), *Burning for the Dead and Scratching for the Poor* (1995), *Please Do Not Touch the Indians* (1998), *Looking into the Eyes of My Forgotten Dreams* (1996), *Shake* (2003), and *Buried* (2008).

DAVIS, LAUREN B. (b. 1955) was born in Montreal, Quebec, lived in France for over a decade, and now resides in Princeton, New Jersey, where she is Writer-in-Residence at Trinity Episcopalian Church. *Rat Medicine and Other Unlikely Curatives* (2000) was her first collection of stories. *The Stubborn Season* (2002), was chosen for the Robert Adams Lecture Series. Her novel, *The Radiant City* (2005), was a finalist for the Rogers Writers Trust Fiction Prize. *An Unrehearsed Desire* (2008) was long-listed for the Relit Awards. Her short fiction has also been short-listed for the CBC Literary Awards. Davis has taught fiction writing at the WICE (Paris), The American University of Paris, The Geneva Writers' Conference, and Seattle University's Writers' Confer-ence in Allihies, Ireland. Davis has also lectured on writing at Trent University, Rider University, Humber College and The Paris Writers' Workshop, and has done numerous readings.

FAVEL, FLOYD (b. 1964) is a Plains Cree theatre and dance director, playwright and journalist. He earned his dramatic credentials at the Native Theatre School in Ontario, the Tuak Teatret in Denmark (a theatrical school for the Greenland Inuit, the Sami of Scandinavia, and Native Americans), and the Ricerca Theatre in Pontedera, Italy. He is one of the founders of the Centre for Indigenous Theatre which is a theatre training program for Indigenous People. His work and methods have been presented at the Denver Art Museum, National Museum of the American Indian in Washington DC, Santa Fe Institute of American Indian Arts, The Globe Theatre, University of Victoria/Australia, Enowkin Centre, UBC-Kelowna, Santa Fe IAIA, New Dance Horizons. He is currently Vice President of the Native American Church of Canada.

HIGHWAY, TOMSON (b. 1951) was born on the Manitoba/Nunavut border to a family of nomadic caribou hunters. He enjoys an international career as playwright, novelist, and pianist/songwriter. His best-known works are the plays *The Rez Sisters* (1988), *Dry Lips Oughta Move to Kapuskasing* (1989) and *Kiss of the Fur Queen* (1998), and the children's books *Caribou Song* (2001), *Dragonfly Kites* (2002), and *Fox on the Ice* (2003). For many years, he ran Canada's premiere Native theatre company, Native Earth Performing Arts (based in Toronto), out of which has emerged an entire generation of professional Native playwrights, actors and, more indirectly, the many other Native theatre companies that now dot the country. Among the many awards he has won are the Dora Mavor Moore Award for Best New Play and Best Production (three-time winner, five nominations), the Governor General's Literary Award for Drama (two nominations), the Floyd S. Chalmers Canadian Play Award (two-time winner), the Toronto Arts Award (for outstanding contributions made over the years to the City of Toronto cultural industries, the National Aboriginal Achievement Award, and the Order of Canada.

IPELLIE, ALOOTOOK (b. 1951) is an Inuit illustrator and writer. His published works include *Paper stays put: a collection of Inuit writing* edited by Robin Gedalof with drawings by Alootook Ipellie (1980), *Arctic dreams and nightmares* (a collection of drawings and stories) (1993), *The Diary of Abraham Ulrikab* (2005), *Abraham Ulrikab im Zoo: Tagebuch eines Inuk 1880/81*, a German translation of *The Diary of Abraham Ulrikab* (2007), with David MacDonald *The Inuit thought of it: amazing Arctic innovations* (2008), and with Anne-Marie Bourgeois *I shall wait and wait* (2009).

KING, THOMAS (b. 1943) was born to a Cherokee father and a mother of Greek and German descent in California, but is a Canadian citizen and has spent much of his adult life in Canada. For ten years, he was a professor of Native Studies at the University of Lethbridge and he is currently a professor at the University of Guelph where he teaches Native literature and Creative Writing. His creative and critical writing has been widely published, and his books include *The Native in Literature: Canadian and Comparative Perspectives* (1987), *All My Relations: An Anthology of Contemporary Canadian Native Fiction* (1990), *Medicine River* (1990), *A Coyote Columbus Story* (1992), *Green Grass, Running Water* (1993) was nominated for the Governor General's award, *One Good Story, That One* (1993) and *Truth and Bright Water* (2001).

MOSES, DANIEL DAVID (b. 1952) is a registered Delaware Indian, and grew up on a farm on the Six Nations lands located on the Grand River near Brantford, Ontario. He currently teaches in the Drama Department at Queen's University, in Kingston, Ontario, and pursues independent writing projects. His published works and productions include *Delicate Bodies* (1980), *The Dreaming Beauty* (1990), *Almighty Voice and His Wife* (1991, 2009-10), *Coyote City* (1989, 1991), *The White Line: Poems* (1991), *The Indian Medicine Shows* (1995, 2002), *Big Buck City* (1998), *Brébeuf's Ghost: A Tale of Horror* *in Three Acts (*2000), *Sixteen Jesuses* (2000), *Kyotopolis* (2008), and the nonfiction collection *Pursued by a Bear* (2005).

NOLAN, YVETTE (b. 1961) was born in Prince Albert, Saskatchewan, to an Algonquin mother and an Irish immigrant father. Raised in Winnipeg, Manitoba, she lived in the Yukon and Nova Scotia before moving to Toronto to serve as Artistic Director of Native Earth Performing Arts. Her plays include *Annie Mae's Movement* (2006), *BLADE* (2010), *Job's Wife* (2003), *Traps* (2004), *The Starlight Tour, Two Old Women* and *Video* (1995). She is the editor of *Beyond the Pale: Dramatic Writing from First Nations Writers and Writers of Colour* (2004), and *Refractions: Solo* (2010), with Donna-Michelle St Bernard. She was the president of Playwrights Union of Canada from 1998–2001, and of Playwrights Canada Press from 2003–2005.

ROBINSON, EDEN (b. 1968) is Haisla, of the Kitamaak Reserve in B.C. Her published works are *Monkey Beach* (1997), *Traplines* (1998), and *Blood Sports* (2005).

SINCLAIR, NIIGONWEDOM JAMES (b. 1976) has had critical and creative work translated into several languages and can be found in periodicals such as *Prairie Fire, Canadian Literature, The Goose, Urban NDN, Canadian Dimension*, and *The Winnipeg Free Press.* In 2009, he co-edited (with Renate Eigenbrod) a double-issue of *The Canadian Journal of Native Studies* (#29.1&2) focusing on "Responsible, Ethical, and Indigenous-Centred Literary Criticisms of Indigenous Literatures." Other short stories and essays have appeared in *Tales from Moccasin Avenue* (2006), *Across Cultures/Across Borders: Canadian Aboriginal and Native American Literatures* (2009), *Stories Through Theories/Theories Through Stories: North American Indian Writing, Storytelling, and Critique* (2010), and *Troubling Tricksters: Revisioning Critical Conversations* (2010). Originally from St. Peter's (Little Peguis) First Nation in Manitoba, he now lives in Winnipeg.

VAN CAMP, RICHARD (b. 1971) is a proud member of the Dogrib (Tlicho) Nation from the Northwest Territoris. He is the author of a novel, *The Lesser Blessed* (1996), which will soon be a movie with First Generation Films, as well as two children's books with Cree artist, George Littlechild, *A Man Called Raven* (1997) and *What's the Most Beautiful Thing You Know About Horses?* (2003) as well as a collection of his short stories, *Angel Wing Splash Pattern* (2002). He is also the author of the baby book, *Welcome Song for Baby: A Lullaby for Newborns* (2007), which was given to every newborn baby in British Columbia in 2008 through the Books for BC Babies program. Van Camp's new collection of short stories is called *The Moon of Letting Go* (2009). His first comic book, *Path of the Warrior* (2009), is out with Cree artist Steve Sanderson. His second will be *Kiss Me Deadly.*

VERMETTE, KATHARINA (b. 1977) is a Metis writer of poetry and fiction. Her work has appeared in several literary magazines and compilations, most recently, *Home Place 3, Prairie Fire Magazine*, and Heute *Sin Wir Hier / We Are Here Today*, a collection of Canadian Aboriginal writers, compiled and translated into German by Hartmut Lutz and students of Greifswald University. A member of the Aboriginal Writers Collective, and 2010-2011 *Blogger in Residence* of thewriterscollective.org, Vermette lives in Winnipeg, Manitoba.

(cover painting) NORVAL MORRISSEAU (1932-2007) was an Anishinaabe artist. Known as the "Picasso of the North", Morrisseau created works depicting the legends of his people, the cultural and political tensions between native Canadian and European traditions, his existential struggles, and his deep spirituality and mysticism. He founded the Woodlands School of Canadian art and was a prominent member of the "Indian Group of Seven."

Permissions

Robert Arthur Alexie "The Pale Indian" is excerpted from *The Pale Indian* (Toronto: Penguin, Canada, 2005) and is reprinted by permission of the author and Penguin, Canada. Joseph Boyden "Born With A Tooth" is reprinted by permission of the publisher, Cormorant Books. Richard Van Camp "Love Walked In" is reprinted by permission of the author. Joseph H. Dandurand "Please Do Not Touch the Indians" is reprinted by permission of the author. Lauren B. Davis "Rat Medicine" is reprinted by permission of the author. Floyd Favel "Governor of the Dew" is reprinted by permission of the author. Thomson Highway "Hearts and Flowers" is reprinted by permission of the author. Ipellie Alootook "After Brigitte Bardot" is reprinted by permission of the author. Thomas King "Coyote and the Enemy Aliens" is reprinted by permission of the author. Daniel David Moses "King of the Raft" and "The Witch of Niagara" are reprinted by permission of the author. Yvette Nolan "Scattering Jake" is reprinted by permission of the author. Eden Robinson "Queen of the North" is reprinted by permission of the author. Niigonwedom James Sinclair "Trickster Reflections" originally appeared as "Trickster Reflections (Part II)" in *Troubling Tricksters: Revisioning Critical Conversations* (Eds. Deanna Reder and Linda M. Morra, Waterloo, Ontario: Wilfrid Laurier Press, 2010) and is reprinted by permission of the author. Katherina Vermette "what ndns do" is reprinted by permission of the author.

All attempts were made to obtain permission from all copyright holders whose material is included in this book, but in some cases this has not proved possible at the time of going to press. The publisher therefore wishes to thank these copyright holders who are included without acknowledgement, and would be pleased to rectify any errors or omissions in future editions.

FSC
www.fsc.org
RECYCLED
Paper made from
recycled material
FSC® C005834